CW00495295

ENEMIES TO LOVERS

PORTIA MACINTOSH

Boldwood

First published in Great Britain in 2023 by Boldwood Books Ltd.

Cover Design by Alexandra Allden

Cover Illustration: Shutterstock

A CIP catalogue record for this book is available from the British Library.

Paperback ISBN 978-1-80426-690-8

Large Print ISBN 978-1-80426-689-2

Hardback ISBN 978-1-80426-691-5

Ebook ISBN 978-1-80426-687-8

Kindle ISBN 978-1-80426-688-5

Audio CD ISBN 978-1-80426-696-0

MP3 CD ISBN 978-1-80426-695-3

Digital audio download ISBN 978-1-80426-693-9

Boldwood Books Ltd
23 Bowerdean Street
London SW6 3TN
www.boldwoodbooks.com

For my amazing family
I'm so lucky to have you all

1

'Are you nervous?'

I glance up at Sonny, who is sitting on the sofa opposite me. I swallow hard, feeling the muscles in my jaw tighten as he flashes me one of his trademark cheeky grins.

'I'm not nervous,' I insist. 'This isn't my first time, you know…'

Sonny nods, his smile still firmly fixed on his face.

'Okay, sorry,' he replies, not sounding all that sorry. 'You just seem a bit… on edge. Like you're not quite sure what's waiting for us inside the hotel room, or like you don't know what to do once you're in there.'

I don't say anything.

'Lara,' he says, trying to catch my attention.

'I know what I'm doing,' I insist firmly. 'To be honest with you, I would much rather we waited in silence. Do you think you can manage that?'

Sonny raises his fingers to his lips and pulls closed an imaginary zip. He then takes an imaginary key, twists that inside an imaginary lock and throws it over his shoulder, his mouth finally seemingly sealed shut – he still manages to grin, though. Unbelievable.

I glance around the private hotel lounge, trying to distract myself. I have done this countless times before, but Sonny's words are in my head now. I seem edgy? Do I seem edgy? Now that he's mentioned it, I do feel a little on edge, but that's him. That's Sonny. This is what he does to me.

This place is beautiful, not the kind of place I could ever afford to stay in, but given that it's a five-star hotel in Central London favoured by the rich and famous, that's no real surprise. I just about make enough money to live a Tube journey from work – a longish tube, and in a not very big apartment with two room-mates – so I doubt I'll be staying anywhere this fancy in the near future either.

We're waiting under what is, frankly, aggressively romantic ambient lighting for 2 p.m., as smooth jazz pumps from the speakers, so softly and delicately it almost tickles your ears.

The furnishings boast that sleek, minimalist aesthetic you often see in expensive places – where less is always more – with plush sofas upholstered in a luxurious shade of deep emerald green, and cushions, so many cushions (another strong indicator of wealth, I find, is an abundance of cushions, especially ones that don't do anything). The big, plush ones are nice, though; squashy things that beckon you deep into their soft embrace.

Sadly, I'm not here to relax.

There is a low wooden coffee table in front of me, thoughtfully set out with an arrangement of freshly cut flowers and carefully selected magazines, so I grab a copy of *Tatler* and mindlessly thumb through the pages, not truly reading or absorbing anything, because I can see Sonny's eyes still on me.

'So, what's the plan?' he pipes up. He must have had a spare imaginary key, it seems. 'Talk about favourite sex positions and why we're all going to be wearing blue this summer?'

'Is that what you think women care about?' I ask him, slapping the magazine closed, as one of my eyebrows raises curiously.

Ugh, he's got me to bite. Why do I always rise to it?

'It's what I think you think women care about,' he replies.

'Well, it sounds more interesting than talking about how to trick women into sleeping with you, or how many raw eggs to wash your steroids down with,' I clap back.

I am so blatantly rattled but Sonny finds this exchange ever so charming.

'Erm, less of the steroid talk,' he ticks me off playfully. 'But it does take a fair amount of protein to feed these.'

Sonny playfully flexes a muscle. He's wearing one of those fitted long-sleeved black T-shirts – well, I assume it's supposed to be fitted, it's that or the material is just stretched so tightly over his big arms and his muscular frame.

Sonny's physical presence is hard to ignore. He's tall, with broad shoulders and a muscular build resembling a Greek statue, and not only is he fit, but he knows it. He radiates a casual confidence, turning heads wherever he goes – although this could be something to do with the fact that he is at least 6'3 – because women can't seem to resist his trademark pairing of rugged handsomeness mixed with an untamed mop of tousled sandy-blonde hair. Well, I say untamed, but I highly suspect a lot of time and effort goes into his 'effortless' man bun. He usually wears his hair tied back, revealing a strong jawline and a pair of piercing blue eyes that always seem to be harbouring a mischievous sparkle. It suits him, suits his energy, he's like a golden retriever: big, energetic, always in your personal space, trying to show you what a good boy he is. I say women can't seem to resist him, but I absolutely can.

Blonde hair is about the only thing Sonny and I have in common. I'm almost a foot shorter than him, which doesn't help when it comes to ignoring him, because he seems like a giant in my presence. My hair is much longer than his, brushing the small of my back, but it pains me to admit that his colour is more natural, and as such his ends are in much better nick. My eyes were blue when I was younger, but they're green now. I don't know when they changed, but I'm not ruling out some kind of Incredible Hulk-style response, one that years in Sonny's presence may have triggered in me. My round face is anything but chiselled, my muscles are notable by their absence, and while I'm hopefully as stylish as he is, we're very much opposite ends of the spectrum.

Sonny likes loud, in-your-face, quirky clothes that come in bright colours and dizzying patterns. I'm more of a classic dresser. I prefer understated sharpness to eye-catching conversation starters. Think black, with variety coming in the form of greys and, well, slightly darker blacks. I use pops of colour here and there, to make subtle statements, but ultimately I'm always going to be the little one who blends into the background, and Sonny is the main character whom everyone loves. And, boy, does it show, in all areas of life.

'If you must know – and I'm only telling you this so that you raise your expectations – today we're focusing on men and social media,' I explain. 'What it's like for men on Instagram and the like, and the pressures they feel.'

Sonny makes a face, a subtle admission he's impressed, but not much.

'Sonny Hale?' a man, who seemingly appears from nowhere, says.

Of course he's first.

'Yep, that's me,' Sonny tells him. Then he turns to me. 'Good luck.'

One last smirk and then he follows the man into the hotel room. Oh. My. God. Sonny makes my blood boil, honestly, and frustratingly I am around him all the time.

Sonny and I are kind of like work rivals. We don't work together (for which I am so, so thankful) even though we both work for the same parent company, and in the same building, but the fact that we have the same job at our respective publications means we wind up at all the same jobs and events – like today, when we're both here to interview pop star Troy Reeves, but obviously Sonny somehow finds a way to make sure he goes before me.

I'm a writer for *Stylife*, a glossy women's magazine – one that Sonny seems to think is all 'try this sex position to keep your man' and 'only eat orange foods if you want to be size 2' but we strive to do better than that. Sure, we have some fun stuff – the love and dating team are especially and hilariously hands-on when it comes to writing their features – but we're trying to create more political and social content.

It's worth noting that, when I say 'we', I mean the magazine generally, it's not exactly an area where I'm getting to make a difference given that I'm the showbiz writer. I think the role of showbiz will always be to attract people with gossip, salacious headlines, behind-the-scenes drama and things like that. I'm trying to ask deeper questions but, annoyingly, Sonny is right. No one really cares about Troy Reeves's position on women's rights, they just want to know if he's single again and when his next album is out.

Sonny works for *Mach* (as in macho, which I find kind of gross) which is sort of like our sister (or brother, I suppose) magazine. I would like to say it's all 'how to get thighs so big you can't sit down' and 'do this with your beard if you want any woman to sleep with you' but, I have to admit, they're trying to do more too, raising awareness around important issues like mental health. However, like me, Sonny is the showbiz writer there, so his contributions are similar to mine.

So whether it's interviews like we're doing today, premieres, or parties, I'm always there, and he's always there, and we're always competing, always trying to one-up each other, and that is a full-time job in itself.

I pick up the magazine again and, *again*, I still don't read it. Eventually, Sonny reappears.

'I think that went really well,' he announces proudly.

'Oh, I'm sure,' I say sarcastically as I pull myself to my feet, ready to be called in next. I walk over to where Sonny is standing.

'That's the way you roll, when you work for a decent publication,' he continues, potentially a little tongue-in-cheek, but I clearly can't get enough bait.

'Absolutely,' I agree, somehow turning up the sarcasm even higher. 'How you guys didn't win the Pulitzer Prize for that article on how masturbation is anti-ageing is beyond me.'

'Looking for tips, were you?' he teases, standing just a couple of feet away from me, so close I can smell his aftershave.

'That's your secret, is it?' I reply through a smirk.

'Lara Bailey?' the man calls out upon his return.

'Here,' I reply.

'I guess I'll see you back at HQ,' Sonny tells me.

'Not if I can help it,' I reply.

I'm shown into a hotel room where I find Troy Reeves sitting, waiting for what I'm guessing is his final interview of the day.

'Hi there,' he says politely, but like he's said it a million times today already.

'Hello,' I reply. 'How are you?'

'Very well, thanks,' Troy replies.

'Am I your last interview of the day?' I ask.

'You are indeed,' he tells me. 'Video interviews were first, I did a bit for the radio, and you're the last of the journalists.'

'I'll try to make it quick,' I say with a smile, hitting record on my iPhone before setting it down on the table between us.

Troy was on a TV talent show back in the late noughties and, despite not winning the show, he's gone on to have a great career as a successful solo artist. To be honest, I'm not even sure I remember who won the show that year, but I don't think they're still around. Given that he's been on the scene for fifteen years now, he's reached that status where he knows who he is, and what he is. The thing I've liked about Troy when I've interviewed him before is that he still seems like such a nice, down-to-earth guy.

I ask him a few questions about his new album and his forthcoming tour – the same questions he's probably been asked all day – and you can tell he's reeling off the same replies he's given to everyone else. With those questions out of the way, I can finally ask him something original, something interesting. Something that will get him talking and hopefully give my interview that little something extra that makes it worth reading.

'So, I wanted to ask you about social media,' I start. 'If you ever feel at all affected by what you see online, if you think men have any different struggles to women that perhaps we might not know about, and so on, if that's okay?'

Troy sighs heavily.

'Yeah, okay,' he says. 'Sure, go ahead.'

I'm picking up on something, like perhaps he doesn't want to talk about it.

'Are you sure that's okay?' I ask him. 'If you're not comfortable...'

'No, no, it's not that,' he reassures me. 'I'm just knackered and I've been answering the same questions all day.'

'I'd hoped this might be something a little different for you to talk about,' I say.

'Yeah, absolutely,' he replies. 'But you're not going to believe it, the last guy who was in here asked me about the exact same topic so... I guess I can say it all again.'

I take in a sharp breath. Sonny, bloody Sonny. I should have known, when I told him the angle of my interview, that he would steal it from me. Just when I think he can't stoop any lower.

'Oh,' I say simply. 'That's okay, we can talk about something else.'

'No, honestly, it's fine, I'm sure I can say it all again,' he insists. 'Let's do it.'

It's not that I worry he can't say it all again (although, if he's said it once, he'll probably say less the next time he talks about it) it's more that it's not unique now, it's not worth reading my article over any others, because my angle has gone.

I'm heading back to the office, when I'm done here. Sonny had better hope I don't see him there. I'd say I can't believe he's done this but, truthfully, this sort of thing happens all the time. And I'm really starting to get sick of it.

2

Stylife, the magazine I work for, is a part of Mediworldwide – yep, the big, bad mass media and communications company. As the owner of multiple newspapers and magazines, a publishing house, a rolling news channel and multiple radio stations, Mediworldwide like to keep all of their businesses in one place, so all operations are run from here, The Cactus, an iconic building in the London skyline. The reason they call it The Cactus is because of its curved, green-framed windows, although, if you ask me, it's almost the opposite of a cactus, given that most of its pricks are on the inside.

I mean, I'm sure the world of journalism isn't special, it's probably like any other big business. Everything is so corporate – so important too. Your job isn't allowed to simply be your job, it's supposed to be your life and, as such, I work long hours and I haven't been on holiday in years. Oh, and I'm single, because who has the time to find a seemingly normal one? But this is what I signed up for, what I studied for years to do, the reason I have a chunk of student debt I need to work to pay off. I asked for this but, I don't know, sometimes I feel like there's got to be more to life than working into the early a.m. writing up the favourite food of the cast of the latest comic-book movie.

I head up in the lift, to the *Stylife* floor, where I try to make my way across the office to my desk quickly and quietly. It's a game I play every day, trying to get from the door to my desk without catching the attention of my editor.

'Hey, Lara.'

I'm relieved when I realise that it's Lauren, my friend, calling me over.

'Hello,' I reply, pulling up the nearest chair, plonking myself down next to her.

I exhale so deeply I swear her long, wavy blue hair dances in the breeze, rippling like the ocean. It's quite fitting, I guess, that she is *Stylife*'s travel writer.

'Didn't it go well?' she asks curiously, reading a combination of my mind and my body language. 'Ugh, what I'd give for a one-on-one with Troy Reeves. How could it not go well? Unless... God, you didn't do something to embarrass yourself, did you?'

She says this like I've got form for it. Honestly, you spill a drink down yourself in the VIP section at the Rockin' Radio Summer Roadshow, just feet away from rock royalty, one time and suddenly you have a reputation for embarrassing yourself.

'Oh, no, nothing like that,' I quickly insist. 'Quite the opposite, really – I might have made more of an impression if I had humiliated myself. No, it was just really boring, really flat, and he had already answered every question under the sun.'

'You've got to hate when that happens,' she replies sympathetically, reaching out to squeeze my knee.

'It didn't help that I made the mistake of telling *you know who* what the focus of my interview was going to be,' I add. 'He went in before me and talked Troy's ear off on the subject. He was over talking about it by the time I got to him.'

Lauren narrows her eyes as she smiles.

'What?' I ask.

'What?' she replies mockingly. 'You act like he drives you mad but, I swear, you like it.'

My eyebrows shoot up.

'I like what?'

'You like this, whatever it is, that you have with Sonny,' she replies. 'Even if it's just because it keeps you on your professional toes, but I think it's more than that.'

'Well, you would be wrong,' I inform her.

'Okay. Then you won't mind doing me a favour.'

Oh, she's in there like a shot.

'I wondered where this was going,' I say with a laugh. 'Go on, what do you need?'

'I need you to go on a date with me,' Lauren replies.

My eyebrows shoot up even higher.

'Well, not *with me* with me,' she adds with a chuckle. 'I've got a date tomorrow night with one of the lads from Bytebanter. He seems really nervous and he asked if he could bring a friend. My face must have looked like yours does now because it sent him into a panic. Eventually he explained that he was proposing a double date, not a throuple, and asked if I had a friend for his friend...'

'You want me to go on a date with one of the boys from the tech website?' I say in disbelief. 'Me, who loses files without touching them, and can't make a call on anything that isn't an iPhone?'

Lauren laughs.

'Well, if he isn't cute, and he's boring, then at least you can default to getting some tips,' she suggests optimistically.

I wince.

'Oh, Lauren, I don't know about this one,' I reply. 'I'm not really a blind date kind of girl.'

'Please?' she says, pouting playfully. 'I'm having a crap day too. I just found out my trip to Japan is cancelled.'

'You were so looking forward to it,' I reply. 'What happened?'

'Something in the budget,' she says with a shrug. 'They're sending me to Scotland instead which, you know, is nice, but I was so excited to be going to Japan.'

'When is the date?' I ask, secretly hoping there's going to be some reason I have to say no.

'Tomorrow night,' she replies hopefully.

Obviously I'm free as a bird.

'Go on then,' I reply. 'But only because I feel sorry for you.'

The things we do for our friends, hey? Plus, I know she would do the same for me, if I asked – not that I have much luck finding myself a single date these days.

She laughs.

'I really appreciate it and... Uh-oh, Addison is coming,' she says, quickly changing the subject, lowering her head.

And I'm like a sitting duck.

'Lara, there you are,' Addison calls out. 'Got a minute?'

'Sure,' I call back. Then I turn to Lauren. 'See you later.'

'Yeah, good luck,' she replies. 'It seems like she's pinching the pennies with everyone today, watch out.'

Interesting...

I follow Addison into her office and sit down in the chair opposite her desk. I drum my fingers on the side of the chair as I wait to find out what she wants.

Addison has been running the show at *Stylife* for the past two years, and I don't know if it's her generally aggressive nature or her tall, statuesque figure that commands a petrified respect from everyone, but we're all very much terrified of her. Standing at a formidable six feet in her heels, she has short, sleek blonde hair cut with seriously sharp angles, which perfectly complements her poised and polished persona. I'm not scared of her because she could take me (although I'm almost certain she could) or because she physically towers over me (although that does add to her intimidating demeanour); I think it's because, as bosses go, she asks a lot, and she expects you to do it. Whether it's skipping a night of sleep or putting yourself in physical danger, if Addison asks for it doing, she expects it to be done. She could be about to ask me to do anything.

Addison clears her throat, breaking the silence.

'You're touring that film set tomorrow morning?' she checks.

I nod.

'Yes, well, it's not happening now,' she informs me.

What? No! Why? I mean, it's hardly the same as an all-expenses-paid trip to Japan but, even so, I was actually really looking forward to it. It's the latest Freddie Bianchi movie, a stylish spy flick set in London, and I've been deluding myself into believing that I was going to bump into him and he was going to fall in love with me, despite him not being single, and me obviously being clearly deranged.

'Why?' I ask simply, trying to keep any hint of emotion from my tone.

'Inappropriate inter-office relations,' she replies.

I freeze, like a helpless bunny caught in the headlights.

'...and sexual harassment in the workplace,' she adds. 'The course we're all supposed to take.'

I feel almost relieved to not be in trouble – I haven't even been on a date in months, never mind harassed anyone.

'Can I just quietly give this one a miss?' I ask. 'We have a fully female writing staff, there's no one for me to harass, and I'm too busy, and anyway, I know the rules about dating members of the team so, even if Henry Cavill walked in tomorrow, and was, for some reason, remotely interested in me, I would know what to do and what not to do.'

Addison stares patiently as she waits for me to finish babbling.

'Have you finished?' she asks.

I just nod.

'You already know that this course is mandatory for everyone in the building,' she explains. 'After... recent events.'

Yeah, recent events being someone at pretty much the top of the company engaging in sketchy practices with female employees and then sacking them soon after. That's one guy, at the top of the food chain, who probably isn't even sitting through the course himself. Because of him, and to try to quash the bad press, we're all having to do this waste-of-time course – well, it's a waste of time for me, anyway, because I actually find it quite easy to not sleep with someone and then sack them for not wanting to sleep with me any more. Not all of us need a course to know that's horrendous.

'Lara, you've dodged it long enough,' Addison says with a sigh. 'This is the last session, and you're one of the handful of people in the entire organisation who hasn't attended. I can't let you slide any more. It's mandatory, and I expect you to be there first thing tomorrow, okay?'

'Okay,' I say, sighing with resignation.

'One other thing, before you go, what have you got for me?' she asks, her eyes firmly fixed on her laptop screen.

'What have I got for you?' I repeat back to her.

'Yes, what's coming up, what's in the pipeline, what's happening in the world of celebrity?' she persists.

Do you ever do that thing when someone asks you a question and your mind goes completely blank?

My mouth opens but nothing comes out.

'I hear Sonny has landed an invite to Emmy Palmer's wedding,' she tells me. 'And an exclusive.'

I grit my teeth. That's the problem with having a 'brother' publication, it's like having a sibling, someone for your parents to constantly measure your success against. Sonny is like my over-achieving older brother, one who my parents let run amok, their golden boy who can do no wrong. I'm the little sister who still has to follow the strict rules and can't seem to live up to anyone's expectations.

'I've got a few things cooking actually,' I lie. 'But let me verify my sources before I get back to you.'

'Fine, fine, go,' she says. 'And don't be late tomorrow.'

I laugh to myself as I head back to my desk. A course on office relationships in the morning and then a blind date with a lad from one of the other publications in the evening. It's not as bad as it sounds, though, Lauren said we were double-dating boys from Bytebanter, and there's no rules that say we can't date anyone in the building, each publication is considered its own thing and, like I said, none of the other writers are really my type anyway.

3

We have a yoga studio in our office building – because *of course* we do.

I can't say I've ever been before, or that I've ever tried yoga, although lord knows I could do with the benefits of it. Everyone tells me how it decreases stress, and increases things like flexibility and core strength, but to me that all feels like a real Catch-22 kind of situation.

I've seen yoga, people doing it on TV, and in gyms that I've passed on my way to, well, probably restaurants and bars, and it very much looks like something where you need to have flexibility and core strength to even get involved. Everyone always looks so poised, well balanced and serene as they gracefully move from pose to pose. I, on the other hand, can't even dangle off the bed to grab my phone without hearing my heart beating in my ears, and usually falling flat on my face. Somewhere between the banging in my ears, and the thud of my hitting the floor, I get my very own drum sting, for my slapstick comedy moment – ba-dum-ts! – so the last thing I should do is be myself in a room full of gorgeous, flexible people. Also, and I know it's going to sound stupid, but I'm too stressed to relax. That's the problem, when you're working all the time, never taking a holiday, never even calling in sick. You reach a certain level of stress and you live in it, thrive on it even, to the point where you can't really afford to turn it down, and even if you could, you're too stressed to try. I have an unused lavender candle from a well-meaning colleague to prove it. Well, when do I have time to huff a candle in the hope it chills me out?

I remember reading that in the eighteenth century, doctors would dunk society ladies in the sea, and that a combination of the shock of the cold water and a little low-key drowning would somehow calm their anxiety. While being forcibly dunked in the sea might not sound ideal, I think they were almost on to something. I need a holiday – that will fix me. I need to swim in the sea, sunbathe on the beach, float on a bright pink inflatable in a sky-blue pool with a luminous-looking cocktail in my hand. Oh, and a holiday romance thrown in for good measure. Why not? Oh, right, because I'm always working, that's why.

Take today, for example, when I have a couple of hours off work, but only so I can attend a stupid sexual harassment course, in a yoga studio, that I absolutely don't need. Honestly, you know you're stressed when you would rather spend the two hours working than slacking off in the yoga room, but here we are.

Oh, am I late? Walking through the doors I can see four other people, sitting in pairs, and a frustrated-looking course leader standing at the front. She sighs.

'Sorry I'm late,' I say, looking at my watch, realising that it's only one minute past the hour, but apologising anyway.

'Lara, I assume?' she says and I nod. 'I'm Pauline, your course instructor. It's nice of you to finally join us.'

Her thinly veiled sarcasm doesn't go unnoticed. Wow, this is going to be fun!

I resist rolling my eyes.

'Better late than never,' I joke, taking a seat on my own.

The disapproving look on Pauline's face pretty much confirms for me that she isn't the kind of woman who enjoys a joke, so best I don't waste my time on trying to charm her – seeing as though an almost aggressive sense of humour is the only real tool at my disposal. Well, when life is, y'know, life, all there really is to do is crack jokes and hope it will all be okay.

As Pauline begins her introduction to the course, her eyes dart suspiciously then disapprovingly towards the door as it creaks open again. Another late arrival saunters in, one that I recognise. It's Sonny.

He tries to skulk in, clearly hoping an apologetic smile will see him to a seat, but Pauline isn't falling for the charismatic aura he usually coasts through with.

'Another late one,' Pauline says with a click of her tongue.

I narrow my eyes at Sonny. I want him to think that I'm judging him for being late.

'Sit down there,' Pauline suggests, pointing out the chair next to me. 'The two late ones can sit together. You must be Sonny.'

Sonny smiles at me smugly as he takes his seat and I can't help but frown at how alike we can be sometimes. Both turning up late to a course we've put off until the very last minute. If I'm being truthful, we probably have all of the worst things in common – not that I like to spend too long comparing myself to him in any way.

'Just like old times, huh?' Sonny whispers to me.

I'm not even going to dignify that with a response. It makes it seem like we're old friends, when we're not at all, we just went to university together – and even then, I only saw him for the first year, back when he seemed like he might be a sane person. We actually both did our first-year work placement at the *Daily Scoop* newspaper – Mediworldwide's paper, which in a roundabout way is how we both wound up working here, but that's not a story for now.

Right now, we're learning how not to sexually harass our colleagues – well, we're supposed to be, at least.

'As I was saying before our late guests decided to join us,' Pauline continues pointedly, her tone very much conveying that she's having none of it today, 'this course will focus on the importance of recognising and addressing inappropriate workplace behaviour, particularly related to relationships and harassment.'

'It's bullshit that we're the ones having to do this stupid course and the one person who needs it doesn't have to,' Sonny whispers to me.

'Shh,' I reply. 'You're going to get us in trouble.'

'We're grown adults,' he replies. 'What can she do?'

'Right, you two, up here,' Pauline demands.

I scowl at Sonny.

'This,' I say. 'This is what she can do.'

'One of you on either side of me, please,' she demands. 'If you need to be separated, like children, then that's what we'll do.'

Wow, being made to stand at the front of the class, it's almost like being at school again. I wonder if we'll have to write lines on the board.

I will not have sexual relations with people from work, I will not have sexual relations with people from work...

Unruly children taken care of, and back to the task at hand, Pauline's voice continues to drone on about the intricacies of workplace relationships and the importance of setting boundaries. My attention wavers as I move my attention to my classmates, and the vibe is very much a combination of restlessness and suppressed boredom, with the occasional stifled yawn being about as lively as things get.

I'm jolted from my semi-conscious state as I feel Pauline's sharp elbow purposefully collide with my forearm.

'Now, for our first activity, we're going to review some scenarios involving potential harassment and inappropriate workplace relationships. I need two volunteers to read the dialogue while the rest of the group try to flag any potential issues…'

I'd rather die.

'…and who better to read than our latecomers?' she continues.

My heart skips a beat as she glances back and forth between me and Sonny. Of course, it had to be us, the ones who drew unnecessary attention to ourselves, who are being punished in the spotlight. With an amused glint in Pauline's eyes, she thrusts scripts into our hands.

'Lara and Sonny, if you would be so kind as to read the two characters, please,' she instructs. 'Everyone else, look and listen closely, see if any of their behaviours raise any red flags. Make notes in the booklets provided and we'll discuss after.'

I cast a quick eye over the script in my hand, skimming the first few lines of dialogue, my eyes widening as it quickly becomes apparent what is going on. Oh, you've got to be kidding me. How can Pauline not see the irony, that she is here to teach us all about why we shouldn't touch each other, and yet right now she's giving Sonny (of all people!) a free pass to put his hands on me.

Sonny, of course, is already grinning like a Cheshire cat, blatantly relishing the idea of such an awkward encounter. Honestly, it feels like a big part of his day is devoted exclusively to messing with me. I don't know where he finds the time to endlessly pump up his muscles in the gym, or sit foiled-up in the hairdressers to keep that blonde hair so bright and brass-free, when his number one hobby is winding me up.

Pauline clears her throat, her expectant stare fixed on us. She's looking at us like she expects us to do an Oscar-worthy performance, while somehow also putting across the implication that her expectations are rock-bottom.

'All right, Lara and Sonny, whenever you're ready,' she instructs. 'Oh, and wherever it says "[name]" – just use your real names, for the purpose of clarity. And… go!'

'Lara, hi, you said you needed to see me?' Sonny says with a faux innocence, smiling brightly.

I look at the script, then at him, then back down at the script again. Oh, the little shit, he's reading the part of the woman, which, you know, would be fine, except in doing so he is forcing me into the role of the sexual predator.

Sonny and I exchange glances, him subtly smirking because he knows what position he's put me in, me seething because I can't believe I'm about to say the words I am about to say.

'Sonny, there's something I've been meaning to tell you,' I start, my voice dripping with faux affection. 'I can't concentrate on anything when you're around. My heart races every time our eyes meet.'

Sonny, playing the part he probably wasn't given, drops his jaw with theatrical flair.

'Lara, you're my boss, you mustn't say things like this,' he insists in a high-pitched voice.

'I know I am but… but…' I cough to try to clear my throat, it feels like it's closing, stopping my words from coming out, almost as though I'm having an allergic reaction to what I'm saying. '…but I can't help myself, it's those short skirts you wear and that… and that… that tight little ass?'

My voice shoots up, like I'm asking a question, because I can't quite believe this is the dialogue. I glance at Pauline.

'It's an American script,' she explains. 'And for some reason you're reading the part of the man, but we've come this far. Push on, please.'

'No, please, I'm just here to do my job,' Sonny insists, his character taking an even stronger hold of him. 'I'm your secretary and I'm not interested.'

I frown. I can't help but think this script might be a bit sexist in itself, but I'm not about to open that can of worms, I just want this to be over.

'It says I'm supposed to try to grab his arse,' I point out quietly to Pauline. Obviously, I'm not going to...

'Yes, just try,' she insists encouragingly. 'Don't actually do it, obviously, that's not in keeping with the values I'm trying to instil in you all.'

I glance around the room to look for the hidden cameras. This has to be a prank show, a practical joke, some kind of social experiment to see how far we'll take this. And yet Pauline is encouraging me with a nod of her head. I suppose I could just reach out, because – as per the script – Sonny is supposed to try to stop me. Honestly, you could forget I was a grown woman with a job to do. This feels like some kind of dated high school drama exercise.

I reach out in an attempt to grab Sonny's 'tight little ass' and I try to keep a straight face, but it's a losing battle. Suddenly, everyone in the room is gripped, waiting to see what happens next, and Sonny is pouting at me, batting his eyes, and almost comically offering me his butt to grab – honestly, you can tell that he thinks this is one of the funniest things to ever happen. The sheer absurdity of the situation destroys what little composure I had and I burst into a fit of laughter. I clap my hands over my mouth, to try to suppress it, but it does little good. I'm laughing so hard my chest is bouncing. I feel like I'm on a pogo stick.

Of course, when one person breaks, no one else is far behind them. Sonny falls about in hysterics and the rest of the group follows. Well, everyone but Pauline, that is, because Pauline (allegedly) takes this stuff seriously.

'Right, that's it, you two, if you can't behave, outside,' she demands.

'You're sending us out?' Sonny replies in disbelief. 'Like school?'

'I'm kicking you out,' she corrects him. 'Both of you. Get out of my sight.'

Pauline ushers us towards the door.

'So, can we go back to work?' I ask, conscious that I have so much to do today.

'Go back to work,' Pauline practically demands.

'So... we're good?' Sonny checks with a smile, quietly, so no one else in the room hears. 'Passed with flying colours?'

'If you get out of my sight,' she replies. 'I won't have you disrupting my class.'

It's funny because I think she thinks she's punishing is, by kicking us out, but this is exactly what we want.

The door closes behind us. With only one way to go, we naturally stroll towards the lift together.

'Well, if that's yoga, I can't say I find it all that relaxing,' Sonny jokes. 'Way more butt-touching than I anticipated too.'

'I mean, if the aim of the game is to teach us not to touch one another, I think I've proven myself today,' I reply. 'Although perhaps if it was someone other than you...'

'Yeah, you've got the T-shirt there,' he says casually. 'I was surprised you didn't go in for seconds...'

He's joking about something from what feels like a million years ago, but it infuriates me, so I push it far from my mind and push Sonny back to arm's length.

I step inside the lift, holding out a hand to stop him from following me.

'Get the next one,' I tell him. 'Just in case I can't help myself.'

My sarcasm makes him smile but he does as he's told and lets the door close between us.

Relieved to have got my time back, I head for my desk, keen to squeeze some extra work in, so that I can get out on time later.

Well, I have a double date to get ready for, don't I? Just something else I'm being forced to participate in where, presumably, I won't want to touch anyone's butt either. But, hey, the night is young, I suppose...

4

The air in Barb – the venue of Lauren's (and technically my) date tonight – is fizzing with a post-work release of pent-up energy, the chatter of conversations and the clinking of glasses. It's near work, making it the place Mediworldwide staff often frequent after a hard day at the office – although I tend to avoid it, lest I bump into any colleagues.

As I sit alone at the bar, waiting for Lauren and our dates to arrive, I fidget with the stem of my cocktail glass as I watch the bar staff working their magic, putting on a show as they mix and serve various drinks. Barb is a cool place. The modern, sleek design of the bar, complete with glass walls and exposed steel beams, gives it an intentional office-like vibe, a peculiar fusion of relaxation and work ethic, designed to entice all the busy workers in the area that this is the perfect haunt for them – almost as though it's an effortless transition from their actual offices to this one, where the only thing they need to put on their time sheets is that they're here for a good time.

Why on earth did I agree to this double date? I ask myself the question for what feels like the hundredth time as I shift on my bar stool, my fingers tapping rhythmically against the sleek surface of the bar. My gaze flits to the entrance of Barb as I await my 'date'. He should be here any minute too and it's hard not to wonder what I'm getting myself into. But then I remind myself that I am doing this for my friend.

Lauren has been practically bursting with excitement about this date all day. When it became clear that Jon – the nervous guy from Bytebanter – didn't want to do this alone, and had requested she bring a friend along for his friend, it became quickly apparent that this thing was only happening if I came along. So here I am, on a date I didn't sign up for, but still – for some strange reason – feeling nervous about it, like it's a real date.

I lean back against the bar, my mind wandering to the process of preparing for a date – the careful selection of an outfit (a sleek black minidress and a leather jacket to keep out the cold), the indecisive mirror-gazing, and then the ordeal of executing full hair and make-up without accidentally putting a bend in your hair as you curl it or jabbing yourself in the eye with your mascara wand because you're rushing. It's a ritual I've participated in countless times, although admittedly not recently, and I can't help but feel amused that I've gone through the motions tonight, and that I have the butterflies in my stomach, even though it's not an actual date, and I'm not invested in it at all beyond supporting my friend. I suppose old habits die hard.

As a few more minutes tick by, and the anticipation builds, my mind races through various scenarios. Will he be nice? Charming? Handsome, even? Or could he be like Jon sounds; shy, awkward, and nervous around women too? My eyes dart towards the entrance again, as another parade of strangers arrives. Every time the door swings open, my heart skips a beat. *What if he doesn't like me?* The thought flits through my mind, a whisper of vulnerability that I quickly push aside because it's silly, I'm not here for myself, my sole purpose tonight is to offer support, to be the designated friend who provides a safety net, a buffer against any awkward silences or uncomfortable moments, and to distract the mate's date. Nothing more. And yet... imagine if he's perfect for me. He could be just my type. What a meet-cute this would be – one of the coolest 'how we met' tales to tell in our wedding speeches and... I need to stop. I turn back to face the bar, back to my drink, and back to my usual level of healthy pessimism. I don't know why I'm letting my imagination run away with me this evening.

I sip my drink, the icy-cool cocktail momentarily easing my pre-date (that's not really a date) jitters.

'Drowning your sorrows?' a familiar voice asks me. I jump of out my skin.

My heart sinks and races at the same time. Oh, God, of all the times to bump into Sonny, it just had to happen now. He eyes me with a playful smile, his presence sending an inexplicable wave of embarrassment rippling through me. My brief dance with optimism has turned into sheer mortification. If he knows he's caught me on what is essentially a blind date, I'll never live it down, he'll dine out on it for the rest of the year, teasing me that I can't find a date without it being some kind of set-up. I need to show him that there's nothing to see here, and fast.

'Just enjoying a drink after work, Sonny,' I explain, trying to keep cool, although I can feel my cheeks warming. 'At least I was, until you turned up.'

I try to hold eye contact but his eyes linger on me for a second too long, and I squirm under the scrutiny.

'Ooh, are you meeting someone?' he asks, practically singing the words, like it's London's hottest gossip. 'What is it, huh? Matcher? Tinder?'

'Hilarious,' I reply, still trying to play it cool. 'But I think dating apps are probably more your style. Perfect for preying on unsuspecting women, passing yourself off as normal, before the old date and switch, when they meet you IRL and you're clearly a clown.'

'Hmm,' he says with a thoughtful smile. 'Interesting to hear you've given dating me so much thought.'

I open my mouth, to protest, but as Sonny's friend joins him at the bar, sitting next to me, I take this as my chance to get away from him for the rest of the evening. The only thing that could make this situation worse is bloody Sonny making me feel awkward, cramping my style.

The two of them exchange greetings and settle into their seats at the bar.

'So, how long has it been since your last date?' Sonny asks him.

My ears prick up and my gaze briefly shifts to the newcomer. He's tall, with sharply carved features. He looks pleased to be here but low-key terrified. He lacks Sonny's easy confidence. Still, there's something charming about his awkwardness, in a Hugh Grant character sort of way.

'It's my first one this year,' the man jokes – it's obviously a joke because it's January.

'We'll be fine,' Sonny reassures him.

Okay, what? Sonny, the Sonny I know, is an all-out ladies' man. Believe me. Is he here on a date? Is he on a date with this guy?

Suddenly, it feels impossible to mind my own business. I'm gripped, drawn in by the little snippets of their conversation, curious to know more.

'You're a catch, don't forget that,' Sonny reminds him encouragingly. 'She's going to think you're great. And there's nothing to worry about because I'll be right here with you – you've got the best wingman in the business.'

No...

'I just hope her mate is all right,' Sonny adds.

Noooo! No, no, no. Oh, God. I would scream but I can't. My jaw is on the bar. This guy isn't here for a date with Sonny, not in the way I first thought, *I am*.

'Come on, Jon, relax, it's going to go without a hitch,' Sonny tells him.

Unlikely. So, so unlikely.

'So sorry I'm late.' Lauren's cheerful voice interrupts the moment, before I've had a chance to work out what to say or do. 'It's the strikes – I'm not even sure which one is causing the disruption today – but the city is in chaos.'

She shrugs off her coat.

'You found our dates,' she tells me, sounding surprised. If she's surprised by that, she's about to be blown away. 'How did you...'

Her voice trails off as she realises Sonny is Jon's friend, but she keeps her smile firmly in place. Lauren and Sonny don't know each other, but Lauren knows who Sonny is, just from me talking about him all the time. She once asked to see a photo, to put a face to the name, and then she spent the rest of the afternoon talking about how unrealistically hot he was. And now she's dating his mate. Incredible.

I look at Sonny and watch as the realisation washes over him like a gigantic wave. He's not scared, of course. As expected, he clearly thinks this is hilarious.

'Can we get you some drinks?' Jon asks bravely.

'Ooh, yes, please,' Lauren replies, keeping her game face on. 'Surprise us – we'll just nip to the loos.'

As soon as I stand up, Lauren hooks her arm with mine and practically drags me to the toilets. She doesn't say a word until we get there.

'Lara, I am so sorry,' she insists once we're in the sanctuary of the toilets. 'I just assumed Jon was bringing someone from Byte-banter, not just someone from the building – it never even crossed my mind that it might be Sonny. I feel terrible.'

I shake my head casually, offering her a reassuring smile. I'm not going to ruin this for her.

'It's okay, Lauren, honestly,' I insist. 'I said I would be here for you and I meant it. Let's not let Sonny ruin this. At least I know what I'm up against with him, and I can stop letting my imagination run away with me, that Jon might be bringing some dashingly handsome, rich, famous stud with him.'

Lauren laughs but I can tell she's still cringing.

'Don't let this rattle you,' I tell her. 'I can handle Sonny. You just focus on Jon.'

'Are you sure?' she checks.

'I'm sure,' I reply. 'Come on, let's do it.'

Lauren grabs me, squeezing me tightly.

'Thank you, Lara. You're the best.'

'I'm not sure about that,' I reply with a laugh. 'But I'm here.'

We head back towards the bar and I try not to think about the inevitable awkward atmosphere I'm heading into. Jon and Sonny have already got our drinks, and as we take our seats in the booth they have found for us, my eyes meet Jon's shy smile. It's clear he's nervous but excited, his gaze fixed on Lauren as he does his best to relax. Now I really do need to keep reminding myself that I'm here for Lauren, and that I shouldn't run out screaming, because it's bad enough I have to see Sonny so much at work, never mind socially, and on a bloody date of all things.

Unlike Jon, Sonny very much looks like it's business as usual, he's got that glint of something that's hard to place. I never quite know what it is, beyond his usual level of mischief, but it makes me uneasy. It's as if he's studying me, trying to decipher what's going on beneath the surface, like he's trying to see inside my head and it's taking everything in my power to block his mental advances. I always feel this overwhelming sense of, how can I put it? Like this town – or industry, at least – isn't big enough for the both of us, and that one day something will have to give. But, more pressing than that, tonight this booth isn't big enough for the both of us. Our shoulders are touching. I keep trying to edge away, to put a bit of distance between us, but it's no use.

Jon's nervous smile brightens as he presents Lauren with a delicate pink cocktail.

'It's called an English Rose,' he tells her. 'I thought it would be perfect for you.'

Lauren's eyes sparkle gratefully as she accepts the drink.

'Aw, that's so sweet, thank you,' she tells him.

It really is a lovely gesture. It's cute, romantic and thoughtful.

The two of them start chatting between themselves, the conversation flowing, and suddenly it's like Sonny and I may as well not be here. I can't help but smile.

'And I got you this,' Sonny tells me, nudging a dark purple drink in my direction. 'It's called a Moody Mare.'

My smile drops.

Sonny's eyes lock on to mine and I can see the mischief behind them, dancing like a blue flame.

I take a sip, showing him how unbothered I am – or how unbothered I want him to think I am, at least – and find my smile again.

'It's really good,' I tell him. 'Thank you.'

'I'm surprised you dared to drink it,' he says with a laugh. 'Seeing as though it's from me.'

'Yeah, well, not even you would spike a drink,' I reply. 'Not with a girl you weren't trying to sleep with, anyway.'

He smiles. He knows I'm joking, and I am, but I wish I annoyed him in the same way he annoys me.

'On the subject of me not trying to sleep with you,' he starts, raising his voice slightly so that I can hear him over the music, 'obviously, we're both only here for our friends, and this isn't a real date, but we could always pretend it was.'

'What do you mean?' I ask, concerned this might be the set-up to a joke where I am the punchline.

'I mean, let's pretend we're on a date, to practise our first-date technique,' he explains. 'Well, we have to do something while we're sat here. Ah, come on, it might be fun.'

I sigh, feigning exasperation.

'Okay, fine, but this is solely for entertainment value,' I insist. 'Because I'll bet you're a crap date.'

'Well, you sort of know what I'm like on a date,' he points out.

I pull a face. I refuse to think about that right now.

'You're doing a terrible job so far,' I tell him. 'Is that the best you've got?'

Sonny nods, his expression changing as he rises to the challenge.

'I want to know more about you. What did you study at university?' he asks, seemingly genuinely interested – of course he knows what I studied at university. Which gives me an idea...

'Journalism,' I reply. 'What year did you graduate?'

Sonny narrows his eyes at me for a second.

'I didn't graduate,' he confesses. I knew that, and he knew that I knew that – obviously. But then his smile returns. 'I was actually headhunted, at the end of my first year, meaning I got the job I wanted without having to do three full years of studying, coursework, exams, and all that student debt. I think about how fortunate I am, all the time, to have got the job I wanted so quickly, while other people my age find themselves trying to clamber up the career ladder, years behind me, their student loans weighing them down...'

Okay, it was silly of me to think that I could play dirty, and that

Sonny wouldn't be much better at it than I am. I need to think of something else. Something embarrassing.

'Have you ever broken any bones?' I ask, concealing a smirk behind a seemingly genuine smile.

I ask this because I know that he once stacked it, on the red carpet, in front of the cast of *Mission Impossible* (God knows what number) and not only embarrassed himself, but he broke his leg in the mix.

'I broke my leg once,' he says simply – once again, knowing that I know what happened. 'But a bunch of movie stars sent me get-well gifts, so that was cool.'

'Huh,' I reply. Well, I didn't know that bit.

'Have you ever been wrestled to the ground by police?' he asks innocently.

'Oh my God, that was one time,' I insist, angry that he's playing me at my own game, and winning. 'And he wasn't a police officer, he was an overly vigilant security guard who couldn't see that my backstage pass was underneath my hair.'

He laughs as he drains the last of his beer.

I look over at Lauren and Jon, who are chatting away, getting on so well that they are oblivious to the mess going on across the table.

'Another drink?' Sonny asks me.

'Yes, please,' I reply. 'But then maybe we really should sit in silence, listen to the music, try not to kill one another.'

'Sounds good,' he replies.

As the minutes turn into an hour, Sonny and I find ourselves sitting at the booth, alone, silently, sipping our drinks, probably both wishing this would all be over soon. Lauren and Jon are lost in their own world on the dance floor, having a whale of a time, so at least there's that.

They eventually tear themselves apart, Lauren's laughter

echoing as she approaches our table. Her eyes twinkle mischievously as she addresses the two of us.

'So, we're going to get off,' she tells us.

Sonny can't help but snigger at her choice of words.

'*Head*,' she corrects herself with a cheeky smile.

'I don't think that sounds any better,' Jon tells her with a laugh. 'Come on, let's go.'

'Okay,' I tell her. 'See you tomorrow. Have fun.'

'You too,' she replies as she dashes off.

I pull a face. Me too? Ha. Chance would be a fine thing. And with Sonny, well, that really would be a miracle.

Now, it's just Sonny and me. I finish my drink in a couple of gulps, never one to waste a good cocktail, and then pull myself to my feet.

The dim lights cast a warm glow, giving the table a romantic intimacy that seems to envelop us – one that I'm keen to get out of.

'Well, I wish I could say that it had been nice but, you know, it's been horrible so, yeah, see you tomorrow, I guess,' I say with a faux cheeriness.

'Oh, can't wait,' he replies with a cheeky sarcasm.

I step out into the cool night air. For a moment it feels so nice on my rosy cheeks. But then all at once an icy breeze reminds me that it is January, and with Lauren going off with Jon, that means I won't be staying at her apartment as planned, so I need to get home.

There are no taxis around, which is unusual, so I grab my phone from my bag and fire up a taxi app. There are no cars available right now and... shit. My battery just died.

As I sigh, unable to believe my luck, I watch as my breath makes a cloud in the air in front of me, reminding me once again what a cold night it is. They say no good deed goes unpunished – this is what I get for doing a favour for my friend.

'It's the strikes, I think – although I'm not sure which.' Sonny's voice breaks through my thoughts as he catches up to me. 'Public transport is on its knees.'

'Just my luck,' I reply, shifting on the spot to try to keep warm. 'I was hoping to get a taxi.'

I glance up and down the road. Not a taxi in sight.

'I was supposed to be sleeping at Lauren's,' I tell him, a hint of embarrassment creeping into my voice. 'Not quite sure what I'm going to do now.'

'Listen, I don't live far from here,' he replies, his tone surprisingly earnest. 'Do you want to crash at mine? I've got a futon in the spare room, you can sleep there if you want.'

I hesitate, caught off guard, but I only have to think about it for a second to realise I don't have much choice, and this is actually really kind of him – for once.

'Yeah, that would be great. Thank you,' I reply, the words coming out with a reluctant gratitude.

'Sure,' he replies. 'It's this way.'

We start walking in the direction of Sonny's apartment, the cold air prickling my skin as I wrap my arms around myself. The tension that has been unmistakably there all night seems to have thawed a little, Sonny's act of kindness briefly disturbing the equilibrium.

'You know, I'm really glad to see Jon so relaxed with Lauren,' he says, breaking the silence. 'He's usually so shy around women.'

I nod in agreement, a small smile tugging at my lips.

'Yeah, it's nice to see Lauren dating someone who isn't a bad boy for once,' I reply. 'Someone who won't break her heart.'

It's strange, having a normal conversation with Sonny, seeing this side of him – it's not that it's bad, it's just so unexpected. I keep waiting for the punchline.

Our conversation lulls as we continue on our way, the city's usual energy muted by the late hour. Suddenly, the sound of an alarm pierces the cold night air, drawing our attention to an off-licence across the road. Two figures in balaclavas burst out of the shop, their footsteps pounding on the pavement as they head in our direction.

I freeze in panic but, for Sonny, instinct takes over. He grabs my arm and pulls me into a nearby doorway with him, tucking us safely away, our bodies pressed tightly against the wall – and against one another, as he wraps his arms around me protectively. My heart races in my chest as the robbers run by, their presence a jarring reminder of the reality of being in the city at night, and I'm so grateful to have been with Sonny, to have him protecting me. I might think he's a big, dumb idiot most of the time but tonight, something about his large frame, his big, strong body, and then his kind, sensitive eyes, makes me feel safe and reassured as they stare into mine. Here in his arms, it doesn't feel like anything bad can happen to me.

We hold our position as we wait until the coast is definitely clear, the silence heavy between us. It's an intense moment, the closeness of our bodies creating an unexpected intimacy. I can feel Sonny's breath lightly tickling my lips, and the warmth of his body seeping through our layers of clothing, keeping me warm, soothing my cold skin. For a split second, I feel myself being drawn closer to him, as though there is some kind of a magnetic pull, something impossible to resist.

Before I can fully process the sensation, I snap back to reality, realising where I am and what I'm doing, coming to my senses all at once. I quickly pull away from Sonny's grasp.

He laughs, his voice breaking the tension that had settled between us.

'Were you thinking about kissing me then?' he asks through a cheeky smile.

My cheeks flush, embarrassment washing over me.

'No, Sonny. I absolutely was not,' I snap at him, my words tinged with irritation.

'No one would blame you,' he replies, and I'm sure he's joking, trying to lighten the mood, but I flip.

'Not in a million years,' I insist. 'And, if you're going to be like that, forget it, I would rather sleep on the streets than on your shitty futon.'

'Lara, come on, I was just kidding,' he insists.

'Well, you're not funny,' I tell him as I storm off.

'Lara, please, it was just a joke,' he calls after me.

I don't reply, carrying on my way. Instead, I simply give him the finger as I storm off.

I know, I know, this is just his humour, and it always annoys me, but I usually just ignore it. Tonight I can't, though, because... was I about to kiss him? Whether it's all the cocktails, the fact that he saved me from a scary situation, or even just because I wanted to keep warm – I don't know – but part of me thinks I was moving in closer to him, and I am mortified that he realised.

So, I'll just have to figure out somewhere else to stay, but there is no way I'm going back to his place. I'm not giving him the satisfaction of saving me again.

5

I shuffle across the hotel function room, my tired limbs protesting every step after a restless night on the office sofa. Well, after I fled from Sonny, with no way to get home, and not wanting to splash triple digits on a hotel room (if I could even find one), I didn't have much choice but to let myself into the office. With a yawn and a half-hearted stretch, I pour myself another cup of coffee from the refreshment table. It doesn't smell great but it is desperately needed to try to jolt me to my senses. I take a sip. Urgh, it's not pretty, but neither am I right now.

The room is a hive of activity, with journalists and photographers all buzzing around like bees amped up on cheap coffee. If a bomb were to go off right now, the UK's showbiz gossip columns would all grind to a halt, and then where would we be, huh? Probably all peering down into the rubble, nosily, hardened to anything bleak or gory thanks to a diet of tabloid journalism and true crime documentaries.

I've always had a love-hate relationship with my job. Writing about the glamorous lives of celebrities is fun, and it's so interesting

– and kind of exciting – being part of the behind-the-scenes chaos. But there's a darker side too, one I'm not all that fond of. The incessant scrutiny, the ruthless dragging of people for their mistakes, or just for being in the public eye – it doesn't sit well with me. All I can do is my best, to do the job in the way that I want to do it, but at the end of the day it is a job and I do have to do as I'm told if I want to keep it.

Today I am in the land of make-believe, albeit one created by a clever production team and not actual magic. I'm at the pre-season press event for *Bragadon Forrest*, a hit fantasy TV series where fairies and elves are fighting for the throne of Bragadon Forrest. All of the fairies are petite and beautiful while the elves are gigantic, terrifying creatures – but both have their armies, and are quite well matched, so the fight goes on for season after season, power shifting back and forth between the two, but no one ever really getting anywhere (such is real life). It's a gripping show, if you're into fantasy, and with the new season about to start, everyone is obsessed. So, here I am, to chat to the cast, and help create more hype for the new season.

I take a bite of a croissant, a bigger bite than I was planning, but boy do I need it.

I feel a presence beside me, and I turn to find Sonny smirking at me, amused to see flakes of pastry raining down over my chest.

'Well, if it isn't the poster child for the morning after the night before,' he jokes. 'Good morning.'

I roll my eyes, barely able to suppress a smirk of my own.

'And then there's you, who had all the time in the world to get ready, and still turned up looking like that.'

'Like what?' he laughs.

'I don't know – like a salesman for intermittent fasting and mindful hiking,' I clap back.

Sonny's grin widens.

'It's a purposefully dishevelled look,' he points out. 'Some say my good looks are effortless.'

'Effortless, meaning you don't look like you tried at all, yes, that we can agree on,' I insist.

Sonny has his tousled sandy-blonde hair pulled into his usual man bun, keeping it neat on the top of his head, but he somehow pulls it together in a way that does indeed look effortless. He's wearing another tight-fitting T-shirt that clings to his giant frame (whether it is supposed to or not) and a pair of jeans that he must have to buy from somewhere specialist, to fit his thick thighs. He does always seem to look good (technically, but not to me) no matter what he wears, but I would never give him the satisfaction of me confirming that in any way.

'How are you feeling?' he asks me as he pours himself a coffee. 'Good night, was it?'

The pain in my back from sleeping on the sofa is surely etched on my face.

'Not really,' I tell him. 'I went on probably the worst date of my life last night.'

Sonny laughs.

'That bad, was it?' he replies. 'I went on a date too. It wasn't great but, still, she tried to put the moves on me, but you know, I had to let her down gently.'

'Oh, I'm sure she didn't,' I tell him, still mortified about it, but trying to style it out. 'I know I would never be so bold.'

'Funny, because you kind of look like you're dressed like you're on the pull today,' he points out. 'Confident move.'

He's obviously only saying that to point out that I am wearing the same outfit as I was last night. I shouldn't rise to it, however…

'See, this is exactly why you got kicked off the sexual harassment course, and why I ran off into the night last night, even though I had nowhere to go, rather than sleep at yours, because you, Sonny, are a creep.'

A man clears his throat loudly, interrupting our little exchange, and when I turn to look, I see a figure standing beside him. He's a publicist – I've seen him running about the place – and he's accompanied by none other than Helen Bonas, a towering force of nature known for her role as one of the elves in *Bragadon Forrest*. Helen, an ex-professional wrestler turned actress, stands over six feet tall, muscles rippling beneath her clothing. Of course, she's a lot more attractive in real life, because in the show they make the elves look totally terrifying, but her stature is intimidating nonetheless. She and Sonny are about the same size.

Shit, I wonder how much of that they heard?

The publicist's attention is squarely on me as he addresses me by name.

'Lara, I presume?' he says, his voice polite but brisk, with a professional demeanour that leaves no room for ambiguity or pleasantries.

I nod, suddenly conscious that I'm dressed in last night's clothes, and wearing a face of make-up patched up from the random bits and pieces I found in my desk drawer.

'Yes, that's me,' I confirm brightly.

He motions towards Helen, introducing her with all the enthusiasm of one who has done it a thousand times.

'This is Helen Bonas, who plays Tanithil Glyngella in the show, you'll be talking with her first,' he informs me. 'If you would both like to take a seat over here. I'll be back when your time is up.'

Helen and I take a seat in a corner of the room set up just for interviews. Her gaze is piercing, her presence commanding the room.

'Great. Nice to meet you,' I manage to say, my voice showcasing everything from embarrassment to nervousness to awe.

'Likewise,' she replies with a nod, although her attention momentarily seems to be over my shoulder.

I can't help but look back, to see what is distracting her. It surprises me that Helen's gaze seems to fixate on Sonny, who has been ushered to a nearby waiting area. God, don't tell me she fancies him.

'I overheard some of your conversation with that man over there,' Helen remarks, her voice laced with disapproval. 'He sounds like a real dirtbag.'

I cringe inwardly but then I see an opportunity to get one up on Sonny. If I make sure that Helen doesn't like him, she won't give him a good interview. He'll have to sit in front of her and squirm through the whole thing. That ought to teach him a lesson.

'Oh, you have no idea,' I reply with a heavy sigh. 'He tried to get me to sleep with him last night, even after I walked out on our disastrous date – one I didn't even want to go on in the first place.'

Helen's brow furrows, clearly taken aback.

'Seriously?'

I nod, seizing the opportunity to embellish further. I mean, what I'm saying is not technically untrue, is it?

'And did I hear something about a sexual harassment course?' she asks.

'Yes, he was supposed to participate in a mandatory sexual harassment course – we've had some trouble in the office – but he drove the course leader so crazy she kicked him out for not taking it seriously.'

Helen's eyes narrow, and I can see the cogs turning in her mind, and her blood boiling beneath the surface of her skin.

'Disgusting,' she mutters.

Ha! Good luck getting a good interview now, Sonny.

Not wanting to waste any more time, I swiftly transition into professional mode and chat to Helen about the new season of the show. She relaxes into it, answering my questions, talking about her character as though it were a genuine part of her own personality, and her fellow castmates as though they were one big family. I do notice, every so often, that she glances over my shoulder at Sonny, almost as though she's keeping an eye on him.

As the interview comes to an end, I thank Helen with a polite smile and head back to the waiting area. As I pass by Sonny, who is up next, I can't resist the urge to wish him good luck, and the smirk on my face must register with him, because his own usually confident smile falters for just a second.

I take a seat and watch as Sonny steps up for his interview with Helen. His charming personality is engaged, but it's clear that his charisma is falling flat with the leader of the elf army. I'm gripped, as though I were watching an episode of the show, as I watch him doing the most to try to chat with Helen, but Helen resembles a brick wall in front of him. She's strong, still, silent, giving nothing back.

Sonny seems to dial up the charm even more but, still, Helen isn't interested. She looks unimpressed... furious even... wait!

The sound of Helen slapping Sonny across the face echoes around the room. Sonny's chair wobbles precariously, and he clutches his face in shock, clearly caught off guard.

Security personnel swoop in, appearing seemingly from nowhere, moving swiftly to restrain Helen as she shouts furiously.

'You need to learn how to treat women!' she yells at him. 'Why don't you pick on one your own size?'

I cringe, sinking deeper into my seat. Once again, the rivalry, tension – whatever you want to file it under – between me and Sonny has created a scene. Here in the room, the commotion begins to settle. However, back at the office, I can't see this not coming up. I just essentially got a megastar – and an ex-professional wrestler, no less – to assault Sonny for me. If I was higher up in the company, I imagine there would be a course for this, and we would say no more about it but, being just a lowly writer, I don't know. I don't think I'm going to get away with this one.

6

I'm sitting outside a meeting room, on a cold metal chair, on a corridor that would be silent were it not for the occasional sounds coming from Sonny, on the chair next to me, rustling the bag of frozen peas he's holding against his cheek. Our positions are reminiscent of two naughty schoolchildren waiting outside the head teacher's office, our expressions a mix of trepidation and sheepishness as we await our telling-off and inevitable punishment.

The sound of hushed conversations emanates from behind the closed meeting room door, reminding me that the moment of reckoning is drawing near. Addison, my editor, and CJ, Sonny's editor, are in there together. I can't help but fidget, my fingers tapping rhythmically against my thigh. Sonny hasn't said a word to me yet, which is most unlike him, and I don't really know what to say to him either, so we're just sitting here, waiting – I wonder if he's as nervous as I am?

As we wait, a young woman with a familiar face walks down the corridor. She's a petite blonde with a sympathetic smile just for Sonny. It takes me a moment to place her – she's from YumThings, the food website that is also in our building. I've seen her in their

YouTube videos, she's one of the people who does the cooking tutorials and tries out the lifehacks and stuff like that.

'Hey, Sonny,' she addresses him, her concern evident. 'Are you okay? Can I get you anything? I brought you some new peas.'

I suppose that's one of the perks of having a food website in the building – plenty of frozen peas on hand for when you've been assaulted. Standard office stuff.

'Thanks,' he replies gratefully. 'But I'm fine, really. My ego is more bruised than my face.'

The blonde laughs.

'Oh, you poor baby,' she tells him. 'You should have hit her.'

Sonny raises an eyebrow. I don't think he was expecting her to say that.

'I'm not really one for hitting people, generally,' he tells her. 'Especially not TV stars.'

'I wasn't talking about her,' the girl insists, briefly scowling at me before turning her attention back to Sonny.

A mischievous glint sparkles in her eyes as she leans forward, her lips hovering near Sonny's cheek. My eyebrows shoot up in surprise as she places a light, friendly kiss there. Her smile seems more flirtatious now, and it doesn't waver as she straightens up.

'If you want me to take you home and make you dinner tonight, just shout,' she tells him.

I roll my eyes. Only Sonny could pull in a situation like this.

Before he has a chance to reply, CJ, his editor, emerges from the meeting room.

'Sonny, in here, now,' he commands. 'You too,' he adds, turning his attention to me.

Here we go.

Inside the office, the air is thick with tension, to the point where it's hard to breathe – although that could just be a panic attack. Sonny and I take our seats, opposite our bosses, almost as though we're on opposing sides in a courtroom, and the judges are sitting opposite us. Addison is the first to speak, and as per she doesn't pull any punches.

'So, I suppose my first question is what the fuck were you thinking?' she asks.

Sonny and I exchange guilty glances as we try to work out if she's talking to one of us in particular or both of us.

'Don't answer that,' Addison quickly amends, her frustration palpable. 'We're supposed to report the story, not become the story.'

Addison's gaze zeroes in on me.

'Lara, explain to me how this happened,' she demands, her nostrils flaring with each syllable.

I swallow hard, weighing my options. Honesty is usually the best policy but the truth doesn't sound all that great, does it? Obviously, I never wanted Helen to slap Sonny, I just thought exaggerating the truth slightly would ultimately mean I got a better interview than him – just like he did with me, days ago, when he stole my interview topics for Troy Reeves – but saying 'he did it first' isn't an excuse, is it? Because we're not schoolkids, we're grown-ups, here to do a grown-up job. We shouldn't be letting our personal rivalry come into it.

'It was just a misunderstanding,' I cautiously begin to explain. 'Helen overheard me and Sonny talking, and—'

'I don't want to hear your excuses,' Addison interrupts me, her tone slicing through the air.

I'm confused, which one is it? Does Addison want me to explain how it happened, or not? It's probably best I just keep my mouth shut for now.

'If this were any other day or week, the two of you would both be sacked,' CJ declares, his tone a mixture of exasperation and frustration. His gaze shifts between Sonny and me, but then his eyes fix solely on me. 'You, definitely.'

'Both of you,' Addison interjects, her voice firm and uncompromising.

'Yes, but your girl is worse,' CJ tells her. 'She got my boy assaulted.'

'But it sounded like your boy deserved it, by all accounts,' Addison adds with a pointed look in Sonny's direction. 'Anyway, you're both in luck. No one is getting sacked today.'

It feels like air fills my lungs for the first time since the slap. Oh, thank God, for a moment I really thought our silly games might have ended my career.

That's it now, I've had a lucky escape but today all of this stops. No more playing silly games with Sonny. In fact, no more interacting with Sonny at all. We both need to be mature about it, and accept that we're no good for one another. I'm sure he'll agree.

The feeling of things not being right hangs in the air, like a storm that has passed but could return at any moment. Why do I get the feeling there's going to be a 'but'?

CJ leans back in his chair, his expression turning more serious.

'But you both would have been sacked, if we didn't have an assignment for you both, a joint project between *Mach* and *Stylife*. It's something we've been working on for a while, and luckily for the both of you, you're the only two who can do it.'

Ergh, so much for thinking I would be able to avoid Sonny at work, but I'm sure we can work together to save our jobs. We're not exactly going to mess up a reprieve like this, are we?

Sonny and I look at each other again. He puts down his peas and leans forward in his seat. He looks how I feel – nervous – it's rare to see our two editors in the same room, and it's an even more unusual occurrence that they're assigning us to a collaborative project. Our magazines have never worked on anything together before.

Addison stands up abruptly, her hands slamming down onto the table with a loud thud.

'Pop quiz, Lara,' she says, her eyes fixing firmly on mine. 'What do you know about Duane Fox and Brittany Coleman?'

'Duitanny,' I reply, trying to seem like a professional, offering up the couple's name that the press has coined for them. 'They're the hottest couple of the moment, everyone is obsessed with them.'

Addison's death stare shifts to Sonny, her intensity not letting up at all.

'Sonny, tell me why they're famous.'

'They're the two main stars of the TV series *Blackrock Bay*,' Sonny responds without hesitation. 'The show is huge, mixing the must-watch, water-cooler TV vibes of *The White Lotus* with every sex-stuffed streaming series mummies watch with a glass of wine after their kids have gone to bed.'

Satisfied with his answer, Addison redirects her attention to me again.

'Lara, what is the show about?'

'It's about a mysterious man who moves to a coastal community and starts up an affair with one of the locals,' I explain. 'It's a show full of sex, secrets, mystery, and intrigue. That's why, with Brittany and Duane being a couple in real life, everyone is so obsessed with their real relationship. Everyone wants to know if they have the passion they share on-screen, if they're into the same... things...'

'If that penis is real or a prop,' Sonny interjects, daring to lace his voice with amusement. He's referring to a notorious sex scene featuring Duane Fox, where he unveils an absolute monster of a dong – a sight that has sparked debate among fans of the show, some thinking it's real, others insisting it's fake.

Addison's lips twitch with a hint of a smirk.

'Very good,' she confirms. 'So, you both know how private they are. It's almost as though they're doing it on purpose, and naturally, everyone and their mum want to know something, anything, everything about them. And you two, our star showbiz journalists, never seem to have anything.'

'Well, like you said, they're a very private couple,' I reply, trying to find my confidence again now I know I'm not up for the sack. 'No one knows where they are, or what they're doing.'

'We know where they are,' CJ announces with a grin.

'And we know what they're doing,' Addison chimes in smugly.

I'm speechless. Literally, I open my mouth, but nothing comes out.

'Huh?' Sonny manages to blurt, clearly baffled too.

Obviously, I've been doing my best to work out where Duane and Brittany are, what's going on with them, if they're still together. I've been checking out their usual haunts online, looking on their friends' social media pages, trying to be the first to see what the paparazzi have to offer every day to get in there first but there's nothing.

'They're at Eden,' CJ reveals, the words landing like a bombshell in the room.

I let out a pathetic little gasp. Eden is an exclusive and luxurious couples' therapy retreat. The place is a total mystery, reserved only for the elite of the elite. If you're really rich and/or really famous and having trouble with your partner, you go there – wherever there is. It's that exclusive and mysterious, no one even knows what continent it's on.

'So, how does knowing that help us?' Sonny asks, echoing the question that's forming in my mind too.

'We've got you in,' CJ replies proudly. 'Both of you.'

Sonny and I look at each other in disbelief. This has to be some kind of joke, a punishment, a prank, *something*.

'Wait, what?' I blurt as my brain tries to make sense of what exactly they're expecting us to do.

Addison leans forward, her gaze locking on to mine.

'You're going there, with all the other couples, as though you are one of them,' she explains, her voice steady. 'And you're going to get us the inside scoop on Duittany.'

My mind races as I absorb her words. A joint feature, to be published in both *Stylife* and *Mach*, where we're going to be travelling to one of the most exclusive places on the planet – it's the kind of opportunity journalists dream about. But there's a catch, isn't there? And pretending to be in a relationship with Sonny is a big one.

'So, where actually is it?' I ask.

'We don't know,' Addison admits giddily. 'No one does, that's part of the exclusivity – you could try to figure it out.'

'When is it?' Sonny adds.

'Tomorrow,' CJ interjects, his voice leaving no room for negotiation. 'And it's non-optional.'

The room falls silent as we process the enormity of what's being asked of us. My mind races with questions – surely, we can't pull this off?

'And what makes you think we'll agree to this?' Sonny eventually breaks the silence, his scepticism mirroring my own.

'Because we'll fire you if you don't.'

CJ's response is blunt, unyielding, and sends a chill down my spine. They're really expecting us to do this, aren't they?

'Look, I don't know if you've realised this,' I start, stifling a bemused laugh, 'but Sonny and I low-key hate each other. Look at what just happened today.'

Addison just shrugs.

'Then that makes you perfect for a couples' retreat for struggling couples, doesn't it?' she replies.

CJ tosses a couple of folders at us.

'You can keep your names,' he tells us. 'That will make things easier. Otherwise your profiles are in there. You're both nepo babies. Entitled little fucks who, despite having all the money and opportunity in the world, can't quite seem to love, so your rich sets of parents have handed over a huge chunk of change to get you in there. Of course, we're your rich mummy and daddy, and we really have forked over a small fortune to get the two of you in there, so messing this up isn't an option. Get us everything you can. If not, well, we can always sack you when you get back.'

'Oh, and you'll need to look the part,' Addison adds. 'So you'll both need to head to the swag room, pack your cases – I'll be sending someone down with the keys to the gold room. You're insanely rich so you need to look it.'

I gasp. Oh my gosh, the gold room. I've never even seen inside the gold room.

Being a building filled with various publications which all get sent loads of free stuff, we have what we call the swag room, full of all sorts of things. The gold room, however, is where the super-expensive stuff gets locked away. I've heard all sorts of rumours about what is in there. I can't believe I finally get to see.

'Now, get out, read through your profiles, pack your bags with things that will make you look like rich idiots, then read your profiles again,' CJ tells us. 'You fly in the morning.'

Stunned and speechless, Sonny and I exit the room, dutifully going through the motions as though we have just been tasked with something, you know, normal. We head our separate ways in eerie silence.

You know, it's funny, but I can't help but wonder if being fired would have been the simpler option after all.

7

Wow, I feel like Dorothy, when she first arrives in Oz – not that I'm expecting flying monkeys and wicked witches to be in my future, but the way my week is going, you can never quite rule things out.

The swag room is like a treasure trove, like Ariel's secret cave from *The Little Mermaid* (no, I don't have any real-life points of reference for anything, clearly, but this really is like a dream) hidden within the office's walls. It's like Harrods for freeloaders which, if our profiles are anything to go by, should help us get into character for our nepo-baby personas.

It's quite funny, really, I didn't grow up with much, and neither did Sonny from what I remember him saying. I suppose we're quite similar in that respect, we're just a couple of working-class kids who got into the same uni, who were lucky enough to land jobs at the mass media company where they did their work experience. Yes, we worked hard, but lots of people work hard. I'm well aware of the good fortune that paved the way for me to get here – which is probably why I'm so scared of losing it all, and while I'm standing here watching Sonny examine shoes to take with us on our *couples' retreat*. I still can't believe we're doing this.

The big, burly bloke with the huge set of keys – the gatekeeper, as we all call him – jangles them like a prison guard, giving us his best intimidating stare. I don't know why he's watching us so keenly, when he just told us he had been instructed to let us take whatever we wanted. Whatever we wanted – imagine that.

At *Stylife* the freebies range from cosmetics to skincare products, fashion and accessories and so on – and then, of course, *Mach* have all the same sort of things, but different versions, for manly men, because of the fragility of macho-man ego. Like, they're all for moisturising, but only if the jar is blue. Bytebanter have access to all sorts of tech, which often they're allowed to keep, so there are a whole host of gadgets in the tech section. And then there are all the lifestyle products – everything from suitcases to furniture. You could genuinely furnish your house, fill your wardrobe and update your tech (probably beyond your capabilities of understanding) in here.

We still haven't said anything to one another yet. I don't think we know what to say. It's almost as though it hasn't sunk in, so we're just silently going through the motions to get ready for the trip.

I glance over at Sonny, watching as he sorts through rails and rails of men's clothing, and can't help but notice a theme.

'You're packing for cold weather,' I point out. 'But you don't know where you're going.'

'Maybe I know something about the place that you don't,' he tells me. 'Or maybe I don't.'

He makes a move, as though he's trying to shield what he's doing from me, but I can see him grabbing things like boots, big jumpers, woolly hats – okay, clearly he has some sort of insider knowledge on Eden. I should follow his lead, but not let him see, I'm not going to give him the satisfaction of knowing something I don't.

'I've got things to do, let me show you into the gold room,' the gatekeeper tells us impatiently – he's clearly never known the joy of a free shopping spree, or anything for that matter. 'Once again, you can take whatever you want to fit the brief, just remember to sign it out.'

He unlocks the door and gestures for us to follow him to next door. The door closes behind us as he flicks the light switch, illuminating the room in front of us.

Bright, modern lighting floods the space, and a distinct lack of windows only adds to the surreal feeling. It's as if we've stepped into an alternate universe where everything is luxurious, but free, and nobodies like us can have whatever we want.

The room is a cross between a designer shop and a futuristic tech haven. Wall-to-wall luxury – even the fixtures and fittings look fancy, compared to most of the building. Each corner hosts an array of designer brands and fancy-looking tech items – almost as though a Balenciaga shop had a baby with an Apple Store.

My breath catches as I take it all in. I feel like I've just wandered into a dream I never really knew I had. The soft rustle of exquisite fabrics, the gleam of delicate jewellery pinging light off in all directions like a bunch of tiny disco balls and... oh my God.

'Shit,' I blurt.

'What?' Sonny asks, as though I might have just seen a ghost or something.

'There's a Birkin over there,' I tell him in a breathy voice. 'An actual Birkin, in the classic Hermès orange.'

'A Birkin?' Sonny repeats back to me. 'Isn't that a pubic wig?'

My head turns around like an owl so that I can stare at him in disbelief.

'What? No,' I reply quickly.

'Are you sure?' he replies. 'Google "pubic wig" and see what comes up.'

'Obviously I'm not going to google "pubic wig" – it's a handbag,'

I correct him. 'It's *the* handbag. Do you know how hard it is to get one of these?'

Sonny shrugs.

'It kind of looks like you just walk over and take it,' he says with a shrug, turning to the gatekeeper for confirmation.

'So long as you sign it out, yes,' he says, with a level of chill that makes no sense to me.

'Fuck off,' I can't help but blurt. 'I can take this with me?'

'So long as you sign it out,' he says again. 'I was told you were allowed to take anything to help you look like a rich couple.'

The gatekeeper doesn't flinch as he says this. It's almost as though he fulfils all kinds of weird and wonderful briefs.

'For a Birkin, I'd actually marry him,' I joke, nodding towards Sonny.

The gatekeeper clearly isn't into jokes, although I suppose he doesn't know Sonny, or our history. I would rather be single for the rest of my life than entertain the idea of marrying him. But I can joke about it for a Birkin.

'It kind of seems like you were born for this role,' Sonny says.

For a second, his words mean nothing to me, but then I realise it's a dig.

'Why do you say that?' I ask.

'You're clearly big on material things,' he replies – ironically, as he casts his eye over all the tech on offer.

'Right, because your clothes are clearly so cheap,' I reply – they're obviously not, you can tell by the way he dresses.

'They're not cheap – however you define that – but they're functional and they're not walking billboards,' he replies. 'You're holding a shoe that looks like a sock that has the brand name plastered across it, and you just pointed out a handbag, by name, that must be expensive if you're too scared to even touch it.'

Ugh, he thinks he's so smart, and so moral, and so sensible.

Sonny is the kind of guy who gets his takeaway coffee from a giant coffee chain in a reusable bamboo cup, and takes pictures with trees on hikes – in places he drove to in his diesel-guzzling car. Sure, every little helps, but Jesus Christ, he's not exactly, well, Jesus Christ, is he?

'Says the man lusting over gadgets, knowing full well we're here to pack for our trip, and that we're not even allowed to take our phones on said trip, so you're basically just looking at that stuff for fun,' I point out in retaliation.

Not being allowed to take our phones, laptops, iPads or even our smartwatches is something that freaks me out a little bit. It's not that I'm a millennial, who always has her phone in her hand (although I suppose I kind of do, so it might be fairer to say it's not only because of that), it's because we have no idea where we're going or what we're going to be doing when we get there. We're not allowed to call home – we're not allowed to call anyone. It does make me wonder about what the hell we're getting ourselves into.

Sonny just smirks at me.

'Did you ever think, when you woke up today – wherever the hell you woke up today – that we would be doing this?' he asks.

'Arguing in what is essentially a cupboard?' I reply. 'I'd never rule that out.'

'That's par for the course,' he replies casually. 'I mean working together, taking this trip, doing... whatever the hell it is we're doing.'

'I suppose we'll find out more about what is expected of us later, when we read through the rest of our folders, and I'm sure Addison and CJ will have more to say...' My voice trails off for a second. 'But, no, I never thought I'd be essentially going on holiday with you. And I definitely never could've imagined I would agree to do it.'

'It's amazing what we can endure when it seems like our jobs are on the line,' he muses. 'Oh, by the way, thanks for that. Getting the cheek slapped off me by a wrestler, in a room full of people, and then almost losing my job over it. Just...'

Sonny kisses his fingers like a chef.

I chew my lip thoughtfully. No matter what I think he did or didn't ask for, it was never my intention for him to get slapped, so I suppose I should apologise. If it was anyone else, I would have already. I just hate to give him any sort of satisfaction in any way, because for some reason he always seems to come out on top.

'I am sorry about that,' I tell him, mustering up the sincerity I have deep down. 'She just overheard us talking and jumped to the wrong conclusions, and I didn't correct her, so, yeah... sorry.'

Sonny stares at me for a second, his eyes narrowing before his face dissolves into a smile.

'Apology accepted,' he tells me. 'I'm sure I'll find a way to get you back.'

God, I hope he's joking. Somehow, I think not, but let's hope he waits until after our trip, because this is surely too important for us to mess around with.

'Am I signing out the bag or what?' the gatekeeper interrupts us.

I walk over to it, slowly, like it's a bomb I've been tasked with disposing of. I wipe my hands – not that they're dirty – on the sides of my dress before picking it up. Wow, I don't know if it's heavier or lighter than I imagined, somehow it's both, and it just feels so perfect and the smell, my God, that fresh Birkin smell (as I'll be referring to it from now on).

'She's taking it,' Sonny tells the gatekeeper on my behalf. 'Man, imagine if we could get girls to look at us the way they look at bags, right?'

I laugh to myself, at Sonny, trying to bro-down with the gatekeeper.

I hook it on my arm and admire myself in the mirror. Oh, wow. It just looks... it makes me look... I don't know. It's perfect.

'Right, well, if the two of you can get a move on,' the gatekeeper tells us.

'Yeah, sure, sorry,' I babble. 'Let's grab what we need.'

I grab the large cases I was given and begin scouring the rooms for the things I need. It's great to be able to grab all sorts of lovely toiletries and make-up items I would never dream of buying for myself. Then, when I get to the clothes, I think about Sonny trying to sneakily pack for the cold weather, so I do the same. I wonder where we're going, and if it's somewhere cold, I wonder what kind of place it will be? I'm thinking – or hoping for, rather – toasty log fires, hot chocolates, big fuzzy jumpers. Imagine.

Whatever it is, we just need to make the best of it but Sonny is right, I never would've imagined the two of us doing this in a million years.

With a moment to myself, I sit down on the floor behind one of the shoe racks and grab my phone from my pocket. I open Google and type in 'pubic wig' just to see what Sonny was on about. The first thing that comes up is an article titled 'The Merkin – the pubic wigs used in the movies' – oh, he's such a clown. Something tells me this is going to be a longer week than I first thought.

8

Everything feels so up in the air – quite literally too. I'm on an aeroplane with absolutely no idea where I'm headed.

I glance around what I'm assuming is the first-class section of a commercial aeroplane (although I have no reason to believe anyone else is on board), where Sonny and I are the only passengers. It's just me, him and a couple of flight attendants. It's certainly luxurious – I was worried I was going to feel overdressed in my cosy black and gold Versace tracksuit, clutching at my orange Birkin bag so hard my knuckles turn white when I hold it – but we fit right in. The seats are so plush, and nicely spaced out with dividers that can go up and down if you want privacy. It's like sitting in a little living room – just, you know, one that has been squashed on to an aeroplane.

Everything in here just feels nicer (although the last time I was on a plane, it was a budget airline, so my perspective might be off). The lighting is modern and bright, casting a soft glow over everything inside the cabin, and the air feels cool – and smells great too, almost as though they're diffusing some kind of coconut scent into the cabin to get people in a holiday mood. Well, it's that, or it's the scent of pina coladas on my breath, because I've had two or three already, and boy are they strong.

It's a peculiar sensation to be surrounded by empty seats. It's almost eerie. It's sort of like when you watch a zombie movie, and you see the familiar but in a new way – like an abandoned supermarket. It's sort of like that on the plane, usually cabins are packed with excited holiday goers. This one feels abandoned, like the zombies might not be far away.

Secrecy really is everything, though. We were led from the airport to the plane wearing black plastic visors that only allowed us to see our feet and the tarmac below them. Then, once we boarded, we were seated in here, alone, with no clocks, and we had to have the shutters closed during take-off so we couldn't see where we were going. And then, of course, there's the fact that we had to leave our tech at home, meaning we have no idea what time it is, but we must have been up here a while, because I've watched a couple of movies already. Thankfully, we get to use the in-flight entertainment, otherwise I would be going out of my mind.

It's a bit disorienting, not knowing where we are or how long we've been in the air. We're allowed the shutters open now but there's nothing to see, obviously, just the dreamy expanse of blue sky and pillowy clouds you would expect to see out of a plane window. It's a gorgeous sight to behold, but it also makes me think of how removed we are from the world below. It's almost as if we're suspended in a void, in a place between places, with no idea what comes next. Anyway, judging from how high up we seem, it doesn't seem like we'll be landing any time soon. The only thing to do is sit back and try to enjoy the ride.

I steal a glance at Sonny, who is currently gazing out of the window with a contemplative expression. His features are bathed in the soft light, and for a moment, I'm struck by how surreal this situation truly is. More so than I was five minutes ago. I can't believe, in all of this madness, that he is here too.

I turn my attention back to my screen, to see what other movies are available. I may as well start another one.

I shift in my seat, the plush cushioning beneath me a stark contrast to how generally uncomfortable I'm feeling right now. Well, if you're going to suffer, why not suffer in luxury, hmm?

Sonny plonks himself down in the seat next to me. I wondered how long it would take him to feel so bored that harassing me would feel like something fun to pass the time.

Sonny's appearance is, as always, a balance between effortlessness and intentionality. He's wearing a designer plaid shirt, that hugs his frame on the tight side, and a pair of chinos. He looks smart but relaxed – far smarter than I do in my tracksuit, but we're on a plane, we need to be comfortable, and if we're going somewhere cold then it will be perfect for when we land. Well, coupled with my coat, obviously. I wonder if Sonny might be cold, but I'm sure his winter coat will be up to the job, plus, with his over-pumped muscles, and all the hot air inside him, I'm sure he'll be able to keep himself warm just fine.

'I heard a rumour,' he says in a low voice, 'that they disorient you by flying around in circles after take-off. You know, just to mess with your sense of direction, so you have no idea where they're taking you. We've been on this plane for hours – maybe we're only going to Iceland?'

I raise an eyebrow, intrigued, but with a double dose of scepticism.

'Well, that seems like overkill,' I reply. 'Most people wouldn't notice, or care about the direction they were going in, because they wouldn't know what to do with that information if they had it. Plus, by the time they've blindfolded you, and made you take off with the shutters closed, who even knows if they're north-west or not?'

Sonny chuckles to himself.

'Yeah, I wouldn't have a clue, but this is Eden we're talking about,' he reminds me. 'Eden, where you're not even allowed to bring a watch.'

'What do they think we're going to do with a watch?' I reply. 'Are they a Las Vegas casino?'

As a flight attendant approaches, I try to look casual, even though we both know there's more to our conversation.

'Can I get you any more drinks?' she asks with a polite smile.

'Oh, she's had enough,' Sonny jokes, charming the pants off her with one flash of his smile.

Sonny nudges me gently as the flight attendant walks away.

'We need to be careful what we say, they're always listening,' he tells me, whispering so quietly I almost can't hear him. 'And I'm pretty sure there are microphones next to the speakers in the seats. It seems like they're for calling the flight attendant but better safe than sorry.'

The second flight attendant passes us next. He gives us a friendly smile as he strolls by. Friendly but... is there a look in his eye? Is he on to us? Sonny returns the smile and gives my knee a loving squeeze. I respond with a polite smile, but once the attendant is gone, I snatch up Sonny's hand and practically throw it back at him.

'Oh, yeah, this is going to be easy,' he says sarcastically. 'Love of my life.'

'Urgh, excuse me while I go throw up,' I reply, standing up, because now feels like a great time to stretch my legs and nip to the loo.

Ah, well, as great as first class (or whatever class we're in) is, a plane loo is still a plane loo. Small, claustrophobic, and with a silver loo that looks like it might suck you down into it if you flushed prematurely. Still, they've made an effort to make it nicer, giving it a real towel, and a variety of fancy soaps and lotions to choose from. I guess even the rich need to pee – just don't expect them to wash their hands with something bright green that smells of toilet cleaner.

After washing my hands, I open the door and am taken aback when I see Sonny standing there.

'Erm, hello?' I say, caught off guard.

Sonny doesn't say a word, he simply steps into the tiny toilet with me, essentially pinning me against the sink. I thought it was small when it was just me in here. Now the man mountain is in the mix, I can feel my ribcage digging into my vital organs. Probably.

'Hi,' he says simply, but with a smile. 'I figured this might be our last chance to chat, without anyone hearing, before we get there... wherever there is.'

I keep having these moments, these little blips, when what we are doing really sinks in, and it sets my mind racing.

'This is so surreal,' I say, leaning against the sink for support, but giving Sonny any extra room somehow just allows him to fill it even more. 'I'm trapped in an aeroplane loo, in the middle of nowhere, with my worst enemy – no offence. I'm heading who knows where, doing who knows what, but I know that I basically have to spy on people, which was never part of the job I thought I signed up for but, no, we can't just review gigs and ask actors about their latest movies, we're supposed to hack their emails and rifle through their knicker drawer and... and...'

Sonny, who has his hands on the small of my back, because where else is he going to put them right now, gives me a bit of a reassuring squeeze.

'First, none taken on the "worst enemy" thing,' he tells me, stifling a smile. 'Second, take some deep breaths. You're going to use up all the plane's oxygen if you keep hyperventilating like that.

Look, I get that this is all weird, but we'll figure it out. It's not exactly going to be a walk in the park for me either. I mean, have you met you? If you're not insulting me to my face then you're getting people to hit me in it. But do you know what, I'm going to suck it up and get on with it, because it's my job, and I'm a professional. We went over our backstories, and we're a couple in crisis, so we're supposed to hate each other a bit. Let's just rein it in a little, and play it all by ear.'

His calmness is almost infuriatingly rational.

'You're right, you're right,' I say, breathlessly but calming down a little. 'It's just another bloody work event that you will also be at, pissing me off as per, but do you know what, I'm going to do a better job than you this time.'

'We are supposed to be working together,' he reminds me.

'I mean, we're never supposed to be competing,' I remind him. 'And yet you always try.'

'Well, like I said, it's good that we're supposed to be a couple who hate each other, that we can do,' he points out again. 'So just chill out, let's just go with it, make it up as we go along – we were up almost all night going over our backstories.'

We were, although separately, I hasten to add.

'You never know, you might have fun,' he practically threatens me.

'With you? Ha! We'll see about that,' I reply with a scoff.

As our conversation tapers off, I suddenly feel very aware of Sonny's body being pressed up against mine, the two of us still squashed in this tiny cupboard of a room, like it's a totally normal thing.

My hands are on his chest, because there really is nowhere else to put them – well, I'm not going hook them around his neck, am I? I can feel his hard pecs under my fingertips – not that I'm trying to, I just can. His size and strength are undeniable up close. Ugh, I hate that I'm noticing, that I'm paying any attention to his body whatsoever.

'What?' he teases, grinning like he's reading my mind.

Before I can retort, there's a loud bang on the door.

'Hello?' I hear one of the flight attendants call. 'Hello? Come on out, come on, you can't do that in there.'

Oh, well, isn't that fantastic, the flight attendant thinks we're trying to join the Mile High Club – I would rather jump out of the plane.

My cheeks heat up as I shoot Sonny an embarrassed glance, my eyes widening for effect.

'Oh my God, she thinks we're shagging,' I blurt.

Sonny's grin turns cheeky – of course he finds it hilarious.

'Well, it does add a layer of authenticity to our couple act,' he reminds me. 'It's like I said, let's just go with it.'

As the bathroom door opens, Sonny steps out with a casual grin that seems to further ignite the flight attendant's annoyance. I follow him, my cheeks tinged with an unmistakable shade of embarrassment. Her stern, judgemental glare seems to burn my skin. I feel like a teenager whose parents just walked in on her with the boyfriend she swore she would never invite to her room.

We head back to our seats as the irritated-looking flight attendant watches us.

'Please don't do that again,' she tells us firmly.

Sonny's smirk remains firmly in place, his eyes dancing with mischief as he keeps in character. It's almost as though he's revelling in the misunderstanding, amused by the idea that someone believes the two of us would get up to no good in a plane toilet. I don't know if he finds it so funny because he's just a generally chaotic individual, or because he knows it is something I hate.

Keeping up (these very specific) appearances goes against everything I believe in. I glance between him and the flight attendant. I want to protest, to not only declare my innocence but to stress that I would never in a million years do something like that – and it would be even longer before I would do it with Sonny. I'm trapped between the desire to defend my dignity and the sinking feeling that Sonny is right, that this does lend a certain legitimacy to the idea that we are a genuine couple.

Sonny catches my eye, that mischievous glint ever-present, and it strikes me that maybe, just maybe, it's possible that he's both on to something and enjoying watching me squirm. Maybe he does understand this game better than I do. Maybe there is something in never taking anything seriously, of coasting through life with an air of entitlement. His confidence – and self-confidence – never cease to amaze me. Maybe that's what I need, if I'm going to stand a chance of pulling this off.

I sink down into my seat like a ticked-off child in a sulk. I rest my head on the wall of the cabin, looking out of the window, where there is still nothing to see but a vast sky over a canopy of clouds. Where the hell are we going? I've gone from feeling anxious to impatient. I just want to know now. I just want to get there, get this done and get it over with. Oh, but I don't just want to get it done, I want to do better than Sonny, to prove to everyone that I can be better than him. Why does he always have to get the upper hand? And why does he always come out on top? Because he has since uni and I'm sick of it.

I need to do this, to show Addison and CJ how capable I am, not just for myself, but for our stupid gendered magazines – I need to win this one for the girls. But, as much as I hate to say it, I am starting to realise that even though I might be able to do a better job than Sonny, there's no way I can do this without him. We're going to have to work as a team, whether we like it or not, and even though we are supposed to be a couple on the rocks, we are going to have to sell the idea that we're a couple – that we were in love, once upon a time, even if that couldn't be further from the truth.

So we'll work together. We'll scheme and we will become our characters as best we can, and if it means getting this job done sooner rather than later, then I'll pretend I don't hate him, hey, I'll even pretend I love him. But then, when we've got what we need to keep our jobs, I'll be the one who lands back in the UK smelling of roses, and if I'm lucky, and I play it right, Sonny will be the one who smells like shit.

But we need to get there, and we need to go one step at a time.

One thing is for sure, though, I think we might be the first couple to go to Eden – with its 100-per-cent success rate – and leave hating each other even more than when we arrived.

9

I feel like I've been kidnapped. And I don't just mean that in the sense that my boss has snatched me from my day-to-day life and forced me to go somewhere. I mean before I got off the plane, someone put what I can only describe as a bag over my head and walked me... somewhere. The man leading me – and I assume Sonny too – gave me simple instructions, as he moved me from A to B. I know Eden likes to guarantee absolute privacy but, my God, this really does feel like overkill. I suppose you can't say it isn't an effective system, though. I can't tell you anything beyond the fact that the bag on my head is making my entire body feel absolutely roasting, and the disorientation is making me feel really sick, dizzy and unsteady on my feet. The ground below me doesn't even feel sturdy.

I feel hands near my face, then the bag being slowly removed, and ironically I can't see a thing as my eyes try to adjust to the bright sunlight.

Wow, it really is bright. It's sunny, really warm, in fact, and... oh my God.

Well, it's no wonder the ground didn't feel steady beneath my feet, that's because we're on a boat, and while I may not know where we are, I can tell you where we're not: we're not somewhere cold.

I'll be the first one to admit that geography was not my strong suit at school, but even I can tell you, without a doubt in my mind, that we are in a tropical climate.

The water surrounding the boat is a shade of blue that usually only exists in those overly Photoshopped travel brochures. The sky too, it's almost like they are having a competition, to see who can be the bluest, and despite being different shades, they're both winning. In fact, I once visited a film set, for a movie that was shot almost entirely on blue screen, and even that was less blue than where we are right now.

I glance over at Sonny, who just gives me a bemused smile and a shrug.

The boat – actually, I have to stop saying boat, because now that I'm looking at it, I know that what I should be calling it is a yacht. The yacht is gleaming, the bright white body and the silver details shining in the sunlight. I sit myself down on one of the cushioned seats, while all the new information sinks in. My gosh, wherever we are, it's warm. There's a nice breeze out here on the water, taking the edge off the heat, but I'm still roasting in the thick tracksuit.

There are two people on the deck with us – a minder each, I suppose. I look to one of them for some sort of explanation.

'We are almost at your destination,' he tells me. 'Your luggage will be delivered directly to your suite. However, you will be required to complete a small hike, to get to Eden yourselves.'

'A hike?' I repeat back to him, as though I must have misheard him, because nobody told me any of this was going to involve a hike.

'Sounds good,' Sonny says.

'Sounds like a hike,' I reply.

The man who delivered the hike news must do this sort of thing – and get this sort of reaction – all the time, because his calm, informative demeanour is unwavering.

'We have hike packs for you, with everything you will need for the short journey,' he explains. 'And we will be arriving shortly, if you would like to prepare yourselves to disembark.'

I can't help but marvel at the fact that I expected basically nothing from this trip, given what little information I had, and yet still nothing is at all what I expected. A hike? A bloody hike! What next?

As we near the shore, an old wooden dock that sits in front of a backdrop of nothing but green comes into view. The breeze begins to calm as we get close to the shore, while the temperature appears to turn up.

'Oh my God, I'm boiling,' I blurt.

'Yeah, it is warm,' Sonny replies.

I watch as he unbuttons his plaid shirt before tying it around his waist. Ahh, you've got to love that male privilege, the fact that it's socially acceptable for men to just whip their top off when it's hot, their nipples proudly on display for all to see. If I did the same, even with my bra on, it would be considered obscene.

Sonny stretches his arms out, letting the sun hit every inch of his body. He always looks like he has a tan – I don't know if that's just down to good genetics or if he secretly hits the sunbeds now and then – whereas I'm almost suspiciously pale. People look at me like, is she ill? Is she a ghost? Who knows! And given that it's January, I haven't had a holiday in forever, and the fake tan bottle in my bathroom has a sticky layer of dust on it, I'm about as white as I get. I would probably be lobster red from this trip, were it not for the fact that this tracksuit covers so much skin.

I can't help notice – lord knows I wish I could – that Sonny's muscles are so defined, you can practically see shadows forming in the contours of each perfectly formed pec and architecturally flawless ab. If I pretend that he isn't him for a moment, he's just some guy, not Sonny, the bane of my existence, then I can admit that his body is incredible. Big, strong superhero proportions that he must put a lot of work into maintaining. He's like a sculpture, a work of art – no one is ever going to look at my semi-naked body and say that, not without the word 'Picasso' in the sentence. But that's just it, though, it's all superficial, he's all style but no substance. In fact, his muscles may as well be inflated with air, because that's how little the man has below the surface.

I can't help but stare at his abs, watching them compact tightly as he bends over and... what is he doing? It takes me a moment to realise what I'm looking at. He's doing something to his trousers, at the knee, he's unzipping them – somehow turning them into shorts. Suddenly he is hot-weather ready and I'm standing here, sweating my boobs off, in a thick tracksuit.

'Wow, that's lucky,' I blurt.

'Yep, really lucky,' he replies with a simple smile.

Huh.

'There are your hiking packs,' a man tells us, placing – I don't know what they're called – but those super-long backpacks, the kind that look like they could fit a seven-year-old in them. 'And this card contains the details of how to find your first checkpoint. Directions to the next will be there, and so on – enjoy your time in Eden.'

I really don't see how that can be at all possible.

He boards the boat, which doesn't waste any time in abandoning us. Now it's just me, Sonny, and wherever the hell we are. I turn my attention back to him.

'It's incredibly lucky, in fact, that you wore trousers that zip off into shorts,' I say, my suspicion rising.

'I know,' he replies. 'Although I did know that they zipped off, when I chose them.'

I narrow my eyes at him.

'Sonny, did you know we were going somewhere hot?' I ask him, cutting to the chase.

Even if he didn't say another word, it wouldn't matter, I have my answer. I can see it in the joy in his eyes. Eventually, his lips stretch into a smug grin.

'Now we're even, for the slap,' he tells me. 'Yes, I knew we were coming somewhere warm.'

'You arsehole,' I reply. 'So you were working me, trying to convince me I needed to bring only warm clothing?'

'You brought *only* warm clothing?'

'*Someone told me I was going somewhere cold*,' I snap. 'My God, you're a piece of work. How did you know it would be hot here?'

'I dated someone who knows someone who knows someone who stayed here, and she said they came back with a tan so... yeah.'

Of course he knows through one of his conquests.

'Fantastic,' I blurt sarcastically. 'Come on, let's go, let's...'

As I try to lift my backpack, it feels as though my body stays bent over it, but my consciousness lifts out of me for a second, before snapping back into my body. Wow, I was not expecting it to be that heavy.

'Oh my God, what on earth is inside here?' I say as I open it up. 'Loads of bottles of water – no wonder it's so heavy.'

'Well, we're hiking in tropical weather, so it wouldn't be great if they didn't give us water,' Sonny reminds me. 'Come on, the sooner we go, the sooner we get there.'

I pick the bag up again, knowing what to expect this time, and wrestle it onto my back.

'I assume you're happy for me to navigate?' he says. 'We go this way first, along the beach.'

'Yes, captain, right away, captain,' I say with a sarcastic obedience.

As we trudge along the beach – well, I trudge, Sonny is of course in his element – I feel like I'm a contestant on some sort of horrible reality show where they put regular people, who have absolutely zero to offer in the way of survival skills, in the middle of the wilderness and film them while they try (and usually fail) to cope. I'm not a hiker – I'm barely a walker, unless you count my brief back and forths between where the shops and bars are, and the Underground.

I can't help but laugh, sort of, to myself in my head, at the fact that I'm here, in paradise – in Eden, no less – and yet dragging myself along the beach, the sand slipping under my feet making me unsteady, carrying a massively heavy bag, boiling underneath the hot sun, wearing the warm clothes Sonny managed to trick me into wearing, and the man himself being here too. I can't think of a more accurate definition of hell.

Sonny, on the other hand, is having a lovely time, just strolling along, like he's having a lazy Sunday in the park. Hiking – which I'm guessing is just what you call walking when you think it's fun – is one of Sonny's passions. He's often going on walks in his free time, climbing mountains, posing for photos at the top with a big, dumb grin plastered proudly across his face. And with him being so strong – and dressed appropriately for the weather – carrying his bag seems to require very little effort.

Then there's me. Small, not strong, boiling and resenting every step I take. My bag, the straps pulling down on both my shoulders, feels like a dead weight, and that water, which I know is supposed to help me, feels like the main thing that is holding me back.

'This is the first checkpoint,' Sonny announces, almost excitedly. Urgh, he really is like a golden retriever of a man – which, I know, sounds like it would be a great thing, but believe me, it isn't.

I glance out to sea. It looks like there's an island in the distance – maybe even two. I'm assuming we're on an island, if there's a cluster of them here. Good to know there's somewhere I can swim to, if it all gets too much (but bad to know that I lack the physical strength to make it there alive, obviously).

'Okay, it says we should go this way, into the forest,' he continues. 'Ah, cool. Oh, and... oh my God... look... a lizard.'

He gets down on the floor, on his hands and knees, and follows it curiously. See what I mean? Golden retriever.

The first checkpoint, meaning there are more to come – I wonder how many? Look, I don't want to be that girl, but I'm sweaty, I'm dirty, I'm boiling, there are bugs and critters and I'm just really, really not into this at all. Everything overwhelms me and I slump down onto the sand, clutching my Birkin bag, which suddenly feels more like an anchor than a fashion accessory. I hug it, as though it were my last connection to civilisation. Then I have an idea. I take a bottle of water from my bag and remove the lid.

'Good idea,' Sonny says. 'We should hydrate and – whoa, what are you doing?'

He shrieks with horror as he watches me emptying out my bottle of water on the sand. The sand drinks it up in an instant, not wanting to share a drop with the roasting hot world above.

'I'm pouring it out,' I tell him. 'Well, I'm not exactly going to leave the plastic bottles on the beach, am I?'

'It's for the hike,' he reminds me.

'Which I won't be able to do if I have to carry all these heavy water bottles around with me. Relax, it's just one or two.'

'Lara, have you never seen any survival show on TV?'

He asks this as though it would be weird if I hadn't.

'No,' I practically laugh. 'Unless I've somehow always missed the week on *Love Island* where they force them to live on pool water and flavoured lube.'

'You're such a baby sometimes,' he points out. 'You don't stop to think about the consequences of your actions.'

'Says you,' I clap back.

'You're never going to find me pouring away the only clean water I have, on a hot day, in the middle of nowhere,' he points out. 'But you, no, you're just going for it, without giving a second thought to what will happen when you're thirsty. If you waste your water, and I drink all of mine, you're not going to like the only liquid that's left for you to drink to survive, believe me.'

I didn't think I could get any hotter but my blood boils because he's right. I slump even further, my back against a conveniently placed rock, feeling every bit of my frustration and exhaustion seep into the sand beneath me. I fold my arms like a moody teenager but then my frustration quickly starts to shift into panic as the reality of the situation sinks in. I can't simply refuse to participate, I'm here, whether I like it or not, and it is warm, and I do need to drink. This isn't a sexual harassment course I can slink out of, this is real.

A large shadow forms over me, offering a fleeting moment of respite from the hot sun. I relax into it a little, even when I realise it's just coming from Sonny, towering over me.

Sonny, always so quick to be a knight in shining armour – or plaid, in this case – unties the shirt from around his waist and extends it towards me.

'Take off your tracksuit and wear this like a dress,' he instructs. 'Trust me, you'll feel much cooler.'

I give him a look that is equal parts gratitude and scepticism.

'Thanks,' I say, my tone dripping with enough sarcasm to fill... whichever ocean is next to us. 'I guess I'll just wear this the whole time, seeing as though someone convinced me to only bring winter clothing.'

Sonny allows himself a slight laugh, which fizzles out into a smug smile.

'I'm not completely heartless, you know,' he insists, although the jury is out on that one. 'I might have taken pity on you, just a tiny bit, because, while you did get me slapped across the chops by the strongest person I've ever met, tricking you into packing winter clothes to a hot country felt like a way more impressive stunt.'

'All I hear is you congratulating yourself, while I melt to death on the sand in front of you,' I reply. 'What are you saying?'

'I'm saying I packed you a bag, with everything you would need for a summer holiday,' he replies. 'I had a look at what sizes you were grabbing and just filled my second suitcase with things for you. You're welcome.'

'You packed a second suitcase for me, listen to how mental you sound,' I reply, furious, but ever so slightly relieved he didn't fully commit to the bit.

'Well, I didn't need the second suitcase, because I'm not all that superficial, or materialistic,' he points out with a shrug.

'Are you saying I'm materialistic?' I reply, irritated.

'Look in your hands,' he laughs.

I glance down at the designer bag I'm hugging.

'Just turn around, please, let me get changed,' I plead. 'I'm melting.'

'Why don't you head into the forest?' he suggests. 'Get some privacy there.'

'Because I don't know what kind of creatures they have in there,' I reply. 'Better I get changed out here, keep the creatures where I can see them, but ask them nicely to turn away so, please, will you not look for a moment?'

'If that's you asking nicely...' he mutters to himself under his breath, his voice tapering off before I can hear him say anything that might make me kick off again.

Honestly, what is wrong with the man? Convincing me to pack the wrong things, but then packing the right things for me is like some kind of psychotic power move. At least he said he checked my sizes, although I don't love that he was rooting around my underwear while I wasn't looking.

Despite my obvious irritation, I am grateful he has given me his shirt to wear. I suppose I should thank him sincerely.

'Thank you for this,' I reply.

'You're welcome,' he says as he turns out to face the ocean. 'Just don't get used to it.'

Ha, believe me, I won't. I'll just have to be more careful, keep a closer eye out for his little tricks – he's always been deceitful. Even back when we were at uni, that's why I realised he couldn't be trusted. I can't let my guard down around him, not even for a minute, which is going to be hard when it seems like I'm going to be around him twenty-four hours a day for the foreseeable future.

Slipping into the makeshift shirt-dress, I can't help but let out a contented sigh as the cooler fabric brushes against my skin. With the sleeves rolled up and my legs mostly uncovered I feel so, so much better.

'Okay,' I say as I stuff my tracksuit into the bag. 'I'm done.'

'It suits you,' he says with a smile.

I shoot him a glance and he looks back at me with a mixture of amusement and something that almost looks like relief.

'It does,' he insists. 'You look so much cooler already and I feel like an arsehole so, give me your backpack, I'll carry it for you. Water and all. I'll even carry your handbag, how about that?'

I blink at him, genuinely surprised by his offer, and, if I'm being honest, still pretty suspicious.

'*You* feel bad? Is that even possible for you?' I ask, half joking, half serious. I mean, he should feel bad, but this is Sonny. He'll probably drop my backpack in the forest somewhere, throw the Birkin into the ocean, and then, I don't know, bury me alive? That all seems like something he would feel is a measured response to what was little more than a mischievous misunderstanding.

He feigns a hurt expression, clutching his chest dramatically.

'You wound me, Lara, you really do,' he playfully insists. 'Honestly, you offer to do something nice for a girl, you even say you'll carry her handbag, and this is what you get. They say chivalry is dead but, you give it to them, and they don't want it.'

He's obviously joking but, even so, I want to push him out to sea.

'Okay, thanks,' I reply. 'But this makes us even, yeah?'

'Okay,' he replies. 'From now it can be strictly work. That's why we're here, right?'

'So I'm told,' I say with a sigh.

Sonny, his own backpack firmly but effortlessly resting on his back, picks up my backpack – with so much ease, I would have sworn someone emptied it while I wasn't looking – and holds it under his arm, like it's a yoga mat or something. He hooks my handbag on his free arm and smiles.

'Look at you,' I can't help but say with a smile. 'You look like some kind of hiking demigod right now. Like a caricature of the perfect man – if such a thing could exist.'

Sonny smiles, clearly taking all this as a compliment.

'Only to look at, though,' I quickly add. 'You would be perfect for a calendar, for older women who don't fancy their husbands any more, but less attractive to anyone who had an actual conversation with you.'

'Aw, thanks, Lara,' he says through a chuckle. 'I'm so lucky I have you, to keep me on my toes.'

I watch him as he strides ahead, his broad shoulders shifting effortlessly under the weight of the bags as he bravely leads our way into the forest. I wonder, to myself of course, whether or not I could guilt him into carrying me, as well as my bags, but the thought of him touching me sounds slightly worse than having to walk. I actually think he would love it, if I asked him to carry me, because the only thing he loves more than (literally) flexing is showcasing how much better than me he is. I shudder internally at the image of his smug grin, as he carries me in his arms, probably telling me that I'm not as heavy as I look or something. Nope. No way am I going to give him that satisfaction. I'll take my chances on my own two feet for now.

A tropical forest in a pair of Ugg boots is not the one. I thought they were a perfect choice, for being comfortable on the plane, and would take me effortlessly to my winter destination. Ha. What a clown. Right now, they feel like two hot, squishy pouches of water. I can feel my toes sliding together as I walk, it's horrible. But, still, better than bare feet if there are lizards around. I would ask Sonny for his shoes, were his feet not so much bigger than mine.

I follow in Sonny's footsteps, just far less gracefully. He strides with confidence, happily, like he's in his natural habitat. I flail around behind him, quite literally like a fish out of water, as I try to keep up.

'I've been having some thoughts, about how we should play this,' Sonny pipes up, studying another checkpoint to figure out which way we go next. 'The brief just says we're not getting on like we used to, and that we're wondering if we should stay together or call it quits.'

'Okay,' I say cautiously, wondering where this is going.

'I think we should say you're the problem,' he concludes.

'Ha!' I scoff. 'Me the problem? You're the problem.'

I wince at my own clumsy wording but, my God, he infuriates me.

'No, hear me out, just seeing how you've been, since we got off the boat, you're being moody, pessimistic, complaining and what have you – you're really good at it,' he explains, in a voice that makes me think this is all supposed to be a compliment, and yet it's so, so insulting.

'Piss off,' I snap.

'See what I mean,' he persists. 'You're great at it.'

'Or, how about this,' I start, feeling myself powering up more and more with each word. 'We say that our problem is you, because you're a clown, you never take things seriously, you make everything difficult by turning it into a joke, and you take practical jokes too far.'

'Oh, come on, I do not,' he insists. 'I just like a laugh.'

'No, you like a laugh at other people's expense,' I correct him. 'Usually mine, for some reason. What kind of boyfriend does that?'

He smiles again.

'We're certainly not going to need to practise our bickering, are we?'

'Unlikely,' I agree.

'All I was saying was, your general misery around the situation will make you a more convincing candidate,' he says, trying to be clearer, but still not sounding great. 'Whereas I'm a little more subtle about my feelings.'

Having just sipped my water, I take the opportunity to be funny, and spray it from my mouth as though I've just had the shock of my life.

'You? Subtle? Don't make me laugh,' I reply. 'Your thoughts and feelings are always so obvious. Right now, you're a frankly hilarious mixture of smug and oblivious.'

'And you're being – as I said before – miserable and moody and pessimistic, and I think that's an easier sell, so that's what I'm selling,' he informs me.

'Well, I'll be saying everything I said previously too,' I clap back. 'So we can bicker right in front of them, and watch them questioning why they ever opened this retreat in the first place.'

'I suppose that will have to be the plan then,' he says with a sigh. 'Because we're here.'

Suddenly, there it is – Eden. The name feels so fitting, it's like something out of a movie, a tropical paradise that you look at and think you would love to go to, but it surely can't be real, it's too perfect, and if it is real, well, ha, there's no way you can afford it.

A brilliant blend of the natural wonders of the island coupled with contemporary human design. The architecture of the large building that stands tall before us is somehow striking, while blending seamlessly into its surroundings. A mixture of wooden cladding and glass, everything looks like a tree, or reflects the real ones that surround it. It's almost hidden away, camouflaged – I suppose that makes sense, given how secretive they are.

A tropical haven mixed with a five-star resort, with what is supposed to be the world's best couples' therapy and wellness retreat hiding inside – what more could a couple of entitled nepo babies ask for? Well, when you don't have the usual problems like a job, paying your bills, and cleaning your own loo, why not invent some in your relationship and pay (what is rumoured to be) five figures to fix it, eh? It's a holiday, at the end of the day, and sunbathing is so old, it's been done, let's talk about our feelings and hit each other with foam sticks and shit like that.

My eyes are immediately drawn to the pool area, situated just outside a set of bifold doors. The water sparkles invitingly under the sunlight, framed by pristine loungers and tables that look like they could hold a fair few cocktails. It looks like the kind of place where all your problems can be solved – or at least where Instagram influencers can pretend they will be.

Just beyond the pool area, inside the open bifold doors behind it, I spy an impressive dining room with an enormous table as its centrepiece. Everything looks so chic and modern, and almost too perfect to be real.

'Welcome to Eden.' A young man in a crisp white linen shirt and trousers greets us of all of a sudden. We both jump out of our skin, as he materialises from nowhere. Wow, who knew people could sneak up on you when you're standing in the middle of an open space? We're going to have to be careful here.

'My name is Lucian – you must be Lara and Sonny?'

His smile is friendly enough, but there's a touch of formality in his demeanour that makes me instinctively want to correct my posture.

Lucian appears to be the physical embodiment of this place. He very much matches the aesthetic with his polished look, like he's been dressed by a high-end designer for the occasion. I notice him notice my outfit but, ever the professional, his face doesn't slip.

'Why hello,' I say brightly, too brightly, in fact I give the sun a run for its money. I need to dial it back.

'Hi, yes, I'm Sonny, this is Lara,' my temporary other half explains, with a far more relaxed vibe. 'Don't mind her, she's just excited to be here.'

I'd say Lucian was in his late twenties. He has a smooth, soothing English accent (think Daniel Radcliffe) but I think it's pretty safe to say, even with my limited geography, that we are not in Skegness. I know Sonny said they fly you around in circles to disorientate you, but we were on the plane for what felt like most of the day, that's a lot of laps of our tiny country.

Lucian smiles.

'If you would like to follow me, I can show you to your suite,' he presses on. 'You have a little time to settle in, rest, and to freshen up, before dinner is served later.'

Resting and freshening up sounds like a dream come true to my sore feet and sweaty body. Who knew hiking in designer winter clothing wasn't it? I feel like I've just been involved in a workout for the super-rich. That Birkin did start to feel like a kettlebell, the longer I carried it.

As Lucian sets off with an assured stride, I look to Sonny, as if to confirm that we're really doing this.

'Let's go,' Sonny says with a reassuring smile.

'We dress smart for dinner,' Lucian tells us as we walk. 'But nothing too formal, especially when it's hot. You will find your luggage waiting for you in your suite – we've taken the liberty of unpacking for you.'

'You've unpacked our bags?' Sonny blurts, a little worry detectable in his voice.

'It's necessary, I'm afraid,' Lucian explains. 'We have to be sure that you have only the things you will need for your stay here.'

That's a polite way of saying they search our bags. Hmm, I wonder why Sonny looks so worried – has he tried to smuggle something in? It would be so funny, if he were to get in trouble. Well, unless it blew our cover, obviously, but I'd love to see him get ticked off for making a small mistake. Why, no, I'm not over his winter clothing prank, thank you for noticing.

'Any contraband?' Sonny asks playfully, but I'm definitely picking up on a vibe.

'You both packed appropriately,' Lucian confirms and the flicker of relief on Sonny's face tells me everything I need to know. He's got something with him, something he shouldn't, something good.

'This place is ridiculous,' I say, changing the subject. 'Like someone brought a Pinterest board to life.'

'Yes, many of our guests find it more than suitable,' Lucian confirms. 'Of course, many are used to the finer things, so this place needs to be no exception, even though it's a working break.'

Ah, crap, I forget that we're supposed to be rich. I need to tone the awe down a little, act like I'm at these sorts of places all the time.

'A working break?' Sonny repeats back to him.

'Working on yourselves,' Lucian replies. 'That's why you're here, after all.'

'It certainly is,' I reply with a smile, taking Sonny's arm in mine, giving it a squeeze.

It's hard to play it cool in a place that is so insane it seems like CGI.

'Did you enjoy your hike across the island?' Lucian asks as he leads us down a long hallway with several large wooden doors off it.

Oh, so it is an island, take that, Year 7 geography teacher whose name I can't remember.

'We did,' Sonny says. 'It's a beautiful island.'

'I always say that the couple who hike together stay together,' Lucian muses.

'And there's me thinking it was a shared Netflix account that did the trick,' I quip.

Sonny looks at me and purses his lips. Right, because we're rich, so who cares?

'What island is this?' I ask, changing the subject, but actually really curious to know.

'Eden is a privately owned island,' Lucian tells us.

'Whereabouts?' I ask innocently.

'The location not being disclosed was in the contract,' Lucian points out. 'Next to the part about us helping you to unpack.'

I can tell I'm annoying him with my line of questioning.

'Are we allowed to know the continent?' Sonny practically jokes. 'Or the hemisphere?'

'Southern, right?' I check optimistically. 'Seeing as though it's clearly summer here.'

'That's not exactly how that works, darling,' Sonny corrects me, politely, because we're in company, but he just loves being right. 'There are plenty of hot countries north of the equator. Do you think it's snowing in Dubai?'

I ignore him and turn to Lucian.

'Are we in Dubai?' I ask with a smile.

'I am sure I won't get in trouble for confirming that we are not in

Dubai,' Lucian says. 'The reason we keep our location a secret is for your privacy, and to keep you focused on why you are here.'

It's funny he should say that because I am beyond distracted by trying to work out where the hell we are.

'This is your suite,' he tells us. 'Suite Four.'

'How many suites are there?' I ask, sounding more like a journalist than a guest.

'For guests, there are four suites,' he replies.

'So only four couples staying here at a time?' I can't help but ask. Ugh, I can't help myself.

'Correct,' Lucian replies. 'Would you like to see your room?'

'Yes,' I say quickly, trying to show a balanced amount of excitement. Imagine if I gave myself away, before I even got through the door.

Lucian leads us through the door, and the moment it swings open, I'm captivated by the beautiful blend of modern elegance and how the nature outside has been carried through into the room. Almost every wall is glass, allowing the outside world to meld seamlessly with the interior. Soft mesh curtains sway gently in the breeze that wafts in from our private deck, carrying with it the natural scents from outside – like a fancy diffuser but, you know, the actual smells, not a bottled version.

The room itself is a masterpiece, sleek sophistication from wall to, well, window, with contemporary furniture that somehow still effortlessly melds with our natural surroundings. Muted tones of beige and ivory create a soothing palette, and tasteful minimalist artwork is strategically placed, adding a touch of personality to an otherwise blank canvas of a space.

I pop my head through the only other internal door and marvel at the swanky bathroom, a lavish mix of marble and glass. A large walk-in double shower dominates the room. The double sink doesn't exactly look like an afterthought either – it's bigger than my bathroom back at home. My God, even the loo looks fancy.

Back in the bedroom, the first thing that catches my eye is the gigantic bath – a bath that is definitely big enough for at least two people, although it's hard to imagine circumstances in a place like this where you could end up with more than that. But pretty much everything in the room centres around the bed that sits at its heart.

It's at least a super-king bed (I don't know if they go bigger than that, but it looks it). The pristine white linens contrast against the polished dark wood frame – I could climb into it right now, if these two weren't here. A thought flickers through my mind, one that I've been fighting off: Sonny and I are going to have to share this bed. We're adults, professionals here to do our job – surely we can handle sharing a bed. It certainly looks big enough that we won't exactly be entangling our limbs all night long.

'Clean up, rest up, and we'll call you for dinner in due course,' Lucian says, his voice breaking through my thoughts, his professionalism unwavering as he tells us what to do. He's mentioned us getting cleaned up twice now – I'm starting to worry about what we look and smell like. Relax, shower and dress for dinner – he makes it sound like we're here for a leisurely afternoon at a luxury holiday resort. I wonder when the actual couples' therapy-type stuff will start. Perhaps they give you a day to arrive, get settled in, get a feel for the place and relax into the surroundings.

Lucian heads out, leaving us to our own devices. When it's just the two of us, the walls of the room seem to start closing in, emphasising that it's just me, Sonny and the big bed we're supposed to share every night. I wonder if he feels as awkward as I do, as uneasy in these unchartered waters.

I clear my throat and chew my lip, my eyes darting around the room for an escape.

'I'll shower first, if that's okay?' I suggest as I head for the bathroom regardless.

'Go for it,' Sonny says simply. No snark, no jokes, no digs. I think he wants space just as much as I do right now.

I close the door behind me and, for a moment, I just breathe. I kick off my boots and feel the cool tiles on my feet as I take deep breaths. I glance at my watch – another phantom notification that comes from years of wearing Apple watches. It's going to be so weird without it, and without my phone. Even just the ritualistic checking of it, or using it as a prop in awkward situations.

Somehow I feel like I'm going to have a week full of awkward situations ahead of me, and it's going to take a lot more than a phone to take the edge off.

10

As Sonny and I make our way along the corridor, heading towards the dining room we saw earlier, I have a fury simmering below the surface that I'm worried I won't be able to keep a lid on. This was never going to be easy, and pretending to be in a relationship with Sonny sounded bad enough, but I thought that him also pretending to be in a relationship with me might force him to be a normal human for a while. Sadly, no such luck.

I should have known I was getting off extremely lightly when he told me that he had packed a case for me – of clothes that he assured me were in my size. I was so relieved to have something other than winter clothes that I didn't stop to think about what he might actually pack for me. At the time, I was worried I didn't seem grateful enough but now that I know what he's done, even a glimmer of gratitude seems like it was too much.

After a blissful shower, elated to feel clean and more relaxed in my fluffy white robe, I walked over to the wardrobe, jazzed that all my things had already been unpacked and put away for me – so jazzed that I briefly forgot I didn't actually know what clothes were waiting for me. I opened the doors and reality hit me like a ton of bricks – a bright pink ton of bricks. Yep, Sonny, ever the comedian, knowing full well that I tend to prefer muted tones (and a lot of black), decided to pack me exclusively pink items. Pink clothes, pink shoes, pink underwear, pink socks. Everything is bright frigging pink, in all sorts of different shades, but nothing any less pink than the thing next to it. An eye-watering array of 'it's a girl' pinks. It looks like he packed my case in Barbie's Dreamhouse.

'I thought we were all still obsessed with the Barbie aesthetic,' Sonny quips, breaking the silence, his lips curving into an amused smile as he reads my mind.

'You're an actual arsehole,' I seethe through gritted teeth, suppressing the urge to go back to the suite and toss every single item of clothing he has into the sea. But we're here now, so I need to shift back into character.

As we step into the dining room, I can practically feel everyone's eyes burning my skin as they look to see who the final guests are. With three other couples already sitting at the table, we're clearly the last to arrive.

A tall, slim woman who I would guess is in her forties approaches us.

'Hi,' she says, her American accent washing over me as she greets us. 'Let me show you to your seats.'

American, eh? I think I can safely say we are not in North America. Honestly, it's as though they employ people with different accents, just to add to the confusion.

The dining area is bathed in an ethereal glow, courtesy of delicate crystal chandeliers that hang from the high ceiling. The long wood table, with guests seated on either side, is laid out with the works, looking like something out of a lifestyle magazine – well, almost the works. It has everything but food on it.

The room hushes as we approach the table, all eyes upon us. The staff member who is seating us gestures to our seats at the table, inviting us to take our places with a nod of her head. Her eyes linger on my attire, only for a second, but I can't help but feel a fresh wave of embarrassment wash over me. My face is probably the same colour as my hot pink minidress. Oh yeah, not only is everything pink, but it's daring, in-your-face and, surprisingly frequently, covered in glitter for the most part. This Barbie is in a relationship crisis.

'Please make yourselves comfortable,' the staff member instructs us, her tone purposefully soothing. 'Dinner will be served shortly. In the meantime, feel free to chat among yourselves.'

I settle into my seat beside Sonny, and plaster my best smile across my face.

'Hi,' I say.

'Well, well, well, look who we have here!' a forty-something Australian man exclaims, his grin as huge as his level of self-assuredness. 'The Norse god himself, Thor!'

His words are accompanied by a chuckle, as he very much enjoys his own joke. He slaps Sonny on the back, as if they're old friends.

'I bet you get that all the time. Absolutely the spit of Chris Hemsworth, you are,' he continues.

Sonny just smiles. Even I know he gets that a lot. It's his superhero build, his good looks and his longish blonde hair. I don't know about him looking exactly like Chris, but he could pass for a Hemsworth brother or play Thor so maybe, all things considered, that'll do it.

'Bloody hell, you took your time,' the Aussie continues. 'We're starving.'

'Sorry,' Sonny says. 'We came right here.'

'No worries, Thor,' the man replies.

Ugh, that's going to get annoying. I hope he doesn't keep that one up.

'I'm Heath,' he says, offering Sonny a hand to shake. 'Heath Scott.'

He makes the introduction but it's pointless really. I think everyone with an internet connection knows who Heath Scott is. He is the forty-something CEO and self-proclaimed mastermind behind AIbotixx Inc – a tech company that I'm not smart enough to understand, but I know broadly that their speciality is robots and artificial intelligence. Heath's slightly dishevelled hair and cool-guy clothing screams that he is trying to look young. He has what they call a dad bod, and the people of the internet are often making fun of him for holding his stomach in for photos. My God, who cares? He's a billionaire. The trolls of the internet thinking that the biggest problem with him is that he's not quite thin enough need to touch grass. I imagine Heath tries to keep looking younger for two reasons. One, because lots of people in the tech industry are young innovators. Two, because of the woman sitting next to him.

'Good to meet you, buddy,' Sonny replies. 'I'm Sonny, this is my girlfriend, Lara.'

Oh, God, hearing him say that out loud makes me throw up in my mouth a little.

'Hi,' I say, still trying to find my character.

'I'm Kellee,' Heath's wife tells us. 'His better half. Not that he usually remembers.'

Sonny and I both smile and wave but, as showbiz journalists, we already know exactly who she is.

Kellee, a Canadian child star turned pop princess now in her mid-twenties, has an air of glamour that accompanies her every move. Her glossy brown hair cascades in waves around her shoulders, framing a face that's graced countless magazine covers over the last decade or so.

The two of them tied the knot a year or so ago, to everyone in the world saying it wouldn't last, questioning what on earth the billionaire and the hot young pop star saw in one another. I suppose, given that they're here, things must not be great between them.

As Kellee extends a manicured hand in our direction, her eyes twinkle with a mix of amusement and intrigue as she appears to linger on Sonny, holding his hand for a second or two longer than you would expect. Heath appears to notice, but tries to pretend he doesn't.

The attention of the table shifts, like a spotlight moving to illuminate the next freak show – because let's face it, we're all *here*, we must all be mad. The young couple to introduce themselves next are the youngest guests, they can't be far into their twenties.

'Danny,' the man introduces himself with a bluntness that makes me think he might be a bit shy. I'm guessing he's from Manchester, based on his accent. Definitely northern, that's for sure.

'And I'm Izzy,' the girl next to him announces brightly in her Liverpool accent. What Danny lacks in confidence, Izzy more than makes up for. She has poker-straight hair, a mixture of honey-blonde chunky highlights over a light brown base. She's wearing a purple body-con dress that looks like it came from the same shop as what I'm wearing, to be honest. You can tell she's a fan of cosmetic procures – fillers, Botox, and what can only be described as an intimidating boob job. Good on her, if that's what she wants. I decided I wanted a nose ring last year but chickened out at the sight of the needle, so she's a lot braver than I am.

'I'm Danny's fiancée,' she explains. 'And if you think you recognise Danny, you do, he's Danny Parry, Liverpool City's *best* player.'

Her revelation hangs in the air for a moment.

'All right, Iz, I don't think this lot are into football,' Danny tells her, blushing slightly.

Danny does look, funnily enough, exactly like a footballer, and

Izzy is doing her best to be a glamorous WAG – and nailing it. She pulls off a bright dress far better than I do.

I smile to myself, their regional accents seem to lend an extra touch of authenticity to everything they say, and somehow it makes me feel less detached from home.

Finally we all turn our attention to the last couple at the table, the reason Sonny and I are here – Duane and Brittany.

'I'm Duane,' he says simply. 'Good to meet you all.'

'And I'm Brittany,' she adds with a smile. 'Hi.'

Wow, even in person they give nothing away.

Duane is a big bloke, but his muscular build is offset by his soft features and his approachable face. He's got kind eyes and his big shoulders look ready to be cried on. He has a brooding look, one that makes him seem like he has a sexy secret, although perhaps I've just watched too much *Blackrock Bay*.

Brittany is the ultimate girl-next-door. Her eyes sparkle, her smile seems so genuine, and she's so beautiful – both of them are. Sometimes you remind yourself that everyone on TV looks great, but in real life they look a lot more normal. Not these two, they're two of the most attractive people I've ever seen. They make one hell of a good-looking couple and, even though they're keeping themselves to themselves, trying to blend into the background, they stand out more than I do in my hot pink dress.

The atmosphere around the table begins to grow restless as the minutes tick on. Heath leans back in his chair and gazes around the room, his brows furrowed in mock confusion. He drums on his stomach with his hands.

'I don't even know what time it is, but it must be late,' he announces, unable to hide the frustration in his voice. 'I mean, how long does it take to serve a meal?'

I imagine, being a billionaire, there isn't much Heath can't have the second he wants it.

'Mate, I'm starving,' Danny, whose appetite has clearly been growing with each passing moment, agrees with an enthusiastic nod, his tone a blend of light-heartedness and genuine hunger.

'It's been a long, tiring day,' Heath replies. 'We need some grub in us. Especially us fellas.'

Ick. I'll let that one go. I'm here to play the game, not bash the patriarchy.

Izzy releases a dramatic sigh, leaning back in her chair, rubbing her own super-flat stomach for effect.

'All I want right now is to eat and then crash into bed,' she says. 'Hmm, if I could have anything right now, anything in the world, I'd smash a Big Mac.'

'Honestly, Iz, you come all this way to… wherever we are, and all you want is a bloody Maccies,' Danny teases her.

Izzy's playful expression falls into a pout. She glances to the side, wounded.

I think we would all love a Maccies right now. I think we'd all love anything.

'Honestly, I could eat anything at this point,' I confess, vocalising my thoughts, trying to join in with the group. 'I'm so hungry that even foods I don't particularly like suddenly all sound delicious.'

As our stomachs all practically grumble in agreement, I glance across the room and notice the presence of the staff members once again. There's Lucian, who showed us to our room, standing with an air of composed patience. Beside him there's a woman I'd guess was in her thirties. And then there's the American woman who initially showed us to our seats, her calm demeanour unwavering amidst the growing restlessness. They're all just standing here, silently, like statues. The kind you see in art galleries that make you start to wonder if their eyes might be following you around the room.

'Ah, this is ridiculous,' Heath says. 'If I had the chopper here, I could probably fly to Maccies and get back with Big Macs for everyone before this lot could fry an egg.'

'If there's no sign of it, I'll pop to the toilet,' Duane says. Both he and Brittany have that perfect RP accent many English actors have.

'Yeah, I could do with a wee,' Izzy says, in stark contrast, 'but I'm gonna wait, in case the food comes.'

'I'll come with you,' Sonny says as Duane pulls himself to his feet. 'I don't know where the loos are yet.'

'Going to the toilets like girls,' Heath jokes, not that anyone else finds it funny. I can't imagine the reception holding him back from cracking more corkers in the future.

Seeing a chance to chat with Brittany, I take the opportunity to shift seats, briefly moving to Duane's seat while he's away.

'Did you enjoy the hike earlier?' I ask her, to strike up a conversation.

'To be honest, I'm not a big fan of hiking,' she admits, her voice warm and friendly, her honesty like a hug.

'I feel exactly the same,' I reply. 'If Sonny hadn't carried my backpack for me, I don't think I would have made it.'

'Oh, that's sweet of him,' she says. 'I just about managed to carry my own bag. It's a workout my personal trainer has me do, to get me in shape before filming.'

'Ah, nice,' I say. I wonder if I should ask her more about her job. I don't want to seem too journalist-y too quickly, though.

'What do you do?' she asks me before I get a chance to say anything else.

I take a moment to recall the cover story Addison gave me. This is it, my first real test.

'I'm an influencer,' I say with a confident smile, fully aware that everyone else at the table is tuned into our conversation.

'That's not really a job, you know,' Heath's voice, in all its bluntness, interrupts me.

'Yes, it is,' Izzy corrects him. 'I'm trying to get into doing it full-time too.'

'You can't do it full-time, because it's not a job,' Heath corrects her. Then he turns to me. 'What do your parents do?'

I summon the details of my fabricated backstory.

'My family own racecourses,' I tell him.

'There you go,' he says with a dismissive scoff. 'You sound like a nepo baby without a real job.'

Jeez, say what you see, Heath. Don't pull any punches or spare anyone's feelings.

'Says the asshole who inherited his dad's business,' Kellee says, not letting his rude comment slide. She clearly isn't afraid to stand up to him.

'I made that business what it is,' Heath corrects her. 'He was little more than a lawnmower salesman.'

The return of Sonny and Duane thankfully prevents the conversation from escalating further.

'Thor, what do you do?' Heath asks him.

'Nothing, man. My dad is an actor,' Sonny replies, unashamed, very much in character.

'Ooh, anyone we've heard of?' Izzy asks curiously.

'Yeah, but my mum isn't his wife, so we have an agreement that I won't say,' Sonny tells her.

'Old dog,' Heath says, clearly impressed. Oh, and it would seem that it's just fine for Sonny to do nothing for a living, but not me.

We all chat among ourselves for a little longer, sometimes in pairs, sometimes as a group, but even though time is ticking by, there's still no sign of any food coming our way.

The exhaustion from the hike and the long flight has left us drained, and the lack of food only amplifies that we're all feeling absolutely knackered.

'You know what, this is a joke,' Heath announces. 'I thought this place was supposed to be five-star. We all paid enough. The least they can do is bloody feed us.'

He turns around in his seat to address the staff members, who are still just standing there.

'Oi, where's dinner?' he demands, unable to hide his frustration.

Silence.

'I said what's the hold-up?' he demands, his voice practically a growl as his patience wears thin. 'I could cook faster than this.'

Kellee rolls her eyes.

'You can't cook,' she blurts.

'And I could still cook faster than this,' he tells her. He turns his attention to the staff again as his tone intensifies. 'What's going on?'

The staff members, standing by like the king's guards, remain unmoved. Their lack of any sort of reply gives the scene an eerie atmosphere, like something out of a suspenseful thriller. It feels like something is going on, this isn't normal.

'Is there anything we can snack on while we wait, perhaps?' Duane asks tactfully.

'Yeah, I'd take a breadstick or something – anything. I'm supposed to eat a certain amount per day to keep my fitness up,' Danny explains, as though that might help.

But despite the growing restlessness, and pleas for even a snack, the staff members remain unresponsive.

Heath, reaching his limit, pushes his chair back and stands up, as though he's going to take matters into his own hands.

'I'm going back there,' he declares, determination etched across his face. 'And I'm coming back with dinner for all of us.'

'Good,' Kellee says, her own impatience clear.

'Go on, lad,' Izzy cheers him on.

I glance at Brittany, noticing her uncertainty. She clearly feels the same way I do about this situation.

'I'm sure that's not necessary,' I call out, raising my voice above the chaos.

'Yeah, Lara's right. Let's just wait,' Sonny agrees, but it's no good. Heath is a man who is used to getting what he wants.

As the unrest spreads like wildfire, the American staff member who showed us to our seats steps forward.

'Okay, listen up, everyone,' she says to get everyone's attention. 'My name is Dr Hope Henderson, and I am in charge here at Eden.'

The abruptness of her words catches us all off guard.

'I thought you were a waitress.' Heath, ever the outspoken one, voices his incredulity. 'If you're the boss, why are you just standing by while they starve us to death?'

Hope's lips curl into a knowing smile, her self-assured demeanour shining through.

'I have to confess to an assessment,' she begins to explain. 'A social experiment, of sorts, to see how you all behave when you're uncomfortable – individually, and as couples.'

I don't think anyone knows what to say to that, not even Heath.

Hope's tall figure radiates confidence and authority. Her physical presence is striking, and you've got to hand it to her, she knows how to command a room. Heath is back in his seat, quiet as a mouse, and she didn't even need to tell him once.

'We will get to know each other better tomorrow,' she explains. 'For now, I will see that your food is brought.'

She says this like it is both a reassurance and a promise.

As if on cue, the silence gives way to the sudden appearance of food, as though it were just waiting in the wings for this moment. Serving plates are placed in front of us, in the centre of the table, laden with a variety of dishes, something for everyone – and with enough variety so as not to tip us off to where we are.

With everyone busy loading up their plates, too hungry to stop and think about how fucked up this all kind of is, I turn to Sonny, talking quietly enough that only he can hear me.

'You went to the toilets with Duane,' I point out.

'Yeah,' he replies. 'He didn't say much, though.'

'I thought you were going to try to catch a look at his business,' I say, as tactfully as I can. 'You did say you were going to find out if it was real or not.'

'Lara, I was joking,' he tells me off. 'Do you really think men stare at each other's dicks in the toilets?'

'Okay, sorry, I was only reminding you that you said it,' I clap back. 'Eat something, you're clearly hangry.'

'Incidentally, I did see it though,' he replies in hushed tones. 'By accident, obviously, but I got my answer.'

I want to know, I can't help myself, but I don't want to ask. Sonny must be able to tell, because he doesn't keep me in suspense for long.

'Definitely a fake one in the TV show,' he replies. 'It's big, but it's not that big. Hell, mine is bigger.'

I almost spit my drink out as Sonny, ever the comedian, reaches across to grab one of the large corncobs from the plate in front of me.

I try to get the thought of what's lurking in Sonny's boxers out of my mind, lest it put me off my dinner. I glance around the room, looking for Hope (ha!) but she's nowhere to be seen.

I do wonder what we're getting ourselves into. Something about this place just isn't right. The secrecy, the strange tasks, the discomfort. Perhaps it's just things seeming strange on the first day, and that it's all just going to take a bit of getting used to, but I don't know.

Suddenly, I'm even more worried about what we've got ourselves into, that's for sure.

11

Sonny and I stroll back to our suite, the soft glow of the hallway lights creating a warm ambience now that the bright sunny day has turned into a much cooler night.

'Well, that was interesting,' I say, when it feels like we're far enough away from everyone else.

'Yeah, I don't know what I was expecting, but not this,' he replies. 'Hope is... I don't know what Hope is.'

'Intense,' I offer up. 'And that stunt with the dinner was... yeah.'

I'm not sure either of us knows what to say. We're in shock.

I think I was expecting to come here, live it up, eat, drink, relax and maybe have a bit of talking therapy here and there. Oh, and I would do my job in the midst of it all, obviously. But long, sweaty hikes and essentially being starved to see how we would all react are not the kinds of things I anticipated. Suddenly, I'm a little worried.

As we approach our suite door, I don't think the lighting changes, but all at once it feels as though it is casting an unsettling glow. It's almost as though it's foreshadowing what is coming next, because as soon as the two of us walk through that door, knackered, ready for a good night's sleep, we are first going to have to address the elephant in the room – or in the bed, should I say – because obviously there is only one bed, but we're not a couple. In fact, we're almost the opposite of a couple. Oh, this is going to be so weird.

I glare at Sonny as we step inside the suite, his annoyingly carefree attitude making him seem like he isn't only unbothered, he's choosing to find this funny instead of awkward. I suppose that's his glass-half-full attitude, whereas I'm looking at it like my bed is only half-empty. I really, really don't want to have to share a bed with him. I can't even share a high-rise office building with him.

'Well,' I say, as the two of us just stand there, both staring at the imposing bed in the centre of the room.

'Well,' he echoes. 'Well, there's the bed or the bath. You would think they would give us a sofa too. But I suppose if this is a place where couples are supposed to fall back in love, they're going to make sure they share a bed.'

Oh, how I wish I could wipe that grin off his face, but nothing I say to him ever seems to do the trick. Everything is a joke to him. This whole situation is like something out of a sitcom, except there's no laugh track to make it less weird, just Sonny chuckling to himself at the absurdity of it all. I suppose it does make things a little easier sometimes, if you can see the funny side.

'How small-minded of them,' I joke. 'It's like they haven't even thought about the journalists coming here, posing as a fake couple, who might not want to share a bed.'

Sonny laughs.

'Okay, what are our options?' he asks. 'And before you ask, no, I'm not sleeping in the bath.'

'That was pretty much all I had,' I say with a laugh.

'It's quite big,' Sonny says, lying on the right-hand side of what is actually a pretty big bed.

I lie down next to him, examining the space between us with my hand. There's some but you wouldn't have to roll over much to collide bodies with the person next to you – something I'm very much hoping to avoid.

'I've actually been in training for this moment for most of my life,' I tell him. 'This sort of thing comes up in romcom movies all the time.'

Sonny laughs.

'Hit me with our options,' he says as he makes himself a little more comfortable.

'Option one: we build some kind of barrier down the centre of the bed – something that will physically prevent us from touching one another. But we would probably have to use the scatter cushions, which will take up a good chunk of the space.'

'And they are the biggest scatter cushions I have ever seen,' he points out.

'Big enough that you could fashion yourself some kind of floor bed out of them?' I ask optimistically.

'Not that big,' he laughs. 'What's option two?'

'Option two is that we roughly decide where the centre of the bed is, we don't mark it out, and we agree on our sides, but then one of us sleeps with our head at the top of the bed, and the other sleeps at the bottom.'

'I imagine the pros and cons to that one are obvious?' he replies.

'Yeah. Pros: we're not actually next to each other in the conventional sense. Cons: we're sleeping next to each other's feet, and if either of us rolls over, we'll probably kick the other person in the head.'

'So, I'm guessing that's your pick,' he jokes.

I smile and shrug. It might be the thing that finally wipes the grin off his face, but I've never been one for violence. Psychological warfare is more my style – but sadly it's Sonny's too, and he finds it much easier to be more ruthless than I am.

'You are missing one obvious option,' he starts.

'Oh, yeah, what's that?' I reply.

'We just embrace the awkwardness, and we spoon all night long,' he jokes. 'I don't mind if you want to be big spoon or little spoon, you can choose.'

'Oh, my gosh, that sounds amazing, I can't believe I didn't think of that,' I say sarcastically.

Hmm, what to do, what to do? As we fall silent for a moment, I realise that I can hear the ocean through our open patio door. The gentle roar is so relaxing. In fact, I can feel my breathing naturally synchronising with it, calming me down, each breath effortlessly drifting in and out like the tide. I have an app on my phone that is supposed to help me sleep, that plays all sorts of noises like rainfall and the lapping of ocean waves. The noise here would be so at home on the app, because it's so perfect it sounds almost fake – in fact, it's beyond perfect, because here (in what I'm told is real life, and not some sort of purgatory) you also get the breeze creeping in through the doors and all the dreamy smells coming in from outside. They say the sea air tires you out – imagine that coupled with a long-haul flight and long-ass hike. I am well and truly shattered. All the more reason to figure out what we're going to do here.

'So, what's the plan?' I ask.

I give Sonny a few seconds to reply but, when he doesn't say anything, I turn my head on my pillow to face him. And... he's fast asleep. He looks so comfortable, and so peaceful, and somehow watching him sleep makes me feel even more tired because a huge yawn escapes my body like an exorcism.

I am comfortable, lying here, and Sonny isn't that close to me. It's the first night, we're both shattered, I suppose I could just close my eyes too, drift off – even if it's just for a bit – until one of us wakes up with the energy and the brainpower to figure out what we do about this situation.

Yeah, we can sort it later, or in the morning, or whatever. But now – I yawn again – now I think I just need to sleep. I'm sure everything will seem easier in the morning.

12

I jolt awake with a start, my heart pounding like when you wake up from a nightmare, except I'm waking up in one – fun!

The room is shrouded in soft light, and for a moment, I'm disoriented. Then it hits me – along with another blast of a blaring horn-like sound that is coming from a speaker somewhere in the room. I instinctively clutch at my ears, because it's too early for that. The second one wakes Sonny, his expression pure bewilderment as he sits upright in bed.

'What the hell is that?' he asks sleepily. 'Is it a tsunami warning system?'

'I don't know, it's—'

'It's breakfast time.' Hope finishes my sentence for me, her voice booming through a speaker that I can't get eyes on, but that must be somewhere in our room given the volume of it.

'Tell me she isn't going to do this every day,' Sonny mutters, rubbing the sleep from his eyes.

'Could guests report to the dining room immediately for their breakfast,' Hope continues. 'We have a short window to eat before a busy day ahead of us.'

Hope sounds so calm – but it's hard to feel calm with her when it seems as though she's saying if we don't go get breakfast now, we might not get any at all.

I glance around the room, realising that we're both still fully clothed in our outfits from last night, and that we are still in the exact same positions we fell asleep in – no barrier required, my body must know to keep away from him, even in my sleep. My make-up is probably a mess, and my hair is definitely in no shape for public viewing.

'I'm not missing food,' Sonny says, springing to action, jumping to his feet and shrugging off his clothes.

'Yeah, it seems like we need to get it while we can,' I reply, pulling myself up.

We both rush to make ourselves presentable enough to go eat breakfast. I slip into a summer dress – a bright pink one, of course – that I find hanging in the wardrobe, and throw on the pair of chunky pink Crocs Sonny packed for me. Ahh, no, these I can get on board with. Next, I quickly fix my make-up in the bathroom mirror, trying to salvage whatever's left after a night of sleep in it. Some of the old comes off, some new goes on – it's a balancing act I've done before. In fact, I did it just this week, after my disaster of a double date with Sonny.

'Do we have a strategy for today?' he asks me as we hurry down the hallway.

'I think perhaps we need to see what the hell we're in for first,' I reply.

As we hurry to the dining room, the hallway seems eerily quiet as usual, the only sounds being our own footsteps echoing against the walls. It feels really early, although I have no idea what time it is. I don't feel like I got much sleep, though. The lack of clocks at Eden is both intriguing and unsettling. It really does feel like we've stepped out of reality, but I suppose we have in a way.

As we arrive in the dining room, we see that the other couples are already here, gathered around a table that looks like it's been laid out by one seriously health-conscious individual (or, more likely, an entire team of them). Fresh fruit juices, yoghurt parfaits, Instagrammable porridges – it all looks beautiful, as a visual spectacle, but as far as eating goes, it's not really my cup of tea. Cups of tea are my cup of tea. Where are the pastries, the toast, the sugary cereals? Hell, I'd even take some kind of healthy seedy all-bran muffin at this stage.

Hope stands at the head of the table, greeting us with that unnervingly pleasant smile – she can't always be that happy, surely?

'Good morning, everyone. Welcome to your first day at Eden. I trust you've all had a restful sleep?'

I exchange a tired glance with Sonny. Restful wouldn't be exactly what I would file it under.

'As you can see, breakfast is served,' Hope continues, gesturing to the breakfast spread set out in front of us. 'We prioritise health and well-being here at Eden. Breakfast is the most important meal of the day, after all. I trust you will have everything you need here.'

I raise my hand. I'm not usually the kind of person to raise my hand but something is missing.

'Is there tea or coffee?' I ask her.

'Not for breakfast,' she replies. 'As part of our wellness programme, we've decided to omit certain beverages that might not align with our philosophy. Caffeine is a toxin.'

Ha. Trust me, with the amount I drink, it would take an enormous amount of caffeine to intoxicate me.

I exchange a glance with Sonny, the caffeine withdrawal practically etched on my face. He grits his teeth playfully. Oh, yeah, it's all fun and games now. Just wait until this evening, see if you all like being around me then.

After Hope finishes her welcome speech, she informs us that we will all be participating in an initial one-on-two session this morning – meaning she is going to talk to us, one couple at a time.

I sip my smoothie. I don't know if it tastes extra healthy or if I'm just telling myself that it does because I resent that it isn't a double-shot caramel latte.

I worry about our upcoming one-on-two session. Sonny and I are going to be under the microscope, presenting Hope – who is supposedly the best relationship expert going – with the completely fabricated facts of our relationship and hoping she somehow falls for it.

'Thanks for asking about the tea,' Brittany says to me quietly. 'What kind of place doesn't have tea?'

'Right?' I reply.

'There are kettles, in the cupboards in our rooms,' she tells me. 'But no tea or coffee. What's the point?'

'Oh, that's just cruel,' I reply. 'I'm pretty sure there is caffeine in Sonny's shampoo. If we get desperate, we can try to brew some of that.'

Brittany laughs.

'It might come to that,' she admits.

As the breakfast continues and conversations start to circulate around the table, people naturally chat within their own couples. I catch snippets of the others' discussions. Duane and Brittany seem to be in their own world, whispering and exchanging glances – I wonder why they are here, what problems they could possibly be having. Danny and Izzy are engaged in an animated debate about their favourite breakfast foods, which is kind of cute, and lets me know that they are my kind of people too. Heath and Kellee really do seem like a couple in a mess, sharing little more than a few hushed words, their expressions more than hinting at the unspoken tension between them.

My thoughts are eventually interrupted by Hope's presence

behind us. She places a hand on each of our shoulders and leans forward.

'Lara, Sonny, I hope you've both enjoyed your breakfast, and that the lack of stimulants didn't present too much discomfort,' she says, kind of rudely, pretending she cares. 'Are you ready for your one-on-two session?'

'We're first?' Sonny says.

'Yes, you're first,' Hope replies. 'I'm very keen to get to know the both of you. I'll be in my office but, when you're ready, that beautiful lady over there is Carmen, she will show you where to come.'

'Great,' I say. 'Looking forward to it.'

All lies. I'm actually even more worried now. Why does she want to see us first? Why is she so keen to get to know us? Is she on to us?

I exchange a quick glance with Sonny, his expression mirroring my own wariness, but in a way that hopefully only I can detect.

'Absolutely,' he agrees.

'Excellent,' she replies. 'You're in for a transformative experience, I promise.'

Hope's smile doesn't waver, but her eyes seem to hold a mysterious spark that makes me nervous.

As she moves on to address the next couple, I lean in towards Sonny.

'Transformative experience,' I repeat to him. 'Best case, it's going to be cringe-inducing. Worst case, we're screwed.'

'It's going to be fine,' he reassures me, squeezing my hand, very much in character. Sonny chuckles softly, the sound oddly comforting in the middle of all this, whatever this is. 'At least we'll have something to laugh about later, whether it goes well or not.'

'There is that,' I reply.

For a moment we just smile together, the absurdity of the situation uniting us in an unexpected way. Dare I say it, life is so much easier when the two of us are on the same side.

I remind myself that I need to do what Sonny is doing. I need to keep myself in character and try not to worry. We're here now, I just need to do my best. I mean, so they figure us out, what's the worst thing they can do? They can't kill us or arrest us even. All they can do is send us home which, now that I know there's no tea here, might actually be preferable.

13

Sonny and I hover outside another nondescript door. It isn't the first time this week we've hovered outside an office together, waiting to see how much trouble we're in exactly, and if I thought the last time was nerve-racking, oh boy, it was practically mindful meditation in comparison to how I'm feeling now. My palms are sweating and it isn't just down to the tropical heat. I don't know why it didn't cross my mind that we would have to do something like this, that I would need to essentially perform under the microscope, but here we are, with nothing to do but give it a go and see what happens.

It's our first private session with Hope – our one-on-two, as she calls it – and while I am absolutely terrified, I am a little curious too. The door opens, revealing Hope's large office, but as I step inside, I can't help but raise an eyebrow.

Hope's office is suspiciously minimalist (then again, that might be how I would describe Hope herself), like she's intentionally designed it to reveal as little as possible about her. She's getting in your head, but no way are you getting in hers. Her walls are covered with abstract art that probably holds a deeper meaning than I'm qualified to decipher. I hope she doesn't have us say what we see, like when they show serial killers inkblots – I honestly feel like anything could happen in here. The furniture is sleek and modern, but almost clinical in its design. I'm half expecting her to enter wearing a lab coat and carry a clipboard, but she's dressed in her usual floor-length lightweight beige dress. It isn't the exact same dress as yesterday, but it's the same in basically every way you could think to describe it.

On the outside, Hope presents as anything but clinical. She is elegant and sophisticated, her blonde hair falling in waves around her shoulders, then stretching down all the way to her hips. She greets us with a warm smile that doesn't quite reach her eyes.

'Welcome to your one-on-two, Lara, Sonny,' she says. 'Please, have a seat.'

Aside from her desk, the only other visible pieces of furniture in the room are the leather sofa, which she instructs us to sit on, and her large wing-back chair that sits opposite. She takes a seat there, making her look a little like a supervillain.

We try to settle on the sofa across from her. Wow, with her chair being so much higher, seeing Hope almost looming over us, I really do feel like a specimen under a microscope. Hope's gaze is steady, her eyes not even blinking as she stares at us. I try my best not to squirm, not wanting to give anything away.

'Let's begin,' she says brightly, her tone composed and measured. 'Why don't you tell me about yourselves in your own words – I hate these files.'

I exchange a quick glance with Sonny, looking for confirmation that I should speak first, and then I clear my throat to buy myself a few more seconds.

'So, I'm Lara,' I start, my voice steady. 'I'm an influencer and also the heir to a series of racecourses in the UK. That's the family business, I'm not really anything to do with it, and I'm not exactly sure I want to either. I think horse racing is cruel.'

Ha. That last bit wasn't in the brief, it just flowed out of me.

'And I'm Sonny, the son of an actor, not much more to say than that,' Sonny jumps in, his tone casual as ever.

Hope nods, her scrutinising stare unyielding.

'Interesting. And how long have you two been together?' she asks.

Sonny looks at me, and I'm momentarily caught off guard by the intensity in his stare, so I just gawp at him until he answers.

'A couple of years,' he replies.

'So, what makes the two of you love each other?' she asks curiously.

I suppress a scoff and try to look at Sonny with adoration.

'He's very funny,' I say, slowly, as I try to muster up something else. 'Very funny and a lot of fun. Nothing is serious in Sonny's world.'

'Okay, Lara, I asked you why you love Sonny, but it sounds to me like you're criticising him,' Hope points out.

Sonny purses his lips, trying to suppress his smug smile, but you can tell he's loving this.

'Well, I'm just being honest,' I insist. 'Everything is a joke to him. He's a clown.'

This isn't in the brief either, it's just how I feel. Why waste a good therapy session if we're here, eh?

'I think the problem is more that Lara is so serious,' Sonny chimes in. 'Too serious. The clothes you're seeing her in, they're not her usual clothes, normally she dresses like she's on her way to a wake, she has a face like it too.'

'Why did you feel like you needed to bring different clothes?' Hope asks, raising an eyebrow.

I snap my neck towards Sonny.

'Oh my God, it was you who packed me this bright pink bag of crazy, you absolute psychopath,' I remind him.

'See, this is what I mean,' Sonny says, turning to Hope. 'She's losing it, over a bit of pink clothing that I packed to try to cheer her up. But she can't be cheered up, she's just so grumpy and I'm... I'm Sonny.'

He holds out his arms in a ta-da sort of way, his smile beaming like the ray of sunshine he thinks he is, as he slumps back into his chair.

'Interesting,' Hope says. 'Very interesting. Would you say you are a case of opposites attract?'

I sigh.

'In many ways,' I reply. 'But then there are also lots of things we have in common, so... I don't know.'

Christ, this is exhausting.

'Do you talk about these problems?' Hope asks.

'Well, let's just say that communication isn't exactly his strong suit,' I reply. 'In fact, he can be very secretive, and quite underhand.'

Sonny raises an eyebrow, a playful smile quirking his lips. We're so far out of character now, airing our real problems, that it actually makes us seem more like a real couple.

'Oh, because you would never do anything deceitful or dishonest to get ahead,' he replies. 'You think you're better than me but you're not.'

I roll my eyes, refusing to let him get under my skin.

'I don't care if I'm better than you,' I reply. 'You're the one always trying to compete with me, to one-up me, it's no wonder that occasionally I will give a little of that back. You're the one obsessed with being better than me.'

'Narcissist,' he replies.

'Clown,' I clap back.

Hope taps her fingertips together in an almost menacing manner.

'You two have an interesting dynamic,' she points out. 'You're right, that you do seem to clash, but at the same time I sense this bond between you, as though you're always on the same page, and yet you try to insist you're in different books. It's fascinating but it tells me, overwhelmingly, that the two of you are a great fit, you love one another, and you'll be together forever if you can just accept it.'

Well, well, well. That's interesting, isn't it? Hope is supposedly the world-leading expert on relationships, and she thinks Sonny and I are not only the real deal, but perfect for one another. This proves to me that Eden is nothing but shit, a grift to get huge chunks of money from people who are more than willing to part with it because they think they're getting something exclusive and elitist. Ah, well, at least I feel a bit easier about it all now, if that's her read on me and Sonny. Nothing to worry about.

'Well,' I interject, a little more confidently now, trying to keep this freak show on the road. 'Recently, it feels like we're... drifting apart.'

A cliché but a good one.

Hope leans forward slightly, her eyes locked on to ours. She looks at me for a few seconds, then Sonny, then back to me. Her eyes feel like a spotlight. When it isn't on you, you relax. When her beady eyes are back on you, you panic.

'In what way?' she asks.

'Well,' I begin cautiously, feeling the weight of her stare. 'We've been thinking about the future, and I'm not sure if I want a family.'

Sonny nods in agreement, trying to get back to our fake problems, instead of pointlessly addressing our real ones.

'Whereas I know I want a family, but I'm not entirely sure about marriage,' he adds.

Time to dial it up a notch.

'Sometimes it just feels like he refuses to agree with me on anything,' I blurt with a healthy dose of exasperation.

'I don't think that's fair,' Sonny adds.

'See, we can't even agree on whether or not we agree or disagree,' I tell Hope, frustrated. While our romantic relationship may be a sham, our professional one isn't, and I do feel frustrated with him. My God, it feels good to find a way to let it out.

'Sonny, what are your main grievances with Lara in the present? Forget about the future for now,' Hope asks.

Christ, don't ask him that, we'll be here all day.

Sonny leans forward, looking almost as though he is powering up.

'Oh, where do I even begin?' he starts. See! 'How about the fact that Lara can't stand not being in control? Or her refusal to consider any idea that's not her own?'

I clench my jaw as I try to keep my anger simmering below the surface, rather than letting it out into the room. I think, if I were to let that genie out of the bottle, there would be no forcing it back in.

'That's because your ideas usually involve unnecessary risks and end up in nothing but unhelpful chaos,' I reply.

'And there you go again, thinking you're right,' Sonny replies, applauding me.

Hope watches our exchange, her eyes twinkling with something that feels surprisingly close to amusement. Great, so long as we're keeping her entertained. I am so glad I'm not the one paying for this – they're certainly not paying me enough to be here.

'It's fascinating how well you two know each other's quirks,' she muses.

Sonny leans back in his chair, adopting a more serious expression.

'Well, when you've known each other as long as we have, you learn to read between the lines,' he says.

Hope's ears pick up.

'I though you said you had only been together for a couple of years?' she checks.

'Oh, we have,' I quickly chime in. 'But we first met back when we were at university.'

It's best to be honest, rather than trying to come up with a lie on the spot, one that we might get caught out with later.

'Our group session later will be sharing how each of you met, so I look forward to hearing more about it then,' Hope says with a smile, her calm demeanour unchanged. 'For now, though, you both seem to thrive on this dynamic. It seems as though it keeps you both going.'

I raise an eyebrow. Oh, yeah, Sonny makes my world keep turning – give me a break.

'Thriving might be a strong word,' I say. 'More like tolerating.'

'Surviving,' Sonny adds.

'Well, what if I told you that was a real asset?' Hope continues.

'An asset?' I reply in disbelief.

'Yes,' she says, her tone gentle. 'Your ability to challenge each other, to push each other's limits, could be the secret to all of your successes.'

Sonny smirks as that playful glint returns to his eyes.

'Well, look at that, Lara. We're actually a match made in heaven,' he says.

'And yet every second I'm around you, I feel like I'm in hell,' I snap back.

The room falls silent for a second. Sonny's smile drops and I can see Hope judging me. Was that too mean? I don't think it was. I'm sitting here dressed as candyfloss because of him. I don't think what I said was unreasonable.

'Sometimes all it takes is a little push, to help you find common ground again,' Hope says. 'Our session is over, for now, but your homework – which I would like you to do right now – is to go and "sea otter" in the pool. An hour should do it. I'll have Carmen or Lucian routinely check on you, so do take it seriously, please.'

'What does that mean?' I ask.

'Sea otters often hold hands to stop themselves from drifting apart and losing each other while sleeping in the water,' Hope explains. 'If the two of you are drifting apart, then I think that's just what you need.'

I stare at Sonny in disbelief, his expression mirroring mine as Hope calls Carmen into the room, instructing her to escort us to our room to change into our swimwear, and then to the pool for our 'sea otter' session.

Seriously, where the fuck are we right now?

Carmen walks us to our room and then stands in the hallway while we change, so we don't have a chance to say anything to each other.

I sigh and roll my eyes as I take the tiny bright pink bikini from my underwear drawer. Thank you, Sonny. Oh, how I can't wait to 'sea otter' in something I can't quite seem to contain any part of my body that isn't totally flat in.

'This way to the pool,' Carmen says.

Carmen sounds Spanish but, as is always the case with any accent I hear here, I don't think we're in Spain, or even Mexico. Something about the climate and the scenery here, and knowing that we're in January, I just can't quite place where we are. Nowhere makes sense.

'So, how are we supposed to float?' I ask Carmen. 'Just, like, bob around on our backs or...?'

'We have a double air mattress for the pool,' she explains. 'Part of the process will be harmonising your bodies, so that you can keep it afloat together.'

It's not that the prospect of floating around on a lilo for an hour, in a beautiful pool, under the warm sun doesn't sound relaxing. It's the fact that I'm supposed to do it with Sonny, holding his hand, with no escape from his hilarious banter and obnoxious charm.

As we step out into the pool area, the warm sun kisses our skin, and the cool water seems like it will be a welcome relief from the tension that filled Hope's office.

The luxury pool is surrounded by lush greenery, the gentle rustling of leaves creating a soothing backdrop. I should just try to focus on the positives of the moment. At least it gives us time off from our double life.

'There you go,' Carmen says, nodding towards the water.

Sure enough, there is our lilo.

We climb onto the pool float, managing to both get on it together, and I must admit that the sensation of the water beneath us is like a gentle caress – one that is seriously welcome right now. We hold hands, doing as we are told, and while this is incredibly fucking weird, and every reflex I have wants to push Sonny into the pool, the tension between us begins to let up again.

'I'll be back shortly,' Carmen tells us. 'Enjoy each other.'

Sonny waits, until Carmen is gone, before he says anything.

'You really gave it to me both barrels in there, didn't you?' he says. 'I'm almost impressed.'

'You didn't do so badly yourself,' I reply. 'But I suppose acting like we hate each other was always going to come naturally to us.'

'Oh, but didn't you hear?' he says. 'We're in love. She can tell.'

I laugh at the sarcasm in his voice. He's as pessimistic about this stuff as I am. So much for his 'Sonny' attitude.

'Seriously for a second, though,' he says, lowering his voice, adopting a far more serious tone. 'This place is fucking weird.'

'Right?' I reply. 'Starving us, making us pretend we're sea otters – what the fuck?'

'There could be an opportunity in all of this though,' he says. 'We can do what we came here to do, to get the low-down on Duittany, but there's so much more to learn here. Why don't we write a piece about Eden, exposing it? I'm sure the world would love to know about what goes on here.'

'Do you think?' I reply.

'Come on, Lara, this is a freak show,' he replies. 'Don't you think it feels like Hope is screwing with us?'

'So, what, she just bleeds rich dummies dry while she messes with them for sport?'

'Can you think of any other reason she would be like this?' he asks. 'We can see how it goes, it's only our first day, but something isn't right here.'

'I've been thinking that ever since we arrived,' I confess. 'Okay, let's see what we can find out.'

'This just got a lot more interesting, didn't it?' he says – I can tell that he's smiling again.

It certainly has. Just when you think things can't get any weirder, you find yourself pretending to be an otter, with no idea what continent you're even on, cosying up with your workplace rival.

I sigh. Wow, it's a tale as old as time.

14

I don't know what I was expecting from dinner tonight. Somehow this ain't it, and yet it feels like it is exactly what I should have been preparing myself for.

What is it? I don't know.

It's something healthy, obviously. Cooked eggs and vegetables with a smoothie on the side. It's the kind of food that – if you're someone like me – you only ever really make yourself eat when you're on a diet, trying to lose weight. The kind of thing that leaves you with a hollow, dissatisfied feeling in your stomach.

I don't usually mind a smoothie but even that isn't hitting the spot. But, of course, if this wellness retreat isn't going to let us have caffeine, then obviously booze is quite literally off the table too. So thick green goo it is – cheers.

There is plenty of stuff on the table, don't get me wrong, it's just lacking anything remotely comforting. No warm, crusty bread, no glasses of wine to take the edge off the day. Just vibrant colours and a sense of impending, healthy sadness.

Hope is sitting at the head of the table, a serene smile on her face, and I can't help but wonder if she ever secretly indulges in a big sloppy cheeseburger and a huge glass of Coke.

'This evening, I thought it might be nice if each couple were to share the story of how they met,' Hope suggests.

The room falls silent as we all wait to see who is prepared to go first.

Heath leans back in his chair. He laughs, probably at the awkward silence, and then takes a deep breath.

'I guess I'll go first then,' he starts. 'I was attending a film premiere, minding my own business, when someone made a beeline for me because I'm rich.'

'Well, that's funny,' Kellee says, not looking at all amused. 'Because the way I remember it is that you targeted me because I was young and you thought I might make you seem young too.'

'Why would I target you when I had a date with me?' he replies.

'Laura?' Kellee scoffs in disbelief. 'Laura, who we all know has chlamydia.'

'*Had* chlamydia,' Heath corrects her. 'Laura *had* chlamydia.'

The room falls silent again.

Hope, while still keeping her mask-like smile firmly in place, looks ever so slightly rattled by this exchange. I swear I can see a bead of sweat forming on her head. Still, ever the professional, she moves us along.

'Danny, Izzy, how did the two of you meet?' Hope asks them.

Izzy's fingers intertwine with Danny's as they share a look.

'We met at college,' Izzy says, taking the lead. 'It was before Danny signed for Liverpool City, back when we were just normal teenagers.'

'Wow, that feels like a long time ago,' Danny says with a sigh. 'It feels like looking back at different people, if that makes sense?'

That is the most I've heard Danny say, in more ways than the obvious one, since we met. He sounds almost as though he misses his old life. I suppose it can't be easy, being a young footballer, going from college to playing for one of the top clubs (I'm no football fan, but I'm pretty sure that's right) in the country.

And speaking of being propelled into stardom...

'We met on set,' Brittany tells the room. 'It's funny, how many on-screen couples end up being couples in real life. You never think it will happen to you but...'

'...but we just hit it off,' Duane continues.

Wow, they're even finishing each other's sentences. What *are* they doing here?

'And finally, Lara and Sonny,' Hope prompts us. 'How did the two of you meet?'

Aware that all eyes are on us, I clear my throat, ready to take the lead.

'Well, Sonny and I... we first crossed paths at university,' I begin, offering up a little bit of truth, now that it's canon. 'But it wasn't until more recently that we, you know, got together.'

'Oh, wow, so you're kind of like us,' Izzy says with a smile. 'Were you friends back then?'

Ha. We're not even friends now.

Sonny doesn't say anything so I take the lead. He doesn't like me bringing up that we knew each other at uni in front of other people, lest I say too much, preferring to operate a more selective memory. It infuriates me that he thinks he can curate our history when it comes to what other people get to see.

'Not exactly,' I reply tactfully. 'We didn't really know each other until we ended up doing our work experience at the same place, at the end of our first year.'

'That's probably the only work you two have ever done,' Heath quips.

Ah, good old Heath. He must have some seriously redeeming features, hidden deep down, because I can't imagine why Kellee puts up with him. He might actually be more annoying than Sonny, and I can hardly stomach working in the same industry as him, never mind being in an actual relationship.

After the dinner conversation winds down and everyone's plates are clear (or as clear as they will get in my case), Hope takes to her feet.

'I think an early night is in order,' she announces. 'We have a big day ahead of us tomorrow. Go, get to your rooms with your partners, and enjoy one another.'

There's only one thing I would enjoy right now and it isn't Sonny.

'I'll catch you up,' I tell Sonny.

I push my chair back and stand up, stretching my arms above my head, killing a little time while I allow the others to filter away from the table so that I can speak to Hope alone.

'Hi, Hope, gorgeous dinner, thank you,' I start, buttering her up – assuming she knows what butter is. 'I was wondering if I might be able to get a teabag. I noticed that there were kettles and cups in the rooms and, to be honest with you, I've got a bit of a headache. I think you're supposed to gradually wean yourself off caffeine, when your body is used to it so…'

My voice tapers off. She isn't going to care, is she?

'Okay, wait there,' she says. 'I'll be back in a moment.'

I try to contain my grin as she disappears into the kitchen. She returns with one teabag on a tea plate.

'Oh, thank you,' I tell her. 'You don't…'

My voice trails off again. It's a camomile teabag. Somehow I feel like I have even less tea than I did before I asked.

'Go, have sweet dreams,' she tells me.

'Thanks,' I reply flatly.

I take my sad little non-caffeinated teabag to my suite.

'Are you okay?' Sonny asks. 'You look sort of devastated.'

'I can't believe there's no caffeine here,' I moan. 'And I can't believe you're not as upset as I am. I've seen how much coffee you drink.'

I slump down on the bed next to him.

'She just gave me a camomile teabag,' I tell him, showing it to him. 'I'm not even sure what camomile is, but I know that you can't dunk a custard cream in it.'

Sonny laughs.

'Okay, come with me,' he says, pulling himself to his feet. 'I actually know a really good cure for a caffeine withdrawal headache.'

'Are you joking?' I ask him. 'If there's a punchline, can you just get it over with, please?'

'No, I'm serious,' he tells me. 'And, if this doesn't help – I don't know – I'll sleep in the bath, so you can have the bed to yourself.'

My eyebrows shoot up.

'Okay, I'm listening,' I reply. 'It's not anything weird, is it?'

I climb off the bed and head over to Sonny, who is hanging around near the wardrobes. He opens one, filling the kettle, before clicking it on. Then he sets two mugs down in front of it. Honestly, why do they even give us a kettle and mugs? It's almost as though they are trying to torture us.

'So, first step is boil the kettle,' he tells me. 'The next step is – can I have that camomile teabag, please?'

I hand it over reluctantly.

'I'm pretty sure it doesn't have any caffeine in it,' I tell him. 'And it kind of stinks.'

'The next step is we throw this in the bin,' he continues, dropping it in the bin below us. 'And then finally...'

Sonny pulls his suitcase out of the wardrobe. He unzips it to show me inside. It's empty.

'Okay,' I say with a laugh. 'Is this like a placebo thing or...?'

Sonny fidgets with the side of the suitcase before appearing to get his hands on something – a zip I've only just noticed – before he unzips a secret compartment.

'Oh my God,' I blurt.

Inside the secret compartment of Sonny's suitcase there are teabags, sachets of instant coffee, and little plastic packets of UHT milk.

'I would have brought biscuits too, if I had known the food was going to be so shit,' he jokes. 'Anyway, help yourself.'

I don't know how else to describe what I'm doing right now other than launching myself at him.

I grab him and I squeeze him tightly.

'Wow, imagine how happy you would be if I'd brought real milk,' he jokes.

I quickly let go of him, well aware I'm probably making things awkward.

'I just... I'm just... I can't thank you enough,' I babble.

'From one caffeine junkie to another,' he tells me. 'What's mine is yours.'

I laugh.

'You know, when Lucian said he had unpacked our bags, I thought you seemed a bit nervous,' I tell him. 'Now I know why. Oh, thank God he didn't find them.'

'Yeah, I was worried for a minute,' he tells me. 'Anyway, go on, get ready for bed. I'll bring your tea over to you.'

'You keep going like this and we might just fall in love after all,' I tell him.

I know, that joke is a bit full-on, but honestly, this might be the happiest I have ever been in my life. I practically skip to the bathroom, to take my make-up off and put my PJs on, giddy to get in bed and drink my cup of tea.

Suddenly, everything feels like it's going to be a whole lot easier. Then again, it is just a cup of tea.

15

I didn't realise that yoga was going to be such a huge part of being a healthy adult.

While I'm sure that lots of people do enjoy and benefit from it, I am not one of those people. I'm not flexible enough (which ironically I am told yoga will help with) and whenever I've tried, the blood has always rushed to my head or my boobs have found a way to press against my windpipe or I've just generally embarrassed myself.

Needless to say, the worst news I could have been given over my mediocre, fruit-based breakfast was that we would be spending our morning doing 'couples' yoga' – I'm hoping the 'couples' part means that Sonny can do it, and I can just watch or spot him or something. Honestly, he'll love it, look at that man bun on top of his head, he looks like the kind of guy who would climb a mountain, to do yoga at the top, just to find himself. I've already found myself today, at the bottom of a teacup. I can't even imagine entertaining such a thing as 'couples' yoga' without a nice strong cuppa in me.

I don't know what time we were up today. We were woken by the horn again – so to speak – and Hope's announcement that breakfast was ready. It felt early, though. It was still quite cool out and I felt like the remnants of dawn were lingering, although don't ask me how I know that. I'm still finding it so strange, not having any clocks around, but I feel like my body is trying to figure out different ways to keep tabs on the time. For what it's worth, anyway. Time seems to mean nothing here.

Honestly, this place calls itself a wellness retreat, but the only thing it's making me feel is sick – mentally and physically. It feels more like it's designed to torture than it is to heal. My body feels knackered, my headache is still lingering, and while he swung it back around slightly last night by finally revealing his secret stash of tea and coffee to me, I've never wanted to kill Sonny more.

The outdoor yoga area is a great spot for taking in the fresh morning air – if you're into that sort of thing. The space is certainly serene, surrounded by greenery that is so beautiful it looks fake, and the distant sound of wind chimes (although I suspect the sound is coming from a hidden speaker somewhere). Large, colourful mats are spread out in a circle, each with a pair of small cushions placed neatly on them. Nice, let's all face one another, I wouldn't want anyone here to miss me embarrassing myself.

I look over at Duane and Brittany, watching them stretch together, the two of them seemingly so in sync with one another. Everyone always talks about how they ooze sexual chemistry, how you can practically get pregnant by simply standing next to them, but all I feel when I'm around them is love.

In the centre, there's a tall, bearded man – Brett, our instructor – setting up his own special mat.

Brett looks like a pretty zen guy. He's muscular, but he boasts a lean build, a stark contrast to Sonny's buff body and bulging biceps. He's American – given away by his accent – which only seems to make him more attractive.

Izzy and Kellee aren't exactly subtle, giggling like little girls, their laughter kicking up a gear every time Brett bends over.

'I'll just fetch some water,' Brett tells us, grinning, because he can tell the girls are swooning over him. 'I'll be right back.'

'Oh, he could put me in a downward dog any day of the week,' Kellee announces, biting her lip for effect.

'He'd be more likely to put you down,' Heath quips.

'Yeah, those are my yoga goals, right there,' Kellee persists. 'Lara, have you seen those guns?'

Oh, God, don't drag me into this.

'She's here with Thor,' Heath reminds her. 'Her gun quota is met.'

'Lucky her,' Kellee says, quickly shutting up when Brett arrives back with his water, taking his place in the centre of the yoga circle.

'Hey, everyone. I'm Brett, and I'll be your guide for today's session,' he announces. 'Today, we're diving into couples' yoga – a beautiful practice that's all about connection, trust, and shared relaxation. So, grab your partner and let's get started.'

I reluctantly sidle up to Sonny. I honestly think I would rather be partners with anyone else – actually, anyone but Heath. Sonny is marginally more tolerable than him.

'Let's begin,' Brett says calmly. 'Come to a comfortable seated position, back to back with your partner, and slowly but firmly push your backs together. Close your eyes. Take a deep breath in, then out, in, then out. Repeat this for a moment. Feel your partner connecting with you. With each breath in, draw in their love, with each breath out, send love back.'

Ugh, doing this with Sonny is probably poisoning me. I dread to think what he is sending my way.

'Very good,' Brett tells us. 'Now that your breathing is synchronised, I want you to mix it up. As your partner inhales, you exhale. As you exhale, your partner inhales. Next, keeping your eyes closed, reach back with your arms, locking your elbows with your partner, and then take it in turns at leaning forwards, one partner bowing towards the floor while the other fully stretches out their back, and then switch.'

Obviously, Sonny and I both try to go forwards at the same time, that's how absolutely not in sync we are.

'I'll stretch forward first,' he says quietly.

'Ow, ow, I can't do that,' I tell him. My eyes snap open. I feel like I'm on a torture rack. 'You're lifting me off the floor.'

'Okay, let's go your way,' he replies.

Nope, that's not working either.

'Okay, now my boobs are crushing my ribs,' I insist. 'I don't think I'm meant to bend this way.'

I notice that everyone's eyes are open now – and all of them are on us.

'Trust me to get saddled with a useless partner,' Sonny jokes to the room.

He's clearly joking but, yikes, I feel so embarrassed now.

'Let's try something else,' Brett insists. 'Carmen, if you can help me demonstrate, please.'

Brett beckons over a member of staff, Carmen, who seems only too happy to oblige.

'See, it's all about communication and cooperation,' Brett explains.

Brett walks us through various two-person poses. Some are easy enough – simple moves standing side by side, holding hands and so on, which I can just about manage – but then they start to get a bit more involved. Everyone else here clearly does this sort of thing – or some exercise, at least – all the time, and they all have a physical connection that gels. With me and Sonny, it's almost as though we begrudge touching one another.

'And now: flying,' Brett announces.

Well, that doesn't sound good.

'Guys, get down on the floor, ladies, stand in front of them,' Brett instructs. 'Wow, it's getting warm out here now.'

I stare at Brett expectantly, ready to see this move I'm probably not going to be able to do, only to watch him slowly peel off his vest.

Kellee wolf-whistles, causing Brett to blush lightly as he bats it off with a smile.

'Now, this is an acroyoga pose, but a simple one,' Brett begins to explain.

I don't even know what acroyoga is.

'Guys, while lying on the ground, plant your feet firmly on your partner's hips. Girls, reach forward and take your guy's hands like this. Guys, slowly straighten your legs. And then, girls, all that is left for you to do is fly.'

We watch as Brett uses his feet to lift Carmen up into the air. She holds her position high above him, flying, like Baby from *Dirty Dancing*.

'Hold this position and breathe deeply until you're ready to come out of the pose,' Brett continues. 'To exit the position, guys, slowly bend your knees like this. Girls, simply lower your feet to the floor.'

Brett and Carmen are back on their feet – they make it look so easy.

Acroyoga... acro as in acrobat? Because that's what it seems like.

'You were keeping a close eye on Brett then,' Sonny muses as he lies on his back. 'Don't tell me you fancy him too.'

'I was watching to see how the move or the pose or whatever you call it was done,' I reply.

That said – and I can only go off physical attraction, obviously – of course I fancy Brett. He's good-looking, he's chilled, he's got that calming, soothing voice, he's strong, and he's got a body that should be gracing fitness magazines. But I really was just studying the move.

'Well, presumably you won't butcher this one,' Sonny says.

I just pull a face at him as I take my position. Sonny places his feet on my hips, I reach out and take his hands, and then I lean forward. His legs being like actual tree trunks means that he has no trouble holding me up. However, I'm not at all strong, so I slowly start folding at the hips, snapping closed over him like a book.

'Struggling?' Sonny asks me.

'You just focus on not dropping me,' I reply, trying to concentrate, trying to straighten myself out.

As I lean forward, I can't help but feel like I'm about to fall. However, if I lean back, my feet edge towards the floor again.

'Lara, if you—'

'I'm trying,' I snap at him, frustrated. I feel like I'm the only person in the room who can't do it.

Maybe I'm imagining it, but I could swear that the sides of Sonny's mouth are twitching, edging into a grin, like he's trying not to laugh at me, or silently making fun of me or...

All of a sudden, I lurch forward, and I try everything I can think of to correct myself, but I'm toppling over and there's nothing I can do to stop it. It all happens in the blink of an eye. My limbs flail and before I know it, I'm on top of him, straddling him as though I were trying to ride him. Awkward.

There's a chorus of laughter from the rest of the group. I feel my cheeks burning.

'Yoga, Lara, not the Kama Sutra,' Heath calls out. 'Save that for when you're in your room.'

I quickly try to clamber off him but, as I try to gain some momentum to pull myself up, I actually do kind of ride him for a second or two, so, never let anyone say you can't make an awkward situation even worse.

Brett comes running over.

'Lara, are you okay?' he asks me. Then he turns to Sonny. 'You dropped her.'

'No, I didn't,' Sonny scoffs.

'You did,' Brett says accusingly. 'I saw you.'

'It's her core, she needs to work on it,' Sonny insists. 'She couldn't hold herself up. I did my bit.'

Cool, cool, cool, let's all talk loudly about how physically unfit I am.

'Partner yoga is a balancing act – no pun intended,' Brett says. 'A harmonisation of two bodies. You should be one. Look, Lara, come here for a moment, please.'

My gaze snaps to Brett. I point at myself, as if to check he means me, when it's obvious that he does, but this situation has me nervous.

'Yeah, come here,' he says as he lies down on the floor. 'Try to move with me.'

Yay, another opportunity to embarrass myself.

With Brett's guidance, I settle into the starting position again, feeling more at ease this time around. Brett's touch is gentle and reassuring as he instructs me, and when he uses his feet to lift me into the air, it's surprisingly effortless. I'm hovering, held up by his strength and expertise – and somehow my core is up to the job this time, holding my body straight. A ripple of applause and cheers from the group echoes around. I can't help but beam with a mix of accomplishment and sheer surprise. It's a strange feeling, being up here and actually holding the pose, after my previous less-than-graceful attempt. Wow, this is quite relaxing.

'I'm going to get a drink,' I hear Sonny say with a sigh.

'I'll come with you, Thor,' his bestie Heath replies.

'See, it's easy when you work together,' Brett tells me.

'My hero,' I tell him. 'Thank you. I was starting to think something was wrong with me. You can lower me down.'

'I can do this all day,' he tells me with a wink.

Ooh, that seemed quite flirtatious. I'm glad Sonny missed that or he might think we were in it – whatever it is – together.

Brett lowers me down slowly to my feet before joining me, back up at eye level.

'Did you feel it there?' he asks me, rubbing my stomach gently with the back of his hand.

'Erm, yeah,' I just about blurt, a little flustered at his touch, but in a good way.

'I can give you some extra lessons while you're here,' he suggests. 'If you would like to get more confident. You would be in safe hands, I promise.'

'I'd really like that,' I reply.

Kellee sidles up next to us. Actually, she practically steps between us.

'Are you single, Brett?' she asks, coming right out with it.

Brett chuckles, unrattled by her question. He looks like he might get asked that question a lot.

'Yeah, I am,' he tells her. 'There's not much chance of finding love, when you work at a couples' retreat.'

'Ah, but there's not zero chance,' she tells him in a breathy voice before turning on her heel and walking away.

Brett looks at me, widening his eyes.

'It's a shame,' he tells me once it's just the two of us. 'Because sometimes, when you do what I do, and you get up close with people like I just did with you, you feel this powerful connection there. But when you're working with couples... it's a shame.'

'It is a shame,' I say, my mouth moving before my brain can instruct it. I probably shouldn't have said that. I might be single, in real life, but at Eden I am very much a taken lady.

Ugh. He's single, I'm single, we're in paradise. What a perfect place this would be for a holiday romance. And now my imagination is running away with me because a man I just met did a bit of yoga with me. A seriously good-looking and charming man, though. A seriously good-looking and charming *single* man no less. Typical.

16

Wherever we are – the island, the country, the continent – it's beautiful. I'm actually disappointed that I can't come back here under normal circumstances, for a proper holiday. Everything is great apart from the retreat itself – and the company, obviously. But imagine coming here for a vacation. Sunbathing, taking a dip in the pool (without sea-ottering with your sworn enemy), drinking cocktails, eating delicious food, striking up a holiday romance. Ugh, it sounds like heaven. Ahh, well, at least I can enjoy the scenery.

The beach is a picturesque blend of pristine sand and crystal-clear water. The sun beams down brightly above, giving everything a warm glow and sprinkle of glitter. It's a warm day, the kind that makes you want to curl up in the sun and fall asleep. But standing here on the beach, with Hope about to address us, a big pile of wood behind her, it doesn't seem like a nap is what we are here for.

I think we're all tired, sweaty and achy from the yoga earlier – well, I am, at least.

'Good afternoon,' Hope addresses us, her voice carrying over the gentle sound of waves crashing against the shore.

'Hey, Thor, I'm not fancying this much,' Heath says to Sonny under his breath. 'Hopefully it's something we can sneak away from. I fancy a swim in the sea.'

Sonny smiles back at him before turning his attention back to Hope.

'All right, everyone, it's all hands on deck today,' she announces. 'Our challenge is to build a wooden shelter by the beach. Something sturdy and enclosed that will provide sanctuary to those who need it. Some materials will be provided, and the rest must be collected from the surroundings. I'll be assigning your individual jobs now.'

Oh, boy, that sounds physical. Was no one listening when we all discussed my lack of core strength earlier?

Hope stands before us, her presence commanding. She's like a tidal wave that is about to engulf us all, as we wait to see what jobs we're all being given.

Sometimes I forget that we're all paying a lot of money to be here, on purpose; this isn't a rehab or a punishment. It's supposed to be a couples' retreat. I would be livid if I had paid all that money just to come here and do building work for them.

'Sonny, Heath, Duane, and Danny, you will be assuming building duties,' Hope announces, her tone clear and decisive.

The four of them all look at one another, as if to assess if anyone might be used to manual labour, but I don't think any of them feel good about the situation.

Hope swiftly moves on, leaving no pause for any kind of protest, and addresses her next victims – sorry, I mean workers.

'Kellee and Izzy, you'll be going with Carmen to gather materials for crafting some of the items that we will need,' she informs them.

I can't help but admire Kellee's death stare. She's clearly not happy about this but Izzy takes her arm in hers, letting her know it will be okay, and they'll do it together.

Hope's eyes settle on Brittany next.

'Brittany, you'll be joining Lucian to learn how to turn seawater into drinking water,' she informs her.

Brittany looks unsure, like this might be out of her comfort zone, but she shrugs it off and smiles.

'It could be good to learn a new thing,' she reasons. 'I suppose you never know when a skill like that might come in handy.'

A quick scan around the beach catches my brain up to the fact that everyone has a job but me. I'm the only one left. But what jobs are left to do? Oh, God, tell me I'm not on toilet duty. I don't even know what it would entail but I'm not into it.

As Hope's eyes land on me, I try to keep my expression neutral.

'Lara, you'll be gathering fruits from the woods,' she tells me. 'And you'll have Brett's assistance.'

A flicker of something passes between Sonny and me, the mention of Brett's name flagging… something. I don't know what, but I do my best not to react to it. Yeah, fine, cool, it's just me and the sexy yoga instructor going off into the forest together. No big deal.

'When all is said and done, the Eden staff will assess which couples put in the most and least effort,' Hope continues. 'The team that contributes the least will be living in the shelter they build for the foreseeable future. How pleasant that experience will be depends on everyone's hard work, as you're only as strong as your weakest link.'

A collective murmur ripples through the group. I don't think anyone likes the sound of that. I mean, I know I don't, how the hell will I brew my contraband tea out here?

As if summoned by fate, Brett appears by my side with a cheeky smile and an encouraging nod.

'Ready to do this, Lara?' he asks.

'Sure,' I reply. 'Let's go.'

Thinking about it, I might have the best job of everyone – although it would be kind of cool to find out how to turn seawater into drinking water.

My eyes betray me as they briefly flicker over in Sonny's direction. He gives me a half-wave, interrupted by Heath giving him a manly slap on the back.

'Thor, you're on lifting duty,' Heath tells him. 'Let's get a move on because there's no bloody way I'm swapping my suite for this beach, no matter how good a job we do.'

Brett and I walk for a minute or two, away from the group and into the forest, before eventually he breaks the silence.

'Heath seems like a handful,' he says with a laugh.

'Yeah, who knew billionaires were crazy?' I reply. 'I can't quite figure out what his deal is, but I don't think he's overly impressed with me.'

'His wife seems to like me,' Heath replies. 'She came to talk to me again, after our session earlier, asking if she could have some one-on-one time. She's very flirtatious.'

'Yeah, I'm not sure what's going on there,' I say. 'Or here. Or ever.'

Brett laughs.

As we walk deeper into the forest, a strange sensation starts in my stomach and then spreads to my chest. It's almost like first-date nerves, which is ridiculous because this isn't a date, it's an expedition to get fruit for our captor. Maybe it's the unfamiliarity of being alone with someone who isn't Sonny, to be spending time with a man who doesn't drive me crazy, or perhaps it's Brett's calming presence that's ironically unsettling my equilibrium.

The deeper into the forest we go, the greener our surroundings get – and, probably, the more I stick out like a sore thumb in my bright pink shorts and baby-pink T-shirt. The air feels so much fresher here, and the scent of earth and greenery and all the different plants makes everything feel so clean. It's a different world from the pristine luxury of the resort, and a million miles from life in London, where pollution is one of your meals.

'What shall we chat about?' Brett asks.

As we continue walking, I ask the first question that pops into my mind.

'What kinds of fruits can we find here?' I enquire, sounding a lot like a child. What a babyish question.

'Oh, lots,' Brett replies, not exactly sharing my enthusiasm for the subject. 'Mangos, papayas, coconuts, banana figs.'

'Banana figs?' I repeat back to him, my curiosity unashamedly piqued.

'Yeah,' he replies, swiping some leaves away so that we can get through into a clearing.

'Is it more like a banana or a fig?' I persist.

'You'll know when you see it,' Brett says with a laugh. 'Come on, let's keep looking.'

'There aren't any cheeseburgers growing on the island, are there?' I joke. 'Or a pizza, or a bag of crisps even. I am so, so hungry, and whatever a banana fig is, I don't think it's going to hit the spot.'

'Are you not enjoying the food here?' he asks curiously.

'It's just not my thing,' I reply, realising that it's probably very much his. 'I live in London and I work long hours. Fast food is a steady part of my diet.'

'A little fast food never hurt anyone,' he says with a smile.

Curious to know more about Brett, I dare to make my questions a little more personal.

'Where did you grow up?' I ask, alternating between glancing at him and looking where I'm going.

'I'm from Oregon originally,' he says. 'The Pacific Northwest. Nature has always been a big part of my life. I love doing stuff like this.'

'You can tell,' I reply. 'You have a really relaxing vibe about you.'

Brett smiles with his eyes.

'Thank you,' he says sincerely. 'Yeah, I've always been drawn to yoga, mindfulness, and well-being. Even as a kid, I found solace in these practices. It's what led me to work at different retreats, and then eventually here.'

I'm intrigued by his journey, but more than anything else, I wonder what he knows about Eden.

'Do you know where "here" actually is?' I ask.

'Honestly, I don't,' Brett replies, sounding sincere, so I'm pretty sure I believe him. 'I'm not a permanent staff member. Eden rotates its yoga instructors, you guys are actually my last group before I move on to my next adventure.'

'Doesn't it drive you mad, not knowing?' I ask. 'I've only been here a few days and I can't stop thinking about it – that and caffeinated drinks and fast food, anyway.'

'It passes, I promise – you ask a lot of questions,' he says, changing the subject as the realisation hits him.

Of course I do, I'm a journalist.

'I've always been nosy,' I reply, which I suppose isn't untrue.

'Fair enough. Well, let me turn the tables,' he says with a cheeky grin. 'Are you a celebrity? Lots of guests here are celebrities.'

'No, definitely not,' I quickly insist. 'I'm an influencer, I guess. But most of my money comes from my family.'

I sense a hint of embarrassment creeping into my tone, even though the statement isn't true about real me.

'Hey, there's no need to be embarrassed,' he reassures me. 'Money and status don't define us.'

That's a relief because I don't have much of either.

'All my family ever gave me was stress and the feeling that I would never be good enough,' he says through a self-conscious chuckle.

I wasn't expecting his vulnerability and it softens me even more. I offer a supportive smile.

'Well, from what I've seen, you're more than good enough,' I insist. 'Don't let anyone make you feel otherwise.'

'I could say the same to you,' he replies. 'Sonny seems to put you down.'

'Oh,' I blurt, caught off guard.

I wasn't expecting him to say that.

'We just have a strange relationship,' I say. 'Teasing is sort of his thing.'

'Well, that makes him sound like an asshole,' Brett replies, raising an eyebrow. 'I guess you just don't seem very happy with him... if you don't mind me saying.'

I'm really caught off guard now, and unsure how to respond.

'It's complicated,' is all I say – because explaining that we're actually in a fake relationship, and why we're here, probably won't go down all that well.

'Let's simplify it,' he suggests. 'What do you like about him?'

'He's got a good sense of humour,' I say, kind of weakly, because I don't always find him funny. 'And a big—'

'Snake,' he replies.

I blush.

'Erm...'

'Over there,' he says, lowering his voice. 'There's a snake.'

I follow his gaze, and I don't exactly get eyes on it, but I see the long grass moving. He means an actual snake! My heart races for a moment, and I instinctively step back.

Brett's response is fast; he grabs my hand and pulls me well out of the snake's path, and before I know it, my back is pressed against a tree trunk. He stands in front of me, forming some kind of human shield – one that I'm very grateful for.

I let out a shaky breath, a mixture of relief (because Brett is handling it) and lingering unease (because it turns out I'm scared of snakes).

'Okay, well, now I know I'm scared of snakes,' I admit, trying to sound playful, but I'm rattled – no pun intended.

'I guess you have to encounter one, to know if you're scared of them or not,' he reasons. 'But you have nothing to be scared of. I'm here.'

As I try to calm my racing heart, Brett catches me by surprise with an unexpected move. He leans in closer, his breath warm against my skin. The unexpected sensation of his beard grazing my neck makes me shiver. It's an intimate gesture that sends a tingle through my entire body.

'You smell amazing,' he says. 'What is that? Is that perfume?'

'Erm, I think so,' I blurt.

Smooth move, Lara. Great reply. Looking real cool.

Brett finally pulls away, but ever so slowly. His lips hover in front of mine for a fraction longer than usual. Long enough for me to figure out what he's doing: he's giving me the opportunity to kiss him – if I want to. It's a moment of vulnerability, a chance for something more. If this were a normal holiday, I might accept. There's definitely the hint of chemistry between us, like there's something we have in common that I haven't quite tapped into yet, but this isn't a normal holiday, and he thinks I have a boyfriend.

I can't forget that I'm here with Sonny, even if our relationship is a sham. A kiss with Brett, no matter how tempting, would be crossing a line that I just can't get away with right now.

With nothing happening, Brett's lips slowly retreat, and I manage a small smile.

'We should go get the fruit,' I suggest, my voice unsteady. 'I don't want to bump into any more snakes.'

'Of course,' Brett replies, his expression understanding, but with an edge of disappointment. He steps back, allowing the space between us to widen. 'Let's do what we came to do.'

As we start walking again, I can't help but feel mixed emotions. Brett's unexpected advances have left me both flustered and intrigued. He's not like the typical image I had of yoga instructors, especially one working at a couples' retreat. He seems like a bit of a bad boy, like there are hidden depths to him that I'm curious to find out more about.

I'm here to do a job, not to enjoy myself, and even if my relationship is fake, I am in it nonetheless.

It's a shame, really. This was just starting to get interesting.

17

As I sit on the beach, I dig my sore feet into the soft, warm sand and it soothes them a little. My legs are aching too, after an afternoon of foraging for food with Brett. I can't help but feel a genuine sense of pride washing over me, though. It was hard work, but I did it.

The deliciously warm summer evening sun casts a golden glow down over us, bathing us in the best weather of the day. All that's left for the sun to do is set, painting the sky with its usual array of beautiful colours, and I'm actually looking forward to it.

Us girls have all wrapped up our tasks, and the boys are putting the finishing touches on their wooden shelter. I want to say that it's a scene straight out of a reality TV survival show where they send out-of-touch rich kids to try to live the life of real people – a la *The Simple Life* with Paris Hilton and Nicole Richie, a show that I loved, which I should probably be taking inspiration from for my character here – but I feel like, all things considered, we're doing a decent job.

The boys have seriously impressed me. They're all getting stuck in – even Heath, who, despite trying to forge himself a role as more of a project manager type, has sweat on his brow from all the hard work. Then there's Sonny, who is lugging a big piece of wood out of the way, shirtless, sweat glistening on his perfectly plumped and chiselled muscles. Not that I'm looking, per se, just noticing, casually, as you do, no big deal. He looks over at me, noticing me noticing him. He looks a little moody, and I could swear he was shooting daggers at Brett, who is sitting on the sand next to me. You could almost mistake his looks for jealousy, although, stupid me, if we're supposed to be here as a couple, that's exactly what he should be doing.

'Still dreaming of cheeseburgers?' Brett asks me, snapping me from my thoughts.

'Big time,' I say with a smile. 'I've pretty much got a one-track mind.'

'Girls only care about one thing,' he jokes. 'Well, I'd better make a move, I've got things to do. But maybe I'll pop back and see you later.'

'Okay, sure,' I reply. 'Thanks for all your help today.'

'It's literally my job,' he replies with a laugh.

Of course it is, silly me.

'It's finished! We've bloody finished!' Heath announces proudly, snapping me from my thoughts.

We all hurry over, gathering around the wooden hut, to admire the boys' handiwork. Wow, it really is amazing, so professionally done, somehow looking like something so brand new and perfect, but so naturally, blending into the backdrop of the island like it has been here forever. I wouldn't have though this lot would know an Allen key from their arse, but they've smashed their part of the challenge. I'm actually really proud of them.

Hope, ever the ringleader of this circus, stands in front of the hut to address us all.

I find her smirk as unsettling as it is intriguing, and as always, her eyes hint at something, something she knows that we don't.

'Wow, I'm impressed,' Hope declares. 'You might just be the best group we've had yet.'

Heath, who looks knackered and like he can't quite believe he's pulled it off, seems genuinely proud. 'Even I would sleep in this, but I won't because I've worked my arse off today. There's no way we're the weakest couple.'

Hope grins with a hint of mischief in her eyes, the kind of look that makes me nervous.

'You've all done so well, no one will be sleeping in it. In fact, to celebrate your success, we'll be having a party on the beach.' She lowers her voice dramatically. 'A bonfire.'

Everyone cheers as Hope brings out a green glass bottle from behind her back. Oh my God, is that wine? My heart dances for a few seconds, until I look closer, and see the scrunched-up rag sticking out from the top of the bottle. I furrow my brow as I watch curiously, wondering what she's doing. Hope raises her other hand to reveal a lighter. She lights the material in the bottle before throwing what I now recognise as *a fucking Molotov cocktail* into the hut. It goes up in flames in a matter of seconds.

'What the hell?' Heath yells, his voice a mix of disbelief and frustration. 'We worked so hard on that. You've just destroyed it.'

'Are you actually joking, mate?' Danny adds, also sounding frustrated, and kind of devastated.

I look to Sonny, who looks back at me, chewing his lip thoughtfully, as we silently acknowledge how messed up this is.

'That's so out of order,' Kellee calls out.

'Yeah, not cool at all,' Izzy adds.

'The boys worked so hard on that,' Brittany insists, her disappointment as clear as anyone's.

'And now the hard work is done,' Hope says, unbothered by the chaos she's unleashed, seemingly carrying on as if nothing just happened. 'Let's enjoy the bonfire and some freshly caught fish dishes. Relax and have some fun.'

Hope leaves us all standing together in stunned silence, next to the blazing fire, a day's hard work up in smoke. This is insane, unhinged, and I'll bet nothing like the brochure promised. Surely, no one would sign up for this willingly?

'Okay, she's out of her bloody tree, that one,' Heath says to the group now that Hope is gone, pretty much summing up what we were all thinking.

'I don't understand,' Duane, always the logical one, adds as he tries to make sense of it. 'What was the point?'

'I don't know,' Brittany says with a shrug. 'But at least it means none of us have to sleep in it. So, that's a plus.'

I love that Brittany is such an optimist.

'Do you think she does this with everyone?' I think out loud.

'What, like every group who comes here builds one of these, only for her to burn it down?' Sonny replies, raising an eyebrow. 'Why would she do that?'

I know, it sounds mad, but that's what it feels like.

'Look, for me, this is all getting a bit *Wicker Man*,' Heath says, practical as ever, summing up how he feels in one sentence.

I can't help but agree. This whole situation feels like something out of a horror movie.

'We all need to stick together,' he continues. 'Whatever crazy stuff is coming up next, we need to know that, if we need to build a raft or whatever, and blow this freak show, we can all team up together. Agreed?'

'Agreed, mate,' Danny says.

'Yeah, we're with you too,' Duane adds.

Heath looks to Sonny, waiting for a response. He glances at me and I nod in approval.

'Of course,' Sonny says. 'At least we know we have the skills now, hey?'

'Ooh, can we all put our hands in the middle, like when they make a pact in the movies?' Izzy suggests giddily.

'I thought you were all supposed to cut yourselves and put your blood together?' Danny corrects her.

Those two clearly watch different types of movies.

'Hands in the middle is fine,' I quickly insist.

Somehow a blood pact or any kind of weird ritual feels like it's leaning into whatever weirdness is going on here.

'Okay, one, two, three – team!' Heath calls out as we all put our hands together in the centre.

'Dinner is served,' Hope calls out from across the beach.

Sonny sidles up to me as we head over to queue for our dinner.

'Ergh, fish,' I moan. 'And it sounds like it's just fish. Honestly, I'd sooner neck another green sludge smoothie.'

'I'll have yours,' he insists with a grin. 'I'm absolutely starving. I worked my arse off today – for nothing, apparently. Just between us, what do you think is going on?'

I sigh, watching the other guests walking ahead of us, making sure no one else can hear our conversation.

'I have no idea,' I confess, my brow furrowing as I try to wrap my head around Hope's strange behaviour. 'I can't figure Hope out. Sometimes she seems normal, kind, caring even – deep down – but then sometimes she's cold, cryptic, and kind of crazy.'

Sonny nods in agreement.

'And to think, everyone else here is paying for this,' he muses. 'More money than sense.'

'True,' I agree with a laugh. 'I do really like everyone, though.'

'Yeah, me too,' Sonny says. 'It might feel like all of our hard work was for nothing today, but we all worked really well together, and we had a laugh.'

I smile softly.

'Yeah, it's been fun,' I say.

'So how was fruit picking with Brett?' Sonny asks. I can't quite decipher the slight tone in his voice but there's something there.

'It was good,' I reply simply. 'It was nice to see more of the island – it does make me even more curious about where we are. I would love to come back here, under different circumstances, obviously.'

'Yeah, I'm itching to explore the place,' he says as we both pause for a moment and look out towards the ocean. 'More so than I am nosing into the lives of these guys.'

Before I have a chance to reply, Izzy appears at my side and hooks her arm with mine.

'We're grabbing some food, and then we're going to have a girly chat,' she tells me excitedly. I sneak a quick glance at Sonny, who shoots me an approving smile.

'Okay, sure,' I agree, a bit nervous because, despite having a close female friend like Lauren back home, I've never really had a proper girl squad for girly chats, and it feels oddly exciting.

Not fancying the fresh fish, I grab a bowl of brown rice and join the other girls. As we sit on the sand, I can't help but observe our stunning surroundings, the bonfire casting flickering shadows across the beach as the sun disappears before our eyes.

'So, how are you guys finding it here?' Kellee asks, her voice carrying genuine curiosity as she kicks off the conversation. 'Any improvements?'

'Duane and I are doing well,' Brittany, always warm and pleasant, says with a smile. 'It's a strange place, not quite what we expected, but we're making the best of it.'

I nod in agreement. I can't quite get over just how normal Duane and Brittany appear to be, despite their celebrity status. I don't mean this offensively, but there is nothing controversial or especially interesting about them; they're just a young couple in love. It makes me wonder why there's so much media interest in them, or what we could possibly learn about them here that anyone would be bothered to read about.

My appetite vanishes as I pick at my plain, dry rice. I have never felt so disappointed by a food – especially on what is essentially a holiday. I had hoped for five-star dining at this luxury resort, not a rice bowl.

'I miss unhealthy food,' I say with a sigh.

'I miss shopping,' Izzy adds. 'What I'd give to buy a handbag right now.'

'Lara might sell you her Birkin,' Kellee jokes.

I laugh, but it quickly fades as I try to work out how Kellee knows about the bag I have with me. It's not like I've been carrying it around with me while I've been here.

'How do you know I have a Birkin?' I ask, trying to sound casual but wanting to know the truth.

'I saw it in your room,' Kellee says simply, not really answering my question.

My curiosity well and truly has the better of me.

'Why were you in my room?' I ask, cutting to the chase.

Kellee leans in, lowering her voice despite the fact that no one could possibly overhear us over here on our own.

'Sonny took me to your room earlier – oh my God, you look so jealous,' Kellee says with a chuckle. 'You must really love him, or really not trust me, or both.'

I wonder which one it is and if there is a chance it could be both.

'Relax, he took me there to give me something,' she continues. 'To sneak me something, I mean – some sugar.'

'Oh my God, he has sugar?' Izzy replies, her eyes wide with wonderment.

'Yeah,' Kellee continues quietly. 'Little packets, from the plane or whatever. I put a little in some sparkling water earlier, and I squeezed out the lemon slices into it. Honestly, it's almost like soda. I know, it seems sus, secretly getting packets of white powder from a guy, but you guys should see if he'll hook you up. Just don't tell anyone; if Hope realises, she'll confiscate it.'

I'm surprised at how relieved I feel, to learn that Kellee was in the room with Sonny, but that it was only so that he could sneak her a sachet of sugar. So he's sharing his supplies with Kellee too – and there's me thinking I was special. It's funny, back in London, everything feels like it's just a game between the two of us, like no one else in the world exists, in fact it's actually kind of weird how much time and energy goes into our twisted game of cat and mouse. Here, with other players in the game, it feels strange, like I'm having to share him. And, wow, that sounds stupid and crazy. Enough of thoughts like that.

'Can I buy your Birkin?' Izzy half jokes. 'I never really feel like I'm good enough to be the missus of a footballer. Maybe that's what I need, to show that I'm good enough, to be taken seriously.'

'Girl, you are perfect as you are,' Kellee insists, her tone sincere as she quickly dismisses the idea.

'Yeah, you don't need a bag to show the horrible people in the world that you're worth anything,' Brittany adds kindly.

'They're right,' I agree. 'It's just a silly, overpriced bag. I only have one because someone gave me one.'

Which is technically true.

'I'm terrified that I'm not good enough for Danny,' Izzy confesses. 'The papers are always saying it, making fun of me for my working-class background, my accent, saying I'm thick. It feels like there's a day coming where Danny realises they're right, that he can do way better than me now that he's minted, and I've got myself in a proper mess trying to make myself feel worth it. I had an interior designer decorate the house, I've bought designer clothes, trendy dogs – and then there's all my surgeries to look good. I'm in so much debt, from trying to buy things to make everyone take me seriously, to make me seem like I deserve this life, all while there are rags like the *Daily Scoop* saying I should go back to working in Asda just because I tripped up on a red carpet once. It's all so dumb.'

I can't help but feel sorry for Izzy. It's the curse of being in the public eye combined with the despicable behaviour of some journalists.

'You need to ignore all that silly noise,' I tell her softly. 'The people who say stuff like that are jealous, trying to knock you down, to make them feel better about their lives. Danny clearly adores you; there's no way he would think he could do better – how do you do better than a childhood sweetheart? Someone who has been with you since before you were rich and successful is the ultimate person to put all of your trust in. No one can compete with the history you guys have.'

Izzy seems comforted by my words, offering a grateful smile, which is a relief. I can't help but feel like part of the problem, even if that isn't my style of journalism.

'I'm sure you're right,' she says. 'It's just hard to ignore it all.'

'The *Daily Scoop* are truly the worst,' Kellee tells us. 'They said I was fat after I had my wisdom teeth removed, and my face swelled up for just a short while.'

Brittany shakes her head in disbelief.

'And I don't even know where to begin with the rubbish they write about me,' she says.

The mood only drops for a moment before Izzy breaks into a smile, clearly feeling uplifted by the support of the group. I guess sometimes, just feeling like you're not alone goes a long way.

'Thanks, girls,' she says gratefully. 'I'm so lucky to have you here. I should talk to Danny, tell him the secret I've been hiding from him, and that I'm feeling under pressure. You're right, I'm being daft; he won't leave me, will he?'

'He would be mad if he did,' Brittany reassures her, leaning over to give her knee a squeeze.

'And I'd kill him if he did,' Kellee adds, her voice strangely calm despite the sinister undertone of her sentence.

I'm engrossed in our heart-to-heart, guilt lightly nibbling away at me, when Brett suddenly interrupts, making me jump for no real reason.

'Lara, have you got a sec?' he asks, looking a little apologetic. 'Hope just wants to make sure we didn't pick the bad bananas.'

'Oh, okay, sure,' I reply, my curiosity piqued. Like I'm going to be the authority on that.

I follow Brett, expecting him to head over to the food table. But instead, he guides me into the woods. I trail behind him in silence, my mind racing until we reach a clearing in the trees and he stops in his tracks.

I follow his gaze and I can't believe my eyes.

'Oh my God,' I blurt out, staring in disbelief. 'Is that a mirage or...?'

Brett grins mischievously.

'That's a cheeseburger and fries, just for you,' he informs me. 'And a chocolate shake, which I highly recommend you dip your fries in.'

I could cry. My jaw hangs open, and for a moment I'm lost for words.

'I just... Why? How? Why would you...?'

Brett chuckles, like this is some sort of everyday scenario, but to me, it's a miracle.

'Staff get to eat whatever we want,' he explains with a casual shrug. 'Only guests have to eat the garbage. And I kinda like you, I feel like you're my buddy here, and you seem like you need to catch a break, so, yeah, here you go. Enjoy.'

I can't contain my gratitude. I grab Brett and squeeze him tightly, but not for long, because my cheeseburger and fries are calling my name. I pounce on my food like a lion that's just caught up with its prey, and dig in like I might never get to eat again.

Brett grins, clearly pleased with – and slightly amused by – my reaction.

'And there's plenty more where that came from if you wanna keep hanging out,' he offers.

I just about manage to speak between mouthfuls of food.

'I would love that,' I reply.

But I'd probably say yes to anything right now.

18

Lying in bed, I feel beyond shattered after the whirlwind of a day we've had. I'm not used to being so active and outdoorsy. The closest I get is charging around at music festivals but, even then, I'm mostly in the comfort of the press area.

The cool sheets and the soft glow of the room's ambient lighting somehow soothe my aches and help me to unwind. That said, I think the cheeseburger that Brett smuggled to me, and the contraband cup of tea Sonny just made me, have been a big help. The home comforts really make a difference, and I could definitely get used to having multiple men running around after me.

I'm not planning on telling Sonny about Brett sneaking me food. Well, knowing Sonny, he might do something to ruin it, just for sport, and even if he didn't, he would want in on the deal. If Brett couldn't smuggle enough food for two, that would be it, he would cut me off, and I can't have that. Plus, it's kind of nice, hanging out with him, and I have to admit that I do like the feeling of sort of getting one up over Sonny.

A contented sigh escapes my lips. Still, I can't quite get over what a day it's been.

'I still can't believe Hope burned down your shelter,' I blurt to Sonny, who is lying in bed next to me.

It's interesting, how sharing a bed isn't really much of a thing at all. I thought it would be awkward, that he would annoy if not terrorise me, but it's actually been all right.

'She looked unhinged,' he replies. 'Did you see that crazy look she had, as the flicker of the flames reflected in her wide eyes?'

I can't help but laugh now, as I recall the scene.

'Yeah, I half expected her to start cackling manically,' I tell him.

Sonny smirks.

He shifts a little, making himself comfortable as he snuggles down deeper into the bed now that he's finished his cup of tea.

'She had this grin on her face, like... I don't know. Like she'd been waiting for that moment forever. And her eyes... they were so alive. The flames were reflecting in them, making them dance. It was like she was part of the fire.'

'It was weird,' I agree. 'Definitely premeditated. I feel like she knew, before we had even started, that she was going to destroy it. It makes you wonder why you tried so hard.'

'I swear she was getting some twisted pleasure out of it,' he continues. 'We all worked so, so hard on it. I actually felt quite sad, watching it burn down, because I had a lot of fun building it. And it turns out I'm good at stuff like that.'

'Oh, well, you're good at everything, aren't you?' I tease.

'Honestly, I surprised myself,' he insists. 'If only I could get a job building wooden huts on tropical islands, I think I would be much happier.'

'Well, I'm glad you had fun with it,' I say. 'For what it's worth, you did a good job, even if it was short-lived. I'm not sure I would want to forage for a living. There are muscles aching that I didn't know I had. But I did have a really nice time this evening, especially chatting with the girls, they all seem so lovely.'

As we chat, I notice his eyes drifting to something beyond me.

'I had a chat with Danny today,' he starts cautiously. 'He has a big secret that he's keeping from Izzy. It sounds like his newfound fame and wealth might be getting to him – I think he has a gambling problem. I don't think he knew what else to do with his time or money and it's all got a bit out of hand now. He's terrified to tell Izzy. I think that might be why they're here, because they both know something is wrong, but he can't bring himself to tell her what the problem is.'

I roll over onto my side to face Sonny, shocked to hear what he has to say, but with a revelation of my own.

'Wow, he told you that?' I blurt.

'Yeah, it just slipped out,' Sonny replies. 'I don't think he was planning to tell me, but I think he felt much better when he did.'

'Izzy confided in me too,' I admit. 'It seems as though she's got it into her head that she's not good enough, that she's not "WAG" material, so she's spending a fortune on cosmetic procedures, designer clothes, pedigree dogs – the works. It sounded like she had spent a lot of money, but she didn't know how to tell Danny. Gosh, if he's spending a lot too, they really need to sort this out. They're so young. I can't even imagine the pressure they must be under.'

We share a knowing look, the pieces of the puzzle fitting into place, and the gravity of the situation playing on our minds.

'They're too inexperienced to navigate something like this, especially if it plays out in the public eye,' Sonny points out. 'If the tabloids got wind of any of this, they'd have a field day.'

'And Danny and Izzy's new life would be over,' I add. 'I think, without these problems, they would be so happy. It seems like maybe the pressures of fame have got to them. Living life in the public eye can't help – with vultures like us, prying into their lives.'

'Come on, we're not that bad,' Sonny insists. 'What we're doing here feels different, not that we had much choice in the matter after

"Slap Gate", but most of what we do is planned and collaborative. It's more entertainment than gossip. We're nothing like the tabloids.'

'I guess,' I say. 'But I do see that line – the line – creeping up in the distance every now and then. And we do work for the people who own the tabloids so...'

'I know, and I feel the same way,' he confesses. 'The constant need to pry, instead of report, to expose, to invade people's lives. I couldn't live my life like that, not for all the money or fame or anything.'

I nod in agreement, a heavy sigh escaping my lips.

'Totally agree,' I reply. 'It's like we're no longer just telling stories; we're digging into people's personal lives, sometimes ruining them in the process. Maybe not us specifically, but our industry, for sure. We might not be the part of the machine that's the biggest problem, but we're a part nonetheless.'

Sonny runs a hand through his hair, frustration etched on his face.

'Exactly. And the worst part is, it's what the readers seem to crave,' he replies. 'The more sensational the story, the better.'

'And it's like we're feeding the public's appetite for drama,' I add, continuing our shared rant. 'I try to do what I can, to not be the worst. Sometimes I edit out things from interviews just to protect the person I'm writing about. They trust us to tell their story, but then we twist it to fit our narrative. I might not do that but someone else could read their words and use them against them. I know that seems silly, and counterproductive to our job...'

Suddenly, I feel like I shouldn't have told him that. Connecting with him like this, finding something we agree on, has eased my guard down. I need to remember that Sonny is essentially my work rival. What if he uses this against me?

I'm expecting a smirk, even a sneaky one, but his expression softens further.

'I get that,' he tells me. 'I really do. I once made up a source to squash a rumour.'

Wow, I can't believe he's admitting that to me. I feel instantly relieved, now that we have an unspoken pact of mutually assured destruction between us, but it's also good to hear that it isn't only me who feels this way.

'You made up a source?' I repeat back to him.

'Yeah. There was this rumour swirling around about an elderly actor having some sort of meltdown on set,' he tells me – I instantly know who he's talking about. 'There was speculation that he might have had some sort of dementia – which it later turned out, when he sadly passed away, that he had been trying to hide. I just had a bad feeling about it so I made up a source called Benedict Armhand – someone supposedly on set at the time who would go on the record as saying it was made up if we didn't put his name in the magazine. I had the idea in real time, in a meeting with CJ, so I came up with the name on the spot. I actually said Benedict Armband, the first time I said it, but quickly corrected myself when I realised that didn't sound like a real name at all.'

'Yeah, I haven't heard of the Armband family,' I reply with a laugh. 'But that was really good of you. I like to think I would have done the same just, you know, with a better fake name.'

'Cut me some slack, I panicked,' he laughs.

'As journalists, we're supposed to be seekers of truth, but in reality, it's often more about twisting things, or straight-up making things up, to entertain people,' I go on. 'I love the writing part, and the stories, but I hate that there are always real people at the heart of them. What I would love to do is maybe shift into writing fiction. I could inform my writing with everything that I've experienced over the years, to give readers the gossip and drama they want, but present it in a way that was fictionalised, that didn't hurt anyone. I would actually love to do that, I think about it all the time.'

'Yeah, that's the way to do it,' Sonny agrees. 'For me, I think the part of the job I love the most is the travelling. Going new places, experiencing things, meeting people – if I could do all that and then write about it afterwards, or even do it as a video blog, that would be sick.'

We both fall silent for a moment and it's as if the world outside our room fades away, especially as I let my mind wander to what life might be like if I could tell my stories without hurting anyone. Then reality sets back in.

'And yet we're here, with a job to do, and coming back with nothing didn't sound optional, did it?' I eventually say.

'No,' Sonny replies with a sigh. 'And all we have right now is the Danny and Izzy story, so we really, really need to find something else.'

'I agree,' I tell him. 'There must be something we can find, that will do less damage.'

'We're supposed to be finding something on Duane and Brittany,' he reminds me. 'But Duane hardly says a word. What about Brittany?'

I shake my head.

'She's really nice, but she's very quiet too,' I reply. 'It seems like something might be on her mind but nothing that she's sharing with the group. They don't even seem like a couple in crisis, to be honest.'

'No, I thought that,' he replies. 'Well, that just leaves Heath and Kellee.'

'I feel sorry for Kellee,' I'm quick to insist. 'But I don't like Heath. Try to find something on him.'

'I think it's all bravado,' Sonny tells me. 'He seems insecure.'

'An insecure billionaire,' I say in disbelief, but Sonny might be right. 'You know what, you're right, none of them deserve it.'

'We'll just have to try to find something that we're okay with using,' he says. 'If we team up, we'll get there. Anyway, we should get some sleep. Goodnight, Lara.'

'Yeah, goodnight,' I reply.

Sonny reaches over and dims the lights.

It's moments like these that remind me why we've managed to work together for so long, despite our rivalry. Because when you strip it down to moments like this, we are on the same page, doing the same things, trying to make the same difference.

We were close, once upon a time, but then something happened and we drifted apart – more than drifted apart, really. I put up a big wall, a fortress, determined that I would never let Sonny in again. By the time we were working together again, I don't know, I was hostile from the get-go, and I guess he put up walls too. The rivalry, the competition – they've become ingrained in our dynamic, shaping our interactions at work and beyond. Yet here, in this quiet moment, those walls seem to fade away, leaving just the two of us, talking openly and honestly.

It's nice, to call a ceasefire, even if it is just for now. But who's to say we have to go back to the way things used to be when we go home? Perhaps this could be the start of something more liveable.

19

Another morning on the island, another beautiful day. But with it comes another breakfast that leaves a big hole in my heart (and obviously my stomach).

I'm trying my best, really I am, and having a good old cup of tea in me goes a long way to helping me start my day, but I just can't seem to get into eating seeds for breakfast. I even tried covering them with almond milk today, like some kind of sad cereal for squirrels, but you won't be surprised to hear that it didn't work out. Chocolate Hazelnut Krave it was not.

I'm yet to see Brett walking around today. If I had, I would have asked him for something, anything, for my breakfast. A pastry, a biscuit, some chocolate – anything like that. But he's nowhere to be seen and now Hope is standing before us. Ugh, what fresh hell today at Eden?

Hope is on her usual top form, radiant and full of enigmatic energy, her facial features paralysed in that position, as though she were so over the moon to be getting her Botox, it froze her that way.

'Good morning, everyone,' her voice carries through the air.

'Today is Intimacy Day – a day dedicated to forging deeper bonds between you and your partners.'

Intimacy Day? I exchange glances with the other girls – which is interesting, but we do feel like a bit of a squad already – as a ripple of nervous intrigue passes through the room. The thing with Hope is that she says it is Intimacy Day, but with her that could mean anything. She could be expecting us to cut each other open and take a look at our partner's beating heart, or we might just have to hug for half an hour. All bets are off.

Hope's instructions swiftly guide us – the girls are to follow Carmen while the boys are led away by Lucian. I am as curious as I am nervous, wondering why she has separated us from the boys.

'Hello,' Hope's voice sighs over one the speakers that seem to be hidden everywhere on the island. 'First of all, take off your clothes.'

What? Is she for real?

'Just your clothes,' she continues. 'Until you are down to your underwear.'

Her words hang in the air, a mixture of surprise and apprehension gripping the room. We all exchange nervous glances, but there's an unspoken understanding that we're all in this together.

'I suppose it's no different than being in our swimwear,' Brittany says, her voice breaking through the tension, offering a hint of reassurance that makes everyone feel a little better.

I don't want to do this. I mean I really don't want to do this, I'm not here to heal through new-age therapies and pretty much genuine torture, I'm here to do my job. But I suppose, today, this is what my job entails, so I take off my bright pink sundress to reveal my bright pink lacy underwear. Honestly, I never thought I would say it, but the pink is kind of growing on me now, especially as I'm getting a little bit of a tan – I think it suits me.

Hope's sickly-sweet but super-smooth voice continues, guiding us through the next steps of Intimacy Day. She explains that we'll be placed inside something called intimacy pods with our partners, where we'll spend time in complete darkness, fostering a unique sense of connection – whatever the hell that means.

'Let me assure you that there are no cameras or microphones inside the pods,' she insists, which eases the tension slightly, although I can't say I love the idea of being in one with Sonny. The thought of standing next to him, in such close quarters, in total darkness in nothing but my underwear, makes my heart race for all kinds of reasons – all of which I'm working hard to keep out of my head right now.

'However, there are speakers in the room, so I will be able to guide you through the process,' she adds.

Carmen, ever the model employee, excitedly blindfolds us before escorting each of us inside a pod. I hear the door close behind me, then nothing, until...

'Without saying a word, remove your blindfold, and simply stand in the darkness for a moment,' Hope says. 'Inhale deeply, knowing that it is only the two of you who share the air – the rest of the world no longer exists.'

I really don't like the darkness, or being locked in what I'm imagining is a small space, so add those to my list of fears along with snakes.

'Now I want you to silently feel your way across the room, find your partner by seeking out their energy, and take them in your arms,' Hope continues.

As I follow Hope's instructions and navigate the dimly lit room, my arms extended tentatively, I allow my fingertips to search for Sonny. I do want to find him, if only to confirm that I'm not alone in here, but I don't fancy colliding bodies with him.

My heart skips a beat as my hands encounter another pair of hands. Sonny takes the lead, running his hands up my arms until he can pull me close, his touch making my skin tingle in anticipation. But as he cups my bum with both hands, a jolt of confusion runs through me. Something doesn't feel right. This just doesn't feel like the Sonny I know. It doesn't smell like his aftershave and, as I place my hands on his shoulders, the hairs creeping over from his back are definitely not his.

A low chuckle reaches my ears, but it's not Sonny's familiar laugh. It's deeper, richer, and tinged with amusement. Suddenly, the lights come on, revealing the face that matches that laugh. It's not Sonny who's holding me – it's Heath, his grinning face inches from mine, as he realises that I am not his wife.

I quickly wriggle out of his arms, unable to speak because I'm in genuine shock – I was nervous enough about doing this with Sonny, someone I know. But Heath! Ew! And he's wearing the least appealing pair of white underpants I've ever seen in my life – not that a pair of Gucci boxers would have helped. My bright pink underwear suddenly feels like it's emitting neon lights. I cover my mouth with my hands, stifling a horrified squeal, before quickly redirecting them elsewhere on my body, where I suspect they might be needed more.

'Fancy seeing you here,' he says with a grin.

'I thought we were supposed to be in our couples,' I reply.

Heath shrugs.

'Perhaps we're supposed to swap,' he suggests. 'It is Intimacy Day.'

Panic grips me as I realise we're trapped in this small space together, with no internal handle on the door, unable to escape the awkwardness.

'Help,' I call out, which might be a hysterical word to use, but it's the first one that comes to mind.

'Hope said no one would be able to hear us outside the pod,' Heath reminds me – thankfully lacking any kind of sinister tone to his voice. 'We're on our own, Lara.'

I cringe as inwardly as I can.

'Now, here's how the pods work,' Hope's voice interrupts the awkward silence. 'These pods are designed to foster closeness so, at random intervals, the walls will shift, enveloping you.'

My eyes widen as I translate her guff into real terms: the walls are going to move, closing in on us, squashing us together.

Right on cue, the walls begin to move, edging us closer together. I'm hyper-aware of every millimetre of space between us, as my sense of claustrophobia shakes hands with my already suffocating level of embarrassment. I try to focus on anything other than the fact that Heath and I are getting closer and closer.

'Huh, I wonder what tech they use,' Heath muses to himself.

I can't help but feel like a helpless animal caught in a trap, my heart pounding as the walls of the pod inch closer – as Heath in his tiny pants inches closer. I rack my brain, searching for an escape, but the room is well and truly sealed. I can't bear the thought of spending even another second in this confined space – with or without Heath. I'm not actually sure which one is worse.

I open my mouth to call for help again but Heath speaks first.

'Calling for help is a waste of time, Lara, you're only going to waste our oxygen,' he says, his tone overflowing with amusement, which is funny give that he just said something so alarming. 'We're stuck in here, might as well make the best of it.'

'What's the best of it?' I blurt in disbelief.

'I'll give you a million dollars if you have a baby with me,' he says, his tone optimistic, which only makes it all the more absurd.

Huh, it's good to know I have a line, and that there are things I wouldn't do for money.

'What?' I squeak.

'I'm joking... sort of,' he says with a weird laugh. 'We'd make a cute baby, don't you think? Kellee won't have a baby with me, even though she knows I want one – I'm getting old, er, older, I mean. I want a family.'

'Well, Kellee is quite a bit younger than you,' I remind him. 'And she's at the height of her career. She probably wants to wait a while, before she considers anything like that.'

'But with me she doesn't need to worry about money, so what's the point?' Heath asks, and I think he actually wants an answer.

'Right, because money is all that matters,' I reply sarcastically.

'Easy to say when you're an heiress without a job,' Heath claps back.

I open my mouth to reply right as the walls of the pod shift again, pressing us closer together now. I squeak and wince as he touches me – not that he's doing it on purpose.

'I know you think this is funny, but I think you're missing something obvious,' I say, very matter-of-factly.

'What's that?' Heath replies.

'That if I'm in here with you then that means your wife is in a pod squashed up close and personal with Thor,' I point out, borrowing his nickname for Sonny – mostly to just remind him how big and buff he is.

Great, now Heath is calling out for help. I knew that would rattle him.

'Okay, come on, relax,' I insist, unable to stand any more of his shouting. 'Sonny is a good bloke, Kellee is in safe hands.'

'Nah, Kellee flirts with every man she meets,' Heath replies. 'And she's always talking about sleeping with other people. I wouldn't put it past her, to have fucked around behind my back, but I've never been able to prove it.'

'You can't be with someone you can't trust,' I remind him softly, actually feeling quite sorry for him all of a sudden.

'But you can't leave someone you love,' Heath replies.

The walls close in again, this time squashing our bodies totally together.

'Do you want kids?' Heath asks, seriously this time.

'Not right now,' I insist, shifting my body to try to get more comfortable.

'Have you and Sonny talked about it?' he persists.

'Not yet,' I reply.

'Make sure you do, soon,' Heath says. 'And if you're at odds, remember that million I promised you.'

I assume he's back to joking again but, before I can figure it out, the pod door opens behind me.

I hurry out to find everyone else standing there – all looking exactly how I feel.

'Oh, my goodness,' Hope says. 'I don't know how this has happened but it would seem that our couples have been mixed up. Come to the group therapy room, where we can talk together.'

Carmen is standing behind her, a pile of white robes draped over her. I can't help but feel a surge of relief at the sight of them. All I want to do is cover up.

'Robes, everyone,' Carmen announces with a warm smile. 'Please put these on before we start the session.'

'Yeah, because we wouldn't want it to be weird,' Sonny says quietly as he walks up alongside me.

I quickly grab a robe, slipping it on over my underwear. The others follow suit, quickly and quietly, I suspect all a little traumatised by what just happened too.

Soon, we're all seated in a circle, each next to the correct partner now, and the tension is palpable. Even Heath has stopped smiling, as we all wonder what is going to happen next.

'Things may not have gone to plan, but I hope you were able to learn something from the experience all the same,' Hope says, her smile as big as ever. 'What I think we should do now is reflect on where our closeness began. Heath, Kellee, tell me about the first time you were intimate.'

'Does she mean...?' Kellee starts.

'I think she does,' Heath replies.

He fills his air with lungs and then laughs to himself as he recalls the memory.

'She basically would not put out,' Heath starts, not at all romantically. 'She said that I needed to prove myself to her, to take her on dates, buy her shit, shower her in compliments before she would even think about it. I took her to Paris on a private jet on our second date – nothing. Our fourth date, I bought her an apartment – nothing.'

All eyes are on Kellee now.

'I wanted him to show me that I mattered, that I was important, I wanted him to prove himself to me,' she insists. 'And he did, on our ninth date, when he cancelled a boys' trip to come and look after me when I was sick.'

That's actually quite sweet.

'Danny, Izzy, what about you?' Hope's voice turns to them, her tone gentle yet curious.

Danny shifts in his seat, his cheeks turning a deep shade of crimson. He clears his throat, casting a shy glance at Izzy before speaking up.

'Er, we couldn't exactly make it as special as that,' she begins, laughing awkwardly. 'We had to wait until Danny's 'rents were away at their caravan for the weekend.'

Izzy chuckles, a mischievous glint in her eyes.

'He made it nice, though,' she continues. 'He bought me chocolates, got me flowers – and it was the first time for both of us so, yeah, it was dead special.'

If it's even possible, Danny goes even more red, but he smiles at Izzy to let her know it's okay.

Danny seems to exude a quiet shyness, his reserved manner contrasting with Izzy's extroverted presence. He's calm and quiet, ever so clearly always listening, but not always wanting to speak. On the other side of the coin, Izzy wears her emotions on her sleeve, embracing the role of spokesperson for the two. I love that her laughter always seems to fill the room. You can tell Danny loves it too.

'Okay, Duane and Brittany, what about you?' Hope says as she turns to them with an expectant glance.

Duane shifts in his seat, clearly uncomfortable at the question.

'We met at work,' he replies, his tone guarded. 'We don't like to talk about it, though.'

Brittany leans in, smiling warmly as she squeezes Duane's knee.

'It was just a case of life imitating art,' she explains, her words eliciting curious glances from the others. 'But... well, not imitating it too closely.'

Kellee's eyes sparkle with intrigue, her lips curving into a knowing smile.

'I've seen your show,' she interjects with a playful tone. 'I don't think you would be sitting on the chair so comfortably if life *did* imitate art.'

Brittany bursts into laughter, her cheeks tinged with a hint of pink.

Duane chuckles, his expression more relaxed now that their turn is over.

'Yeah, well, reality is a bit more complicated than the scripts,' he admits as he smiles back at her.

I can't help but be drawn into their dynamic – like everyone else on the planet. They just have such great chemistry, their little jokes together, the way they comfort one another. I can't get my head around what they're doing at a place like this.

'Finally, Lara and Sonny,' Hope says, her voice directing the attention towards us. My heart races. I've been dreading this moment since Hope made it clear what she wanted us to talk about.

As Sonny and I exchange a brief glance, it's obvious that he's just as unsure as I am about what to say.

Well, honesty is the best policy, no one can catch us in a lie if I tell the truth, so that's what I'll do. The truth is: Sonny and I have actually been intimate before.

'Well, as you all know, Sonny and I went to university together,' I begin, my voice sounding unsure of my story – even though I know this is all true. 'But it wasn't until we did our work experience at the same company that we started spending time together. First at work, then alone, then one night, at the end of our time there, the people we were working with took us on a big night out and Sonny and I ended up in bed together.'

'So, what went wrong?' Izzy asks curiously, clearly on the edge of her seat for a good bit of goss.

I feel Sonny's eyes on me so I look over at him, passing the storytelling duties on, so that he can explain.

'It turned out that, when work experience was over for the year, they would always pick one person to offer a full-time job to, and that person was me,' Sonny explains.

'That's a shame,' Izzy says with a sigh.

'It's also not the whole truth,' I can't resist informing them. 'Because it turned out that Sonny knew there was a job opening, and he used something we had been working on together to secure the job for himself. So he got his dream job while I had to go back to uni for another couple of years, to even be in with a chance of landing a job there too.'

'Thor, you bastard,' Heath says with an impressed laugh. Obviously, he appreciates a crafty manoeuvre like that. 'And you didn't even keep the job, eh?'

Sonny chuckles, but he looks embarrassed too – perhaps even a little ashamed, which I haven't seen before.

'That's what I like to see,' Heath continues. 'If you ever do want a job, you come to me.'

'I'll keep that in mind,' Sonny says, laughing it off.

'Right, time for lunch, I think,' Hope says, clapping her hands together so loudly it makes my ears ring. 'I believe it's quinoa surprise today.'

Absolutely nothing about what she just said is a surprise. Having to talk about this, today, in front of all these people was, though. I've never told anyone about me sleeping with Sonny – not even Lauren, who knows about our work rivalry. Sonny has made the occasional joke about it, but only ever hinting at it. It's not something we've talked about since and, at the time, well, let's just say I only found out what had happened when I heard it from someone else. And then we didn't even see each other again until I got the job at *Stylife*, and we began crossing paths again. The first few times we passed in the lobby, or were at the same work event, he didn't even acknowledge me – I think he was trying to pretend that he didn't recognise me. He couldn't keep it up for long, though, and we've been (what I will dramatically refer to – because I am annoyed – as) sworn enemies ever since.

It's interesting, to see him look a little ashamed of his actions, but that might just be because we're in a room full of our new friends, and Heath was the only one who found it impressive.

Ah, well, time for quinoa surprise. We'll see what Sonny has to say for himself later.

20

I make my way back to the dining room, having just excused myself to nip to the loos, when I feel a hand on my shoulder. It startles me, given how eerily quiet and lonely this place tends to be, but I relax a little once I realise it's Brett.

Brett's warm breath tickles my ear as he leans in, his voice a hushed whisper.

'What are your favourite foods?' he asks, almost seductively, although I could be imagining that because I'm so hungry – yes, despite being in the middle of dinner.

'Oh, I would do disgusting things for a pizza,' I joke, my cheeks flushing slightly as I cringe at the unintended implications of what I just said.

Brett laughs.

'I see a pizza in your near future,' he teases, putting on a playfully mysterious voice. 'We can meet up at our secret spot if you like. You can tell me all about your fellow guests. It's so boring here, I need some entertainment.'

'And I need a pizza, so that sounds good,' I reply, my smile matching the mischievous tone of our conversation.

'Deal, I'll let you know when I can make it happen,' he says before disappearing as fast as he appeared in the first place.

I take my seat back at the dinner table, my plate filled with what Hope called 'quinoa surprise'. The only surprise I can see is that it's just quinoa, plain and simple, which isn't really a surprise to me at all. I wasn't expecting anything more.

Tonight, Hope has split the couples, with the boys at one table and the girls at another. To be honest, I don't mind at all. I really like the girls, they're a lovely bunch, and I'm having a great time hanging out with them. In fact, I would go as far as to say that if we had some cocktails and pizza, this would be the perfect evening. I wonder what the guys are up to on their table. Every now and then, I hear Heath's booming laughter, and every time he laughs, Kellee seems to wince. It's pretty clear that Heath has taken a liking to Sonny, or, as he calls him, 'Thor'. And it's not just Heath, all the guys seem to be getting along just fine. Danny's a real charmer, and even Duane, who usually keeps to himself, looks like he's having a good time tonight.

Here at the girls' table, we're deep in conversation, and naturally, it's all about the boys. Brittany sighs.

'I just wish Duane would open up more,' she shares. 'He keeps everything inside, even with me. It's so hard to get him to open up these days.'

Izzy nods empathetically.

'Danny is the same,' she says. 'He doesn't tell me anything – I think that's why I'm always worried that he's going to cheat on me, or that he already is.'

'Well, Heath is cheating on me,' Kellee announces, almost casually, considering what she is saying.

'No,' Brittany gasps. 'Surely not.'

Kellee takes a sip of her drink, chewing her paper straw nervously for a second as she considers what she's about to say.

'He is,' she insists, and you can see the disappointment in her eyes. 'He's always "working" late and sneaking around. I did think I was being paranoid at first, until I saw messages on his phone about keeping her a secret – she's called Lilly. I don't know anyone with that name, so at least that's something. I suppose it would have been worse, if it was someone we both knew.'

I can't help but feel so sorry for her. If a stunning, successful pop star like Kellee is getting cheated on, there is no hope for any of us.

'Are you sure you're not mistaken?' I ask gently, trying to offer some hope. 'He seems smitten, and he's here with you, so that's got to mean something, right?'

'I don't know,' she admits, her voice tinged with uncertainty, her shoulders dropping as she lets out a big sigh. 'But, spoiler alert, that's why I'm so flirty with everyone – so if you see me flirting with your men, don't panic. I don't mean it, I just do it to try to get a rise out of Heath. I thought that if he worried he might lose me, he might become a better husband, but, well, it's not working just yet.'

Listening to Kellee, it is obvious that she's fiercely loyal to Heath. She's not trying to hurt anyone, she's just desperately attempting to save her relationship. It's heartbreaking, and seriously infuriating, to see how some guys take their partners for granted. Heath doesn't know what a great girl he's got if he's willing to cheat on her.

All of a sudden, Kellee snaps her head in my direction, her gaze fixed on me almost suspiciously – although I could be imagining the last part, courtesy of my guilty conscience.

'Okay, Lara, come on, time to 'fess up, why are you really here?' she asks, quite abruptly, so, no, I'm not imagining it.

Panic surges through my entire body. Is Kellee on to me? How could she possibly know? I'm terrified, and it's not just over my cover potentially being blown, I'm more worried about my new friends discovering I'm a fraud. I genuinely like these girls, and I really don't want them to hate me – and how could they not, if they knew the truth?

'Come on,' Kellee urges, her eyes probing mine. 'Because as far as we can all see, you and Sonny seem like a perfect pairing.'

Relief washes over me as I realise Kellee isn't suspecting my real motives for being here. I need to say something, to make something up on the spot, but these girls have bared their souls to me, so it's only fair I do the same. Perhaps a little honesty right now might help.

I take a deep breath, my voice trembling slightly as I try to find the right words, to be honest with them, but without blowing my cover.

'The two of us were great, back in the day,' I begin. 'We seemed like a perfect match. But these days, I don't know... We're always arguing, trying to one-up each other, trying to make the other person change, and sometimes, well, it's more like we hate each other than love each other.'

I notice Brittany smiling.

'That's when you know it's still love,' she tells me with a reassuring smile. 'When you fall out of love, you know, because you stop caring. You're arguing because you're fighting for your relationship. If the two of you didn't care about each other, you wouldn't bother with each other, and you wouldn't be here now.'

I smile. She doesn't know how right she is because it really is ultimately our fighting that landed us here.

'If there's one couple who I know is going to be together forever, it's you and Sonny,' Izzy reassures me.

'Yeah, come on, he's literally Thor,' Kellee adds. 'He could have any girl he wanted, and he's chosen you, rain or shine, rough or smooth. He's still here. And he's not cheating on you with a floozy called Lilly, so there's that.'

The girls are right back on Kellee, reassuring her, bigging her up. It's so nice to see. Women supporting women. No bitchiness, no rivalry – they're everything you could want in a group of friends. That's the best thing about women, though. You don't even need to know each other more than a few minutes and you've got a friend, someone you can talk to, someone who will give you a tampon in the toilets or pretend to be your friend at a bus stop so that a guy stops talking to you. It's really, really nice.

I feel a pang of guilt wash over me as I watch them. I hate the idea of betraying my new friends' trust. They've shown such vulnerability here tonight, and they deserve their privacy.

I don't want to lie to them, and I know that I can't go back to work empty-handed, after they've arranged this whole thing, but I'm just not comfortable with it. I'll stick with the plan, I'll keep doing my job, and just hope and pray that in the process I'll find something – something harmless, though – that I can take back with me. And if I can't, well, I don't know what I'll do, but I'll cross that bridge when I come to it.

21

Well, if I am getting a pizza, it doesn't seem like it's going to be tonight sadly.

My stomach grumbles – it's clearly on the same page as my brain – and it seems extra loud, although we are in a library.

Yes, after dinner, Hope appeared briefly to send us all here, to wind down after dinner in our pairs. She told us to reconnect before bed, in a mentally stimulating room, where we could share our thoughts and feelings – or some crap like that.

I do love a good library, though, and the one here at the resort is a serene and spacious room, lit with a warm, ambient lighting that is bright enough to read but soft enough to feel cosy. The walls are lined with rich bookshelves, filled with a diverse collection of books – something for everyone. There are plush, comfortable chairs and sofas scattered around the room to relax in, as well as tables and chairs for those who plan to work.

Sonny and I are sitting on one of the sofas, each hiding behind a book that we're not really reading, like caricatures of spies concealing themselves behind newspapers, watching the other couples closely.

Izzy and Danny are sitting on the floor, surrounded by a pile of hardback books, attempting to play a game of Jenga with them. Heath and Kellee are sitting in separate armchairs, their backs turned to each other, both silently engrossed in their books. I can't tell what they are reading from here, but Heath looks like he's holding some sort of academic journal, while Kellee has her nose in a novel.

Brittany and Duane are perched together at a table, both leaning in over a notebook, taking it in turns to write in it. They look like they're planning something – like how they can escape overnight maybe. They're giggling together, like they're swapping secrets, both clearly having a great time.

'What do you reckon they're up to?' Sonny whispers to me.

'Maybe they're playing noughts and crosses,' I reply casually, suddenly not all that interested in finding out, although Sonny is clearly still on the case.

'Nah, they're plotting something,' he insists.

'Why don't you go ask them?' I suggest.

Sonny stares at me in disbelief.

'All right, everyone, that's enough for tonight,' Hope declares, joining us again.

Then she glances at what Izzy and Danny are doing, her eyes briefly widening, as though her poker face is slipping, but then her fake smile returns.

'Time to call it a night. We've got an early start tomorrow,' she continues. 'Oh, and Izzy, Danny, kindly return those books to where you found them.'

Hope leaves again, and everyone starts to make a move, but as Brittany stands up she nearly trips over her own two feet. Luckily, Duane catches her just in time. Meanwhile, Izzy and Danny stack their books on the table before returning them to the shelves. Sonny and I both shoot each other a look, as we notice that, in all the commotion, Brittany and Duane left their notebook behind, and Izzy or Danny has accidentally stashed it on one of the shelves.

With the coast eventually clear, Sonny and I sneakily linger in the doorway.

'I'm going to find that notebook and see what they're up to,' Sonny tells me. 'Man the door.'

'Man the door?' I repeat back to him.

'Yeah, look, there's a lock, just lock it and stand there, keep an ear out for anyone coming,' Sonny insists.

'And what if someone comes?' I reply nervously.

'Then stall them,' he says simply as he dashes across the room to find the notebook.

I do as he says, locking the door, hoping that he'll be fast and that no one will know that we're here, because I have no idea how we would explain it, if we were caught here, when we were just clearly told we had to go to bed.

Of course, almost instantly someone jiggles the locked door handle from outside the room.

'It's locked,' a muffled voice says.

'Should I go grab the key from Hope?' a woman suggests.

In my moment of panic, with no idea what else to do, there's only one thing I can think of. 'Oh my God, Sonny!' I blurt out, in a breathy, overly sexy voice.

Sonny freezes, like a deer in the headlights, looking at me like I've lost my mind. I desperately gesture for him to keep searching and hurry up. He carries on searching through the books, unable to hide his grin.

'Oh my God, are they having sex?' I hear one of the voices on the other side of the door say.

'Oh my God, yes, yes, don't stop, harder,' I demand as I bang my hand on the wall. 'Psst,' I call over to Sonny. 'Join in so it doesn't seem weird.'

'Yeah, that will make it less weird,' he replies with a laugh before immediately following my lead. 'Yeah, Lara, oh yeah, God, that feels so good.'

I feel my cheeks flush.

'That's it, that's it – that's it,' I say, multitasking, as I notice Sonny lay his hands on the notebook.

'Mmm, yeah.' He continues the charade. 'You like that?'

I watch Sonny thumb through the notebook before snapping it shut and laying it down on the table, joining me at the door.

'Right, let's go,' I whisper.

'What, mid-shag?' he replies. 'Won't that seem more suspicious?'

I laugh and wince in equal measure.

'Yeah, yeah, yeah...'

'Oh... yeah...' Sonny continues.

And then I let out some kind of screech, that I'm sure I don't do in real life, but it certainly makes it all sound impressive.

'And scene,' Sonny jokes cheekily before I reach out to unlock the door.

I fling open the doors, as though I'm not expecting to find anyone behind it, to reveal Duane and Brittany, both grinning because they think they've caught us at it.

'We were just, erm, looking something up before bed,' I explain innocently, thinking on my feet, and for some reason, I feel slightly embarrassed, even though nothing actually happened.

'That's okay, we thought maybe we had the wrong room,' Brittany reassures me.

'Yeah, it's hard to know if you're coming or going around here,' I reply.

'Not for everyone,' Duane jokes through a cheeky smile.

'Anyway, goodnight,' I say quickly.

'Yeah, goodnight,' Duane calls after us, and I can practically hear the smile on his face as we dash off.

As Sonny and I make our getaway, heading towards our suite, we stop in one of the deserted hallways and burst into laughter.

'I can't believe you just did that,' Sonny says between breaths.

I let out a weird little giggle, my heart still racing from the adrenaline.

'Well, I needed to do something,' I say. 'They were about to get Hope to unlock the door. Wow, feel my chest, my heart's still pounding like we were actually at it in there.'

I grab Sonny's hand and place it on my chest so that he can feel my heartbeat. With my hand on top of his, pressing it to my body, I feel my pulse speeding up, not calming down. Sonny looks into my eyes, saying nothing, just feeling my heartbeat. Oh, God, we're having one of our weird moments again. It's fine, it's just like, I don't know, when you stand up too fast and all the blood rushes to your head, I just need to wait for it to pass and...

'Sorry, anyway,' I blurt around the same time Sonny snatches his hand back.

'Yeah, I was just going to say, I looked in the notebook,' he tells me, getting back on track. 'There wasn't anything wild in there. It looks like they're planning on building a house. It looked pretty cool, actually.'

'Right, okay, well, let's get to bed,' I suggest, moving us along. 'Hope said we have an early start tomorrow, and who knows what she's got lined up for us.'

Knowing Hope, it could be anything.

22

As the morning sun beams down over the resort, I stand around impatiently with my fellow captives as we wait for Hope to grace us with her presence.

We're all in our gym wear, as instructed, and of course, mine is bright pink. Between my neon-pink bra top below and the sun shining above, my eyes are stinging.

'I am so hungry. Don't we usually get breakfast before she starts torturing us?' Izzy moans.

I can't help but laugh at her choice of words. That's an excellent way of putting it, although even breakfast feels like a twisted form of torture here.

'Yeah, I like to eat before I do anything strenuous,' Danny adds.

'Well, I like to eat and not do anything strenuous,' Heath says. He raises an eyebrow curiously. 'What the bloody hell is this?'

'An obstacle course,' Hope says, appearing out of nowhere. 'Physical exercise does the body a world of good, and so does working together, both in your pairs and as a wider team.'

'You're not going to set it on fire, are you?' Heath asks suspiciously, although I'm pretty sure he's just making a joke.

Hope allows herself to let out a small chuckle at the suggestion.

'Of course not,' she reassures. 'In fact, your efforts will be rewarded, see.'

We all turn our attention to where Hope is pointing. At the end of the course stands a marquee, and under it, a table laid out with fruit juices, a big pile of croissants and an assortment of jams.

My breath catches in my throat.

'Your reward will be the satisfaction of completing the course,' Hope declares dramatically. 'And pastry.'

'If it's pastry, I'm in,' Heath says with a clap of his hands. 'I've never been so motivated. Honestly, this trip is lowering my cholesterol.'

'Which is a good thing,' Kellee reminds him.

'I'm surprised you think so,' he replies.

'Not with our prenup, hon,' she claps back with a slight edge.

Oof, okay, this is awkward – and that's coming from the girl who faked an orgasm for an audience last night, and then had to share a bed with one of the guys she did it in front of.

We turn our attention to the course in front of us, the thing that is standing between us and a decent breakfast for a change. It's everything you could expect from an obstacle course, and while my physical fitness is severely lacking, it doesn't look like anything I couldn't give a good go. It looks like it's designed for fun and teamwork rather than serious athletic prowess. A few hurdles, nets to crawl beneath, rope bridges to climb over. I think we can do it, even on a hot, sunny day like today, because, y'know, there's croissants over there!

'Is everyone ready?' Hope asks, her voice carrying across the course. We all cheer, raring to go. 'You have an hour to complete the course, which should be more than enough time for you all to finish, and then you can all dig into your prize together.'

'Where do we start?' Sonny says, clearly excited, although he's a man-mountain who does this sort of thing for fun, so obviously he's raring to go.

'Right here,' Hope confirms.

'Where?' Kellee asks, scanning the surroundings for an obvious starting line.

Hope points to a massive wall looming over us. It's a huge obstacle with ropes hanging high above, completely out of reach.

'This wall is the first obstacle,' Hope tells us. 'And... go!'

Well, Hope did say it was teamwork that was going to help us through the course, and at least this gets the hardest obstacle out of the way first.

'She can't be serious,' Heath scoffs. 'There's no way I'm getting over that.'

I glance at Sonny. He's staring at the wall, sizing it up, his mind working overtime to figure out a plan. In a burst of heroic athleticism, he makes a jump for one of the ropes but falls short. It's a jump that would put Spider-Man to shame and he's not even close.

'Well, if Thor can't do it, none of us can,' Heath concludes, throwing in the towel with a dramatic sigh. 'So, what's the point?'

'Give me a leg-up,' Danny suggests to Sonny. 'We're the tallest. If one of us can get up, maybe we can pull the others up after us.'

Sonny helps him up, letting Danny stand on his strong shoulders, but even from that height, the ropes are well out of Danny's reach.

'It's impossible,' Kellee sighs, frustrated.

'Yeah, I don't see how we're going to do it,' Brittany adds, her voice tinged with defeat too. 'Duane, any ideas?'

Duane looks equally stumped.

'Unless Sonny and I can bulldoze through it, maybe knock it down, I don't see how,' he replies.

'That's probably technically cheating,' Izzy points out. 'I don't think we're allowed to cheat.'

Heath laughs, almost menacingly.

'So, let's cheat,' he says. 'There's no way we're getting over this wall. We could spend the whole hour trying and get nowhere. We're not getting that breakfast unless we take it, and I'm starving, so I'm taking it.'

'Go on, lad!' Danny shouts.

'Yeah, that sounds like a plan to me,' Kellee adds, nodding in agreement. 'We've all paid for it already anyway.'

'I'm in,' Izzy chimes in excitedly as she follows the rebellion, bypassing the obstacles, heading straight for the breakfast table.

'Well, if everyone is doing it,' Duane tells Brittany, shrugging.

Brittany nods.

'I'm not usually a rule breaker, but I'm starving,' she replies. 'Come on.'

Sonny and I exchange amused glances.

'We did say we would all stick together,' he reminds me through a smile as he wipes the sweat from his brow.

'We did indeed,' I reply, trying to ignore how low-key sexy it was watching him trying to scale a massive wall. 'Let's go.'

By the time Sonny and I catch up with the others, Izzy is already halfway through a croissant.

'Worth it,' she blurts through a mouthful. 'Totally worth it.'

I don't want to sound like a crazy person, but I can smell the pastries before I'm even that close to them. I practically float through the air, like Mickey Mouse catching a whiff of a pie, following my nose to the breakfast of my dreams.

As everyone tucks in, I grab a croissant and stuff it to the brim with strawberry jam. It's only in my mouth for a few seconds when I notice our chatter die down, one person at a time falling silent, as we realise Hope has returned.

'What's this?' she asks us. 'Finished already?'

You can tell by the tightness of her jaw and the fire in her eyes that she knows we haven't.

'You could say that,' Heath points out.

'Well, I heard it from the rest of the team that you quite literally fell at the first hurdle, and decided that you would take your breakfast anyway, unearned – is this true?'

'Listen, sweetheart, we're a democracy here, okay,' Heath begins to explain and, let me tell you this, I know for a fact that Hope doesn't appreciate being called 'sweetheart' because there is steam coming out of her ears. 'We're hungry, and your course isn't fit for purpose, none of us could do it,' Heath continues. 'Look at Thor, look how jacked he is, he looks like he climbs mountains just to stretch his legs. Even he couldn't do it.'

'No?' Hope says, turning to Sonny.

'I gave it my best,' he tells her. 'But it just seemed like there was no way.'

'So, you all helped yourself to breakfast regardless?' she says, again, but with more anger this time.

I wince. It seems like we're all in big trouble now.

'Then you must all be punished,' Hope announces sternly. 'Return to your suites and I will send for you, a couple at a time, to receive your punishment.'

'Okay, sure, when we've finished our breakfast,' Heath tells her casually.

Kellee smirks, looking on at her man proudly before pouring herself a glass of pineapple juice.

Hope swallows hard before turning on her heel and walking away.

'Nice one,' Danny says.

'Yeah, you showed her, babe,' Kellee says.

'But we're all getting punished,' Izzy reminds us.

'Then I guess we should really enjoy this breakfast,' I point out with a laugh.

We all carry on eating, chatting, laughing together, enjoying our moment of defiance, and the best breakfast we've had while we've been here.

I push the idea of punishment to the back of my mind. For now, let's just take a little victory where we can get one.

23

I would be lying to say I was disappointed to find myself floating around in the pool again, the sun warming my skin, Sonny's hand intertwined with mine for our so-called punishment. It seems that 'sea-ottering' is Hope's go-to form of punishment for me and Sonny and, honestly, it doesn't seem like either of us hate it, or find it especially punishing.

The pool is an oasis of tranquillity, the surface of the water rippling gently under the caress of a warm breeze. The water feels so cool and refreshing against our skin as we float so effortlessly I could almost drift off – to sleep, that is, not to sea.

The air here smells so sweet, like flowers and fruit, and as the breeze dances past us it brings hints of the ocean with it. You can hear the breeze blowing through the leaves, birds chirping away in the distance, if you listen really carefully you can hear the waves lapping against the shore somewhere nearby. I have a relaxation app on my phone that makes sounds like this but it doesn't quite hit the spot in my tiny bedroom, in the middle of the night, in winter when my radiator can't quite seem to get going. Here, though, under the warm sun, every single one of my senses feels soothed.

Sonny and I float together, side by side, holding hands, like two relaxed otters drifting down a lazy river.

'Remind me why this is a punishment?' Sonny asks.

I turn my head to look at him. He looks so relaxed, hiding behind his sunglasses, the sun making his abs glisten. Every now and then he scoops up some pool water in his hands and rubs it over his body to cool himself down. He suits this lifestyle – it's a shame he's not really rich. Well, obviously, it's a shame for both of us.

'Yeah, I'm not sure myself,' I reply. 'All she's giving us is space to relax – and to have secret conversations.'

'Speaking of which,' he says, his voice suddenly much quieter. 'Heath thinks Kellee's been cheating on him.'

I raise an eyebrow and chew my lip for a second.

'Really?' I reply. 'How do you know that?'

'He mentioned it during one of our sessions, when it was just the boys,' he explains. 'He said he's been really stressed at work lately, working all hours, and he's convinced she's seeing other people while he's been preoccupied.'

'Hmm,' I say, the cogs in my brain turning. 'That's interesting because Kellee told me that it's Heath who is cheating on her. She says he's only pretending to work all hours, that he's actually seeing someone else – she even knew her name.'

'Wait, what? Are you sure?' Sonny asks, turning to face me, not that I can read his emotions through his sunglasses.

'Yeah, she told me,' I say. 'And I believe her.'

'Heath seemed really genuine too,' Sonny insists. 'And he's got no reason to lie to me.'

'Oh, really, Thor?' I reply with a chuckle. 'Because it seems to me like he loves you and he would do anything to impress you.'

'Jokes aside, it did seem like he was putting up this cool front at first,' Sonny tells me. 'But when he said this, honestly, if he was lying then I fell for it.'

'That's odd,' I say. 'One of them must be mistaken.'

'Or maybe one of them is lying,' Sonny points out.

'Yeah, maybe,' I say. 'I don't know, though. I feel like being here, under these circumstances, together, it sort of feels like we're all friends.'

'We are all friends,' Sonny says. 'Which helps us to do our job in many ways, but then makes it so much harder in others.'

I smile to myself, touched to hear that he has a conscience too.

'What do you think Heath is working on?' I ask. 'Anything exciting?'

'He's very good at keeping tight-lipped when he talks about work – I suppose he has to be,' Sonny says. 'Whatever it is, it's making him stressed.'

'Who could feel stressed in a paradise like this?' I say, playing with the water with my free hand. 'I mean, us, obviously, given what we're here to do, but if this was a normal holiday for us, it would be heaven.'

'Instead, it's Eden,' Sonny jokes. 'But if this is what happens when we get in trouble, maybe we should misbehave more often.'

I laugh, the sound echoing softly in the open space.

'You're right,' I say. 'Punishment has never been this relaxing. Addison and CJ would never.'

'God, don't even say their names,' he says with a laugh. 'I'm not missing work at all. I'm so deep in character, I'm telling even myself that I don't have a job.'

'If we don't find something to take back with us, we won't,' I dare to joke.

We share a moment of comfortable silence, just enjoying the tranquillity of our surroundings. It really is quite nice, spending time with Sonny like this. No competition, no pretence, just two people chatting and being themselves – I would say being normal, if there was anything normal about 'sea-ottering', on an island, not knowing what continent you're on.

I glance over at him and can't help but smile.

'It's moments like these that make me wonder why we can't always be like this,' I say with a sigh, kind of nervously for some reason. 'Just... normal.'

Sonny's gaze meets mine but, again, I can't tell what's going on behind his tinted specs.

'I know what you mean,' he says. 'It's sort of like we're on holiday from being us.'

As we continue to float side by side, hands gently holding on to each other, I can't help but wonder if this is just a holiday, or if there could be more peaceful moments like this in our future. But for now, I'm just happy with this one, and the break from Eden activities, and getting to enjoy such a beautiful space, in a dreamy location. Even if it's all going to come to an end soon.

24

I never thought there would be a time when I didn't get excited about dinner, but here we are. Surely no one gets excited at a plate of raw vegetables, though. Not even rabbits.

Tonight's topic of dinner conversation seems to be around relationships and the problems we are all having. Hope, our ever-watchful orchestrator, is silently spectating as we take the lead. Well, I supposed that's why we're all here, to fix our problems – in one way or another.

'I think the hardest part is dealing with the fact that so many people fancy my fella,' Izzy confesses. 'It's like, how do you trust anyone when people are throwing themselves at him?'

'You know you can trust me,' Danny reminds her.

'But I can't trust the people around you,' she tells him. 'And that really scares me.'

Kellee laughs, clearly for effect.

'Well, that's a problem I don't have,' she announces. 'I mean, who'd want to fancy Heath, right?'

She nudges her husband playfully, mischief twinkling in her eyes. He's not impressed.

Heath raises an eyebrow and I wince pre-emptively as I worry about what he will say in reply.

'Whereas people do lust after my wife, but it's just because she runs her Instagram page like it's an OnlyFans,' Heath says with a casual shrug.

Ouch.

I wonder what is going on with those two, they're both so suspicious of one another, but one of them must be lying.

'Honestly, I think the hardest thing for us is just the constant media speculation,' Duane chimes in, suddenly sobering us all. 'There was a story about us in the press not too long ago. We rushed to the hospital one evening – my appendix had burst, it was an emergency – but the media reported it as the two of us having some kind of kinky sex session, that had gone wrong, and injured us both. It's disgusting when you can't even see a doctor without some twisted version of events being plastered all over the news.'

'That's out of order,' Heath says, serious for once.

'And on Christmas Eve we were in Edinburgh, and they almost ran us off the road, for what?' Duane says. 'For a couple of pictures of us looking scared in the back of a car.'

'Yeah, the tabloids never leave us alone,' Izzy adds. 'It's great, when you want some coverage, but they don't know when to stop.'

'Absolutely,' Kellee agrees. 'I've had my fair share of crap. Journalists are the scum of the earth, aren't they?'

Well, I feel like an arsehole. I don't even know what to say. I can't bring myself to speak, not even to agree. A quick side glance at Sonny confirms the same.

The rest of the group carries on chatting obliviously. That's horrible, what Duane said about when he had to go to the hospital. No one should have anyone giving them trouble at a time like that.

I spot Brett standing at the other side of the room, where the staff members usually linger, waiting to see if they are needed. He beckons me over with a jerk of his head.

'I'm just going to the loo,' I tell Sonny, satisfied that he hasn't noticed Brett.

'Meet me in the forest later, in the clearing by the old stump,' he whispers as I pass him.

I continue on my way to the toilets, so as not to raise suspicion, but I smile to myself as I go. Well, after a dinner of raw vegetables, I can't wait.

25

The forest, it turns out, is the in place for secret meetings.

It's funny that I knew exactly where Brett meant, when he said to meet him in the clearing by the old stump. It's an area that isn't all that far from the main building, but the cloak of the leafy trees provides absolute privacy.

I'm careful not to be seen, as I hurry to meet Brett, excited by what he might have for me.

'Oh my God,' I blurt when I clap eyes on him, and the first thing I notice is the pizza in his hand.

'I thought we could share,' he says with a grin, clearly proud of himself for sneaking something so big out here.

Wow, I don't know if he looks more handsome than usual, or if I'm genuinely just blinded by the stunning sight of a perfect pizza, but I could propose.

I grab a slice, getting straight down to business, and then take a bite. My stomach grumbles in approval – or perhaps it is relief. I'll bet it thought it was never going to get a pizza again.

We make small talk for a while, before Brett turns his attention to what we were all talking about at dinner.

'Did you catch Duane's story?' Brett asks, sucking his fingers clean in a way that is undeniably sexy or, as I said, I am just that hungry.

'Yeah, about his appendix bursting?' I reply, not even bothering to worry about whether or not I'm talking with my mouth full. 'Scary stuff.'

'He was definitely lying,' Brett informs me.

I take a sip of water, trying to act casual even though I'm dying to know what he's talking about, but not wanting to seem like a news-hungry journalist.

Brett nods.

'One hundred per cent,' he says confidently. 'I led him and Brittany in another partner yoga session early this morning. He doesn't have a scar.'

Okay, now my ears really have pricked up.

'Really?' I squeak.

I was going to say that I must be losing my touch, but appendectomy scars can be quite low down, can't they? And I don't often stare at men from the waist down. I suppose Brett is a yoga instructor, so he has an excuse.

'Yeah, he was wearing swimming trunks – they had just been in the pool – and I could see where his scar would be. See, I have one, right here.'

As Brett pulls down his shorts slightly, to show me his scar, I try to drag my mind from the gutter and focus on what he's telling me.

'So he's lying about why they went to the hospital,' I think to myself out loud.

'Seems like it,' he replies. 'But the question is, why would he lie about something like that?'

I really don't want Brett to suspect that I'm interested, so I laugh it off.

'Perhaps it was something more embarrassing,' I say with a cheeky smile. 'And he didn't want to give us the gory details.'

'Maybe,' Brett replies as he offers me the last slice.

As we chat, I find myself secretly revelling in this newfound alliance. I think I'm going to keep my new information from Sonny for now. Well, I think we all know what he would do if he knew, he would probably go over my head with it, to get a pat on the back, and pretend I had nothing to do with it – why, yes, talking about what happened at uni has picked at the scab again. Perhaps this time it could be me with the golden ticket, with the info that's going to be the most impressive.

Either way, I'm definitely going to keep it to myself for now, at least until I know what's going on.

I take a final bite of the pizza, popping the last bit in my mouth, perfectly full – but I would eat more, if there was more, for sure.

'I'd best get back, before anyone realises I'm missing,' I tell him. 'But thank you so, so much.'

Brett flashes me a charming smile.

'I'll get something else to you, tomorrow – something good,' he promises. 'In the meantime, see if you can figure out what Duane is lying about. I'm suspicious of his intentions.'

'Okay, sure,' I say. Well, I'll say whatever he wants, the man just promised me more food tomorrow.

I navigate my way back to the suite, my steps light and careful. I make sure I'm not seen because, in a worst-case scenario, it might blow my and Sonny's cover. Equally as bad, though, would be if it brought about an end to Brett smuggling me food. If I'm going to be staying here longer, I'm going to be needing that lifeline.

Opening the door, I slip inside and exhale a sigh of relief. The suite is quiet, and the lights dim. It seems like Sonny is asleep. I'm about to kick off my shoes and slip into the bathroom to freshen up when Sonny's voice startles me.

He rises up in the bed, like Frankenstein's monster when it wakes up.

'Lara, where have you been?' he asks. 'I was worried.'

I jump a little, my heart racing for a second. I walk over to him, trying to play it cool. He has a curious expression on his face. I forget how observant he is – obviously he is, it's his job. I try to keep my tone nonchalant.

'Oh, I just went for a walk in the forest,' I say. 'I needed some fresh air.'

'You went for a walk alone in the forest late at night in the dark on a random island,' he replies, laying out the unlikely facts.

'Yeah,' I reply simply, refusing to acknowledge how weird it might sound.

Sonny's gaze narrows a bit, and I'm suddenly acutely aware of my appearance. Oh, God, what can he see? 'Your lips look red,' he points out.

I touch my lips instinctively, a little confused. Then I remember the pizza – the tomato sauce. Shit, why do I have to be so messy?

'Probably just sunburn,' I tell him, subtly edging away from him.

'Sunburn that you got on a walk, alone in the forest, late at night, in the dark, on a random island,' he says suspiciously.

'Mmm,' I reply, pursing my lips a little, anything to hide them, or rub off the last of the sauce. Crap, I wonder if Brett noticed. 'Right, I'm going to get ready for bed.'

Sonny lies back down and I head into the bathroom where I wash my face and brush my teeth, destroying the last of the evidence. I was sloppy – in more ways than one – coming in like this.

Interesting, though, that Sonny wondered where I was, and seemed suspicious about my reply. I wonder if he thinks I'm working without him, or if he's jealous that I might be hanging out with someone else. I guess I'm doing both, but he doesn't know that.

Interesting. Very interesting indeed.

26

Ah, the peaceful, serene greenery of the forest during the day. The rustling leaves, the earthy scents, and the sense of quiet seclusion – still, I prefer it when it has cheeseburgers and pizzas for me. All I need now is for the gods (or Brett, if we're being realistic) to bring me my own coffee shop and cocktail bar and I could stay here forever. I pretended to eat my seeds this morning, like a good girl, and my – whatever the hell quinoa is – for lunch. I don't know how I'll do today, surviving on banana figs, but with a bit of luck I'll be able to convince Sonny to climb a tree and get me a coconut. Coconut milk is the closest I'll get to a latte out here.

Today is what Hope has so cryptically dubbed 'personal amusement day'. I find her choice of words as vague as a horoscope. Sonny, ever the realist, translates it more bluntly: Hope's just too lazy to feed us or come up with actual activities, so we have to do it for ourselves.

Her instructions were simple: go out into the forest, explore, enjoy one another, be alone in nature, and find your own food. Oh, and apparently we're all at different parts of the island, so no chance of us bumping into one another. It might have been more fun, if we were doing it as a group – the boys could have built us another shelter, although I suspect they're all far too frustrated to ever bother building anything again.

As we stroll aimlessly, each step takes us deeper into the forest. But of course, being the unromantics that we are, all Sonny and I really have to talk about is work, and the task we came here to do.

'I wonder what they're all up to,' I think out loud.

'Danny is probably piggybacking Izzy over some dirt – which is essentially the entire floor,' he starts, smiling to himself. 'Kellee is probably flirting with a lizard while Heath does something totally rational in response like, I don't know, uses bits of debris he finds on the floor to craft a robot that will damage the island's ecosystem to the point where all the lizards die – something chill like that. And Brittany and Duane, I don't know, they seem like us, like normal people, not celebrities. They're probably just walking and chatting too.'

I laugh – especially at the part about Heath. That sounds exactly like something he would do.

'You know, I still can't figure out why Duane and Brittany are here,' I say, my voice wobbling as I almost trip over some chunky tree roots. 'They seem so happy, like they're living in their own little universe.'

'Well, that's what I mean, about them seeming so normal,' Sonny continues. 'Spending this kind of money on this kind of treatment isn't something normal people do – not unless their bosses make them, of course.'

'Oh, of course,' I reply with a faux seriousness. 'Totally normal part of any job description.'

When our playful banter is more like this, light-hearted, the way it was when we first met, Sonny is easy to be around. I guess here, working together, we're not really competing. It (temporarily at least) takes our usual tension off the table. I can't believe I'm saying it, but I could definitely get used to it. Our work life would be better if the two of us could just be normal.

'Maybe we can see if the beach is anywhere nearby,' I suggest. 'I want a shell.'

'Yeah, we can try to find it,' Sonny replies. 'It's an island – there's only so far we can walk. Any particular reason?'

'When I was young we would always go on holiday with my grandparents, and my gran would always take me to find a shell, everywhere we went, to add to our collection. She already had so many, from all over the world. She left them to me when she passed and I do my best to keep the tradition going,' I say.

'Then we will get you a shell,' he tells me with a smile.

As we continue our stroll, and the forest's tranquil beauty envelops us, I find myself grateful for this moment of tranquillity and connection. I think this is the first real time I have truly appreciated what an amazing place we are in (wherever we are) and how lucky we are to even be here, no matter what the situation.

We venture deeper into the forest, our steps guided by the little flecks of sunlight that shine through the tree canopy that is always above us – one that I'm thankful for, as it really takes the edge off the sun.

'What the...?'

An unexpected sight catches Sonny's attention. His brows furrow in puzzlement. I follow his gaze, squinting to better see what lies ahead, but my brain can't make sense of it either.

'What the hell is that?' I ask, my voice a combination of disbelief and intrigue.

'Let's go see,' Sonny suggests with a shrug.

We slowly venture closer – the thing ahead of us making more sense as we approach it. It's some kind of self-service bar – a rum bar, it looks like – nestled in the heart of the woods. My eyes widen as I take in the sight: rows of assorted bottles, colourful cocktail ingredients, fresh fruit for garnishing. Why, yes, I am on board for fresh fruit in this format.

Sonny picks up a clipboard from behind the bar.

'It has the names of island staff scrawled on it,' he says. 'Along with what they've been drinking – this must be a secret bar, for the staff.'

'Wow,' I blurt, my surprise echoing in the single word. I knew the staff got to eat whatever they wanted, but a fully stocked bar tucked away in the woods is a whole new level of luxury. Brett never mentioned that.

Sonny looks annoyed.

'You're telling me they have a bar while we're drinking nothing but water – or water with fruit in it?' he asks. 'What next? Is there a KFC on the other side of the island?'

You know, there could be...

I smile and shrug my shoulders.

'Well, it's the best thing I've foraged for,' I joke. 'A rum tree.'

Sonny tilts his head and peers at me, a sly smile creeping on to his lips.

'When was the last time you had a drink?' he asks me. 'A drink-drink.'

I think for a moment, but then it's obvious.

'My last drink-drink was during our fabulous not-date,' I say with a laugh.

'I'm just thinking,' he starts, taking a bottle of rum from the shelf, examining it as he grins to himself. 'Hope did tell us to "amuse and provide for ourselves". And she did say we could use whatever resources we could find...'

'I don't think she meant for us to raid the staff's secret rum stash, though,' I point out.

'Perhaps,' he says as he opens the bottle. 'But she didn't say not to either. Go on, take a seat, let me make you a cocktail.'

'Fine, fine,' I say as I give in to peer pressure with, well, basically no pressure at all.

There are some comfortable-looking cushions scattered around so I drag a few into a pile and plonk myself down on them, reclining slightly as I admire the trees that stand tall above us, protecting us from the hot sun.

Eventually, Sonny drops down next to me. He places a drink in my hand before clinking his matching drink with mine.

'What is it?' I ask – not that I care.

'I don't know, something I made up,' he tells me.

'Okay then, what's it called?' I ask with a smile.

He looks at me with a mock-serious expression.

'A Sea Otter Surprise,' he informs me.

I laugh, unable to contain my amusement.

'A Sea Otter Surprise?' I repeat back to him.

'It's our drink,' he tells me with a smile. 'Come on, try it.'

I take a small sip. Then a big gulp.

'Wow, that is good,' I tell him. 'And strong.'

I pull a face that is supposed to convey just how strong it is.

'Well, we've got some catching up to do, haven't we?' he replies.

Of course, one cocktail turns into two, then three, then you stop counting, don't you? We could have been here for four hours or forty-five minutes. Who can say? That's what happens, when there are no clocks, and you reuse your glasses. You lose all track of your drinking.

I hiccup loudly. Sonny almost sprays his drink from his mouth as I make him jump and laugh at the same time.

The trees around us seem to sway with our laughter. My cheeks feel warm, and every giggle is like a tickle in my chest. The world becomes a touch more vivid, a bit more colourful, and maybe it's because I'm in a good mood, or maybe it's because I'm drunk, or maybe it's both?

'I hope we don't see the UFO,' Sonny muses.

'Huh?' I reply before draining the last of my cocktail. 'What UFO?'

'Did Izzy not tell you that she thought she saw a UFO?' he replies.

'Erm, no,' I say with a scoff – initially more bothered that she told Sonny and not me, more so than I am about the concept of the island having a UFO.

'She was terrified,' he tells me. 'But then she realised it was just a bird.'

I roar at the idea of Izzy, looking up to the skies, thinking we were finally meeting alien life and then realising it was just a seagull.

'She's brilliant, I love her,' I insist.

I go to take another sip of my drink but it's empty, which confuses me for a few seconds.

I lean against the pile of cushions, the buzz from the Sea Otter Surprises making the world spin just a little faster than usual.

'Who is the worst celebrity you've ever met?' I ask curiously. 'Tell me a horror story.'

Sonny's face scrunches up in deep thought.

'You know, it wasn't even for work, I was at this nice restaurant, and guess who was sitting at the next table?'

'Who?' I say as I lean in, eager to find out who it is.

'Alvin Matthews – you know, the "motivational speaker"?' Sonny's tone is exaggeratedly dramatic, if not sarcastic, and I can't help but laugh.

'The one who's all about "finding yourself inside yourself" and "embracing the you who won't embrace you"?' I reply, mocking

Marvin's soothing voice, finding it almost impossible to get to the end of my sentence without laughing at my own impression.

'Yeah, that guy,' Sonny confirms. 'So, I accidentally knocked over my glass of wine, and he noticed, came over, and he turned it into this whole spiritual lesson about how my "body was tired of me drinking so much" and "working me from the inside" – everyone was staring at me, it was mortifying.'

'You? Drink too much?' I say in extremely exaggerated disbelief.

We both fall about laughing again. Honestly, this evening, every little thing is hilarious – my God, is it night-time already? – and even as a bug flies towards Sonny's face, almost landing inside his mouth, we both just think it is the funniest. Unless it happened to me, of course, then it would be a whole thing.

Suddenly, it is as if a switch has been flipped, the laughter fades, and Sonny's expression turns serious, almost vulnerable. He's gone from being the happiest I've ever seen him to looking so, so sad. He's staring at me in a way that worries me. All at once, it feels like the party is over.

'Lara,' he starts, his voice softer now. He puffs air from his cheeks. 'I need to say something. I can't… I can't do anything else until I do. I need to… to apologise, for what happened back at uni.'

I feel my eyebrows practically meet in the middle.

'What?' I say, confused. 'Why? Why now? Because everyone made you feel bad when it came up the other day?'

My tipsy brain is struggling to catch up with the change in tone.

He takes a deep breath, his eyes locking on to mine with an intensity that sobers me up a little – well, almost.

'No, because I've wanted to apologise ever since it happened,' he confesses. 'I'm sorry. I was young, ambitious, and stupid. I thought I needed to do what I did to get ahead, to move up the ladder, but instead of stepping on the first rung, or whatever, I stepped on you.

But I really liked you, back then, I did, and I've kicked myself ever since.'

His words hit me like an empty rum bottle, and suddenly, the alcohol in my system evaporates, making way for something else. I'm gripped, on the edge of my seat, waiting to see what he says next.

'And I wanted to call you, I did, but I was embarrassed – ashamed even,' he continues. 'Ashamed of myself for the way I got the job.'

'Sonny, I—' I try to speak but he cuts me off. The regret on his face looks like it is physically hurting him, and I'm seeing something I've never seen behind his eyes before.

'Everything since then has been like school playground teasing, anything to stay on your radar because I knew you'd never want me as a friend.' He pauses, looking as though he's carefully considering what to say next. 'I'm sorry if I annoy you sometimes, but honestly, the times we spend together while we're working are usually the best parts of my day.'

I'm speechless. And the alcohol is no longer numbing my senses – I wish it would, because my head is spinning, and my emotions are surging. I'm fully present, fully aware of the vulnerability he's showing, my heart softening with every word he is saying, his gorgeous eyes, his lips, his...

Before I can even process a word he just said, before my rational thoughts can catch up, my tipsy heart takes the reins. I lean forward, closing the distance between us, and press my lips against his. My intention was to put my lips on his, kiss him, and then pull back to figure out how it made me feel. Except I'm still kissing him, I'm heating things up, I'm pushing him back onto the cushions and climbing on top of him.

Sonny grabs my bum, his head lifting off the floor as he leans into my kisses. Eventually he's had enough, he scoops me up in his arms and lays me down on the floor before pressing himself down on top of me. As he takes charge, I run my hands over his big shoulders, down his biceps, eventually resting them on his bare back. As he kisses my neck, I feel myself involuntarily dig my nails into his back.

Well, so much for waiting to see how one little kiss made me feel. It turns out I didn't need it, to know just what I wanted.

27

Bang, bang, bang-bang. Bang, bang, bang-bang...

My head feels like a band is having a jam session inside my skull. At first, I put it down to all the rum we drank, giving me one hell of a thumping hangover, but then I realise it is more than that. I can hear drums. Real drums.

My eyes snap open, revealing a familiar scene: Sonny and me, still sprawled on the floor of the outdoor bar where we had successfully drowned ourselves in rum last night. I know it was last night because it was dark then, it's not now. It was dark when we... oh, my, God. I slept with Sonny last night. Not just slept next to, slept with.

Sonny stirs beside me, his eyes squinting in retaliation at the bright sunlight above us.

'Shit, are we late for something?' he says. 'If the drums are anything like the alarms then we're probably missing some mandatory activity.'

'And we're not supposed to be here,' I say, jumping to my feet, my head throbbing extra hard for a moment. Yikes. Why did I drink so much?

I grab a bottle of water from behind the bar and press it against my forehead.

'Okay, I'm up,' Sonny says with a sigh.

He rubs his eyes before stretching, flexing every muscle he has in the process.

'Well, as nights off go, that was great,' he says. 'Back to it now.'

'Sonny, wait a sec,' I say, stopping him in his tracks.

I take a big gulp of water, swish it around in my mouth, and then spit it out. It does little to get rid of the rum aftertaste, but I feel less dry at least.

'What's up?' he asks, looking concerned.

'What are we doing here?' I blurt.

I watch a mixture of panic and tension building in his face.

'Oh, God, no, not us,' I quickly correct myself. 'I know what we're doing here. I mean, here on the island, the job we're here to do.'

'What do you mean?' he asks.

'What I mean is... I don't know... I know what we're here to do but what if I don't want to do it?' I blurt. 'I really like everyone here. I know we haven't known them long but they're our friends, they're confiding in us, trusting us, and we're going to – what – sell them out? What if we didn't? What if we just packed our bags and went home right now, me and you, and then we figure everything else out later.'

I can see the weight of my words pressing hard against Sonny's chest.

'We would be going back to unemployment if we did that,' he points out. 'We know they've thrown loads of time and tons of money into sending us here. You and I are in the same boat, we've put all of our eggs in this basket, we have no other provable skills, no other work experience, and there's no way we'll get a good reference if we mess this up. We'll never work in the industry again –

who knows when we will work again, and doing what? We both have rent, bills, a crippling dependency on food and water...'

I sigh.

'Lara, I'd love nothing more than to pack our bags and head home,' he tells me. 'But we can't afford to lose these jobs. It's all we've got, and this is our only shot at keeping them.'

'I know, Sonny, I know. It's just... it all feels wrong,' I point out, probably naively.

'Well, I'm not going to mess this up,' he says, straightening himself up, locating his clothing and putting it back on. 'I'm going to wherever these drums are and I'm going to do what I've got to do.'

I grab my things so that we head back towards the resort. Stumbling through the warm, sticky forest feels like trying to swim in quicksand. The forest, with its uneven floor and its swarms of bugs, seems to be conspiring with the blazing sun to make my throbbing hangover even worse. Even the happy chirping of the birds is making me feel so much worse. The forest air, heavy with the scent of damp earth, wildflowers, and the occasional whiff of fruit, is usually a dream – today it's a nightmare, one that is making me gag.

I follow Sonny, a few paces behind, shuffling like an extra from *The Walking Dead* (and with the complexion to go with it too), in silence. I don't know what to say to him, and he clearly doesn't have anything to say to me. I felt like we were getting closer, settling down, like we were finally on the same page for once. Now it feels like the book has been slammed shut and chucked onto the bonfire and now I have no idea where we are.

One thing I do know, though, is that, job be damned, I don't feel good about doing this, and I would rather worry about my own problems than publicly broadcast someone else's. Sonny, however, is still the same ruthless arsehole, willing to do whatever it takes to get himself one step further. That's where we differ, where we'll always differ, why we can never be friends.

The path eventually opens up, and the resort comes into view. I notice that everyone is already standing outside, and we're the last ones to arrive.

'Sorry we're late,' Sonny announces as we join the group out by the pool. 'We just went for an early-morning walk.'

'You're here now,' Hope confirms. 'I hope you're all ready for our first activity of the day: drum yoga.'

Because of course it's whatever the hell drum yoga is, when I've got the worst hangover I've ever had, paired so hellishly with a double dose of regret. Of course, I can't use my hangover as an excuse to get me out of it (and any reasonable person would definitely excuse me if they knew) because I'm not supposed to have one, we shouldn't have been drinking last night.

'Not today,' Heath moans. 'I'm not feeling up to it.'

'Yeah, I'm not arsed for drum yoga either,' Izzy adds.

I look around the group and notice that everyone looks a little rough today. The others are probably just tired, or sick of the early mornings and the yoga, but with my hangover I can't think of anything worse.

'Brett, if you would be so kind as to lead the group,' Hope says. 'And I'll be back to check on you all shortly.'

'She's probably going for a full brekkie,' Heath mutters under his breath.

Brett is setting something up, a little way away from the group, so I try to subtly shuffle over to him.

'Morning,' he says with a smile. 'You don't look your usual self today.'

'What a polite way of saying I look like shit,' I reply with a laugh. 'I don't think island life is agreeing with me, and I'm seriously craving a cheese sandwich. Do you think you can sort me out?'

'I'm like a snack dealer,' he jokes. 'But yeah, sure thing. You got some hot gossip for me?'

'Depends on what you've got for me for lunch,' I joke.

'You drive a hard bargain, Lara,' he says through a grin. 'Okay, I'll bring chips too.'

He must be bored out of his mind working here, with hardly anyone else around, I'm not surprised it's turned him into a bored housewife looking for a gossip over lunch.

I make my way back over to the group.

'Are you wearing yesterday's clothes?' Kellee asks through a smirk.

'Thor, you stud,' Heath praises him. 'Out in the wild – that is wild.'

'Yeah, you two love the danger, don't you?' Duane teases.

Brittany rolls her eyes.

'Lara, I'm not feeling all that up to it either,' she tells me. 'Come and stand with me, we can take it easy together.'

I feel my cheeks flushing and it's not because I'm embarrassed that the group think I'm some kind of deviant who gets off on, well, getting off in public places. It's because I'm annoyed at myself because I slept with Sonny – again – and he's screwing me over a-fucking-gain, putting work before anything else.

That's it now, no more working together, it's every man or woman for themselves. I just can't believe I fell for it again. Fool me once, shame on you. Fool me twice – my God, I'm an idiot sometimes.

28

My footsteps crunch on the ground as I make my way toward my and Brett's secret meeting spot.

I am so excited for my cheese sandwich, honestly, it's the only thing that got me through the hell that was drum yoga with the mother of all hangovers. I'm actually fantasising about it, what kind of bread it will be in, what kind of cheese will be inside it. I suppose, given that Brett is American, when he says chips, I'm not sure if he means chips as in chips like in the UK, or chips as in crisps like in the US. My God, even that is exciting. Either would be amazing, and the adrenaline rush as I wait to find out, wow, it's really something.

It's not just about the food, though. Not today. Things are a little awkward between me and Sonny now, to say the least, so hanging out in the forest (ideally with a sandwich) will give me a moment to catch my breath, and work out what is going on in my head.

I turn towards the rustling in the bushes, expecting to see my knight in... shining... sandwich? I don't know, I'm so hung-over and so hungry.

It isn't Brett, though, it's Sonny – shit.

'What are you doing here?' he asks, one eyebrow raised suspiciously.

I blink at him, attempting to feign innocence, but aside from how thick I am probably laying it on, I think Sonny knows me too well to fall for it.

'Oh, just, you know, just enjoying the scenery, taking a walk through nature,' I tell him, smiling, swaying on the spot like a toddler who is just so proud of the balloon she's holding.

His smirk is practically audible.

'Another walk, huh?' he replies. 'Says the girl who – when the lift was broken at work – called in sick.'

'Well, that was a long time ago,' I tell him. 'I've really learned to love it.'

'The same girl who, when we were walking yesterday, sang "I hate walking" to the tune of "I Want Candy" for about eight minutes,' he reminds me.

'Yep,' I manage to say with a straight face.

'Lara, come on,' he prompts me expectantly – and it works.

I huff a laugh, not even trying to keep up the act.

'All right, fine. I'm meeting Brett,' I tell him.

'Meeting Brett?' he blurts, not sounding at all happy about it. 'Why?'

'Just, you know, socially,' I offer up. 'For fun.'

'Lara, what is going on with you?' he asks me, frustrated. 'With us? And with work – suddenly you sound like you're just going to throw it all away. We both know what we were sent here to do – we're here as journalists. At least take that seriously. We need people to keep believing that we're a couple, we need to get our story. And then you can run around with all of the yoga instructors you want.'

He doesn't quite sound like he means that last part.

We stare at each other, only for a second, before a rustling in the bushes jolts us both back to reality.

'Shit,' I whisper. 'Someone was listening.'

'I'll go see who it was,' he tells me. 'Wait here.'

I'm left standing alone, my heart pounding, anxiety intensifying or numbing every sense I have. What if someone overheard us? What if we're about to be caught? What will they do to us? What *can* they even do to us? Panic and paranoia swirl around me until finally, Brett emerges from the trees, smirking, holding a sandwich and a large bag of crisps.

My brain short-circuits for a moment. At first, I'm relieved that it wasn't one of our friends who overheard us, but then it occurs to me that this is so much worse, because Brett is resort staff. We're screwed.

'Hey, I hope you're hungry,' he tells me. 'It sounds like we have a lot to talk about.'

'Sonny and I were just, er, we were just shagging,' I blurt. 'Sorry, hope you didn't see anything.'

'You and I both know that I didn't see anything,' he says, setting the plate down on the stump next to me. 'I heard plenty, though.'

I open my mouth, ready to launch into an excuse or a lie or something. But Brett raises a hand, halting me, telling me not to say another word.

'Don't worry, I'm not here to blow your cover,' he reassures me. 'In fact, I'm sort of in the same line of work.'

My eyes widen with horror.

'What do you mean?' I ask him.

He laughs, a mischievous glint in his eye.

'I'm a journalist too. That's why I'm here, posing as a yoga instructor,' he says proudly. 'I bullshitted my way into this gig by pretending I'm a yoga guru. I had to get a few friends in high places to help me make it legit but, yeah, I've been here for a while, getting the inside scoop on all kinds of people – you wouldn't believe it. Of course, we don't have the internet here, and no phones, so I haven't been able to report back yet. I couldn't believe my luck when Duittany stepped off the boat. I could not have had a better last group. I knew something was up with you guys, though, thought it was weird that I couldn't place either of you – even the soccer player I knew but, wow, I can't believe it.'

My mouth hangs open, and for once, I'm actually, genuinely speechless.

'Well, now we both know why we're here, we both know the truth,' he continues excitedly. 'We can swap notes, work together. I'm based in the US, you're in the UK. We could pull off some incredible stories on our respective sides of the pond.'

Before I can say anything, Sonny arrives back. He's hurrying until he sees Brett. Then he slows down, as though he were approaching an armed man.

He opens his mouth to speak, but I beat him to it, quickly filling him in on the truth before he can make anything worse by lying.

'So, it turns out Brett is a journalist too,' I tell him. 'We just realised we all share a connection.'

I say every word with a smile, keen to keep Brett on side. He didn't have to confess to us, he could have just exposed us, and kept everything he found out for himself.

Brett grins at Sonny, extending a friendly hand.

'Brett Waters. Pseudo-yogi and undercover journalist.'

'Hi,' Sonny says, shaking his hand as though he were meeting him for the first time.

'Listen, I need to dash, Lara can fill you in,' he says. He turns to me. 'Think about what I said. And I'm sure it's pretty obvious why I've been sneaking you food now, but there's plenty more where that came from.'

Brett disappears as fast as he arrived.

'Okay, now you really need to tell me what's going on,' Sonny demands. 'He's been sneaking you food?'

'Yeah,' I say weakly.

'And you haven't been sharing it?' he says, his voice so much higher than usual.

Hilariously, it seems like he's finding me not sharing food with him the biggest betrayal of all.

'Right, listen, Brett has been smuggling me food,' I begin. 'I guess he's been doing it to try to get information out of me. I didn't know he was an undercover journalist until just now. I suppose it makes sense we wouldn't be the only ones to try, everyone is desperate to know all about this place. But it's good that it was him who overheard us, he won't blow our cover – he actually wants to team up. Like some sort of weird transatlantic group project.'

'Well, the main question is: are you going to share that sandwich with me?' he asks.

'Of course,' I say, bobbing my head like a nodding dog.

I push the plate over towards him a little and we take half each. Sonny's eyes practically roll into the back of his head when he takes the first bite.

'My God, bread and cheese,' he groans. 'What else have you been eating? Actually, don't answer that, I'll never speak to you again.'

I open the bag of crisps and nudge them toward him. If it were a small bag, I would tell him that he could have them all, as a sorry, but it's big enough for the two of us.

'Do you think we should actually work with Brett?' he asks me as he begins to slow down with his eating, the initial rush of getting it in seeming like it's passing – I got through two thirds of a cheeseburger before I came up for air, so I get it.

'No,' I tell him honestly. 'I don't trust him to write about our friends, he'll twist everything, make them look bad, make their problems so much harder to deal with.'

'I know what you mean, but it would be good to get some of his information if he's been working here, if he had something for us about someone we weren't friends with maybe,' he wonders out loud. 'But I don't know, there's something about that guy, he gives me a bad feeling. He's dodgy – the way he's just been lying to us all.'

'Yeah, it's not great when you find out, is it?' I say mockingly. 'All Brett has been doing is exactly what we're here doing – we're no better than him.'

'That's true,' Sonny says. 'Maybe we need to find a way to make sure we can be.'

With our sandwich done, we head back to our suite, before anyone realises that we're missing.

The tension from earlier seems to have fizzled out slightly, replaced by our task at hand.

'I think that might have been the best sandwich I've ever had in my life,' he says with a contented sigh.

I laugh, nodding in agreement.

'And a bag of crisps. Don't forget the crisps,' I say.

'Oh, yeah, those life-changing crisps,' he says in a breathy voice.

'Did you notice they were UK crisps?' I point out. 'Are we in the Scottish Highlands?'

Sonny laughs.

'Honestly, if it turned out we were, even though it doesn't make any sense, I wouldn't be at all surprised,' he tells me.

'Me neither,' I reply. 'I'd be booking a holiday here for later in the year too.'

We reach the door of our suite, and Sonny pauses, his expression suddenly more serious again before it quickly dissolves into a laugh.

'You know, before I found out the truth, I actually thought you and Brett were having a fling,' he confesses. 'Now I find out you were just having food.'

I laugh.

'Yeah, turns out I was selling stories in exchange for snacks,' I joke. 'Did you ever hear anything more me?'

Sonny chuckles as he walks ahead of me.

I wonder what he's thinking. Did the thought of me and Brett having a thing upset him? Is he jealous? Or perhaps he's just jealous that I made a link with another journalist before him? Somehow I don't think that's true and, suddenly, I don't want there to be any secrets between us. We're in this together.

'Oh, Brett did say something interesting,' I say as I close the door behind me. 'He overheard Duane's story the other night, about going to hospital to have his appendix out.'

'Oh, yeah?' Sonny asks curiously.

'Yeah, Brett says he had a yoga session with Duane and he doesn't have a scar, so it can't have been true,' I tell him.

'Huh, well, that is interesting,' Sonny muses.

The last thing I want is for any news publication to run any kind of story on Brittany and Duane's private life, but I just don't want the secret to hang over us any more.

Well, I've never been like Sonny, I could never be ruthless. I don't need a tactical advantage, I just want to get this over with, as gently as I can, and then get home. And I'm starting to wonder if Sonny and I might want the same things after all.

29

Hope is on top Hope-y form today, standing in the centre of the room, her big plastic smile barking soft, silly orders at us.

Now, more than ever, I am sure that if I had paid for this myself, I would be furious. Fair enough, Sonny and I are not a real couple, but you would think I might have learned something from my time here, anything, from at least one of her wacky therapies. If anything, I think I might be leaving here worse off than when I arrived, because I'm going home feeling like shit about my job so, cool, thanks for that.

Her voice may be soft and smooth, but she commands the room like a head teacher on a bad day. She projects her voice with meaning but chooses her words carefully – too carefully sometimes. I'm starting think a lot of it is guff, just flowery nice-sounding stuff that is designed to soothe with no real proof it will work. The thing I can't quite work out yet is whether or not she believes her own hype, or if she's just a grifter trying to get rich while she can.

'Good afternoon, everyone,' she announces with an air of calm authority. 'Today, we're going to embark on an exercise that might challenge you, but it's designed to help strengthen the bonds you have with your partners.'

Challenging is not what I am in the mood for at all today. Christ, life is challenging enough, without Hopc's wild ideas.

'Openness and honesty are the cornerstones of any healthy relationship,' she continues. 'But we all know that it's not always easy to share our deepest thoughts and secrets with the people we care about the most – the ones it should be the easiest to share with.'

She saunters around the room gracefully, her eyes connecting with each of us as if she's peering into our souls, letting us know that she cares oh-so much about us all individually. Wow, I am on a cynical one today.

'Today, we're going to give each other the opportunity to do just that. We're going to confide in someone else – share a secret, a fear, something you've never told anyone before.'

Ugh, more sharing. I think the people here know more about me than my best friend does, and I'm supposed to be here under a false identity.

I can feel the collective tension in the room as we all brace ourselves for another day of sharing. Well, if I know anything about this lot, it's that they're all overflowing with secrets, but none that they are all that keen on sharing with anyone. And, ironically, while it might do most of them the world of good to talk about their problems, the last people they should be sharing their secrets in front of are a couple of journalists.

Hope smiles gently.

'But remember, when you share your secrets, you're placing trust in someone else, and that trust is reciprocated. This is about leaning on each other, finding balance, and forming deeper connections.'

Mutually assured destruction. I appreciate that.

She gestures toward a row of confession-style booths that have been set up at the edge of the room.

'Ladies, please choose a booth first,' Hope instructs us. 'I will assign your partner to a booth that is not yours. After the first round of confessions, I will direct half of you to a new booth, to talk to a new person. You will all get the chance to talk to a man and a woman – who is not your partner – so if there is anyone you would feel comfortable with, you have an opportunity to talk it out. Take turns confiding in one another. Speak from the heart and listen with an open mind. Let's heal each other today.'

I'll save my eye-roll for the privacy of my confession booth.

As we make our way to the booths, I feel sort of strange. I've never been in a confession booth but, being here, hearing celebrities talk freely about how they feel about the press, it's made me feel a little dirty. If anyone needs to confess in this room, it's probably me.

I take a seat and make myself comfortable, ready for my first conversation.

'Er, hello,' a voice says – an Australian man's voice. Hmm, I wonder who it could be?

'Hi,' I reply.

'Is that Lara?' he asks.

'Yep.'

'Lara, it's Heath,' he says, as though I never would've guessed. 'Was this supposed to be anonymous?'

'I doubt it,' I say, stifling a laugh.

'All right, if we're doing this, listen, there's something I've been keeping from Kellee, something that will change our future, but I don't think she's going to be happy about it,' he tells me.

For once, Heath actually sounds serious, worried – genuine. My heart goes out to him.

'Heath, whatever it is, you should talk to her,' I reply honestly.

'Secrets always have a way of coming out but, before they do, they appear as all sorts of different things, things that they are not, but we're human, we're inquisitive. If we know there is a secret, we'll try to work out what it is, and land on all sorts of wrong answers in the process. Don't let her wonder, be honest with her.'

Heath sighs heavily.

'You know what, Lara, you're right,' he eventually says. 'I know I should, but I'm scared of how she'll react, and I'm scared about what she might be keeping from me.'

'Just know that she loves you,' I tell him. 'What else matters?'

'You're right,' he says. 'Again. Listen, I'm not great at this stuff, but I can listen. Tell me what's on your mind.'

'I guess I'm a bit worried about things with me and Sonny,' I tell him, deciding to be honest, because if Heath can let his guard down with me, then I owe him the same.

'How so?' he asks. Bless him, I can tell he's doing his best to listen and be attentive. For a second, I worry that it might just be Sonny in there doing an Aussie accent.

'I'm worried that he will always try to betray me, if it comes down to it,' I confess. 'That he will clamber over me, to be better than me, to always come out on top like he did when we were at uni.'

I pause for a moment, reminding myself that I need to keep my story straight.

'What I mean is that, if he sees something he wants, and I'm in his way, he won't care if he hurts me to get it,' I tell him.

'I know a lot about what it takes to succeed, and a lot about Sonny too, and I don't think he's that kind of guy,' Heath reassures me. 'I don't think he ever was. He was a kid back then, right? That's one mistake, more than ten years ago, that – let's say I had some insider information on – I'm certain he's regretted every day since. No one gets to the top without stepping on people. He was an ambitious kid who made a mistake. He doesn't seem that way now, and he doesn't seem like he's looking for someone else, or like he thinks there's someone better for him out there. How long does a person deserve to be punished, for something they have probably regretted since the day they did it?'

Wow, I can't believe I'm saying this, but Heath is right. Sonny was a kid back then – I don't even think he was twenty at the time. It's easy to say now (and I probably said the same at the time), that I would never step on anyone like that, but who knows what I would have done, if I'd known there was an opportunity for the taking?

'Thanks, Heath,' I tell him. 'That was actually really helpful.'

'I have my moments,' he replies.

'Okay, time to switch,' Hope announces. 'I will be leading some of you to a new booth, to talk to someone else.'

I hear the door next to me open and close, then the silhouette of someone else taking a seat on the other side of the screen.

'Hello?' I say.

'Lara, is that you?' I hear Brittany ask.

Okay, I'm not sure why we're hiding our faces, when we can all tell who we're talking to, but we move.

'Hey, Brittany. Yeah, it's me. This is weird, isn't it?' I say, hoping she can hear my smile.

'You're telling me – I just had to talk at Danny for the whole thing. I only knew it was him because he didn't say a word,' she jokes. 'I feel sorry for whoever ends up talking to Duane. He's not the kind to say much either.'

We share a laugh, the absurdity of the situation squashing the tension between us. I really like Brittany, she just seems so down to earth and normal. I feel like I could be friends with her in real life, had we met under absolutely any other circumstances.

'So, do you want to share your deepest, darkest secret with me?' I joke.

'Actually, yeah – maybe,' she says, her voice suddenly much more serious. 'I trust you, Lara. And I need to tell someone. The other girls are so young, I don't think they'll get it, but something about you just makes me feel like you'll understand.'

Wow, this actually sounds serious, and while I want to scream at her to run out of this room with her hand placed firmly over her mouth, it seems like she really needs another girl to talk to.

'Of course you can tell me,' I assure her. I feel sick saying the words, but she can tell me, I'm listening as a friend right now, not as a journalist.

'Duane and I aren't actually having any problems with each other, that's not why we're here,' she explains.

I already know that. You can tell that the two of them are crazy about one another.

'The reason we're here is because we needed a break from the press,' she continues. 'Honestly, they have been hounding us, never giving us a moment of peace. We knew that this place was super exclusive, and super private, so it felt like the perfect place for us to come and just get some time to be us, with no one watching, no one trying to get any dirt on us.'

'That makes sense,' I reply.

'I don't think anyone realises just how bad things are,' she says. 'I know the others get press attention, of course they do, but with me and Duane they're just taking it too far at the moment. The more we try to be private, the more they pry. Duane was lying, covering for me when he said that we were at the hospital because his appendix burst.'

Brittany's voice cuts off suddenly. I don't say anything, giving her a moment to catch her breath, letting her carry on in her own time.

'It was me who needed to go to hospital,' she continues. 'I, erm, I had an ectopic pregnancy and, well, I'm sure you know how it goes.'

'Brittany, I'm so sorry,' I tell her sincerely.

'Thanks,' she replies. 'It was hard enough but when the press started turning up at the hospital, reporting that the two of us had been hospitalised after some bondage session gone wrong or something silly like that, God, it just made it all the more difficult.'

What on earth can I say that's going to make any of this any better? My God, what the two of them must have been through together. I wasn't one of the people at the hospital hounding her, and I never would be, but I'm a cog in a machine that hurts people.

'I'm so sorry,' I say simply.

'It just feels good to be able to tell someone,' she says, sounding like she's almost laughing with joy. 'Someone I can trust. And this place really has been a great place for us to heal, we've had so much fun, and made so many new friends.'

'I'm glad that you felt you were able to tell me, and that you feel better for talking about it, but I probably wouldn't tell anyone else here,' I say. 'Just... you never know. I'm always paranoid about who might be listening.'

'Yeah, me too,' she says. 'But something about you just made me think it would be okay to talk. You have to trust people sometimes, don't you? And just hope that they don't let you down.'

'You do,' I say with a sigh.

Perhaps I need to take that advice more than anyone else here.

Brittany sounds relieved, her voice lighter, and that makes me happy but, hearing what I heard, wow. It was like a punch to the stomach. No matter what happens, no one in this room, or outside of it, should ever know what happened to her. It's Brittany's life, and not only do I need to protect her privacy but, you know what, I don't want to do this job any more. Not just this assignment – if that is even the right word for whatever this fucked-up situation is – but this whole job.

'If I could have everyone's attention for a moment,' Hope calls out. 'What you don't know is that today you will be taking part in "the final challenge" – the last piece of the puzzle, the one event that will ensure everyone leaves here happy.'

Wow, that's a bold claim.

'I'll be taking each couple one at a time so, we'll finish up here, and then we'll call you one at a time. Stand by.'

'Final challenge?' Brittany says. 'That sounds... scary.'

'It does,' I reply. 'And, well, final.'

Is this it? The last obstacle of the trip? The thing that's going to make everything okay? If only.

One thing it does tell me for sure is that this is almost over, time is up – and I don't need a clock to know that.

30

In a turn of events that is absolutely not terrifying – please note my sarcasm – I am currently standing on the edge of a cliff with Sonny. The view before us (or should that be below us) is both breathtaking and daunting – the unfathomable expanse of water below, waves crashing hard against the rocks, weirdly inviting (if it weren't so far away) yet clearly impossibly deep, you can even tell from up here.

Hope stands between us, flanked by Carmen and Lucian. Ha, this kind of looks like a wedding. Oh, God, tell me we don't have to get married.

'This isn't like *Love Island*, is it?' I dare to joke. 'Where they make each couple pretend to get married and say cringey stuff? Because that gives me the ick.'

Sonny laughs, getting my joke.

'I don't know where that is,' Hope says simply.

Hope is as serene as ever, even when she's standing dangerously close to the edge of a cliff.

'We are here for the final challenge – a leap of faith,' she explains, which is a dicey metaphor when you're standing next to a sheer drop. 'All that is left for the two of you to do is jump off this cliff together, into the sea below.'

Sonny and I, perfectly in sync, both burst out laughing. I didn't realise Hope did jokes unless, nope, look at her face, she's deadly serious right now.

Wait, what?

'Why?' I blurt out.

My God, I cannot believe I'm having to even ask that.

'The sea has healing properties,' Hope says, incredibly sure of herself. 'It will cure all your ills – even your emotional ones.'

Sonny and I exchange a look that says it all – this has to be a joke. But Hope's calm expression says otherwise.

'Can it cure the bones you break on impact?' Sonny asks with a raised eyebrow.

'It is perfectly safe,' Hope reassures us, her eyes steady on Sonny. 'It is important that you do this,' she insists.

'It's important that I don't die,' I reply, just as firmly.

'I could do it, but it's not fair on Lara,' Sonny chimes in.

Okay, I'm not switching sides or anything, but I'm not letting that one go.

'You don't think I can do this?' I blurt, the competitive streak I have (when it comes to Sonny at least) igniting.

'It's not that I don't think you can,' he tells me, backtracking quickly, clearly having realised the error in his choice of words. 'But you're not exactly a diver, are you?'

'I've jumped into pools and the sea plenty of times,' I insist, ignoring the fact that none of those times have been recently. On a holiday I'm more likely to dive into a cocktail and a big bag of crisps by the pool, rather than the actual ocean. 'You still think you're better than me,' I snap, my emotional baggage clearly full to the brim with things to bring up in an argument. 'I think you're scared, and you're using this as an excuse to not have to pull the trigger – classic Sonny.'

'I'm not scared,' he replies quickly, his stubborn streak strengthening with each word. 'I've already said I'll do the jump for us.'

'One person can't do a leap of faith,' Hope reminds us with a slight laugh. 'You both need to do it.'

'Is this just something else you want to use to prove that you're better than me?' I can't help but throw at him.

'Why are you making this a competition?' he asks me, frustrated. 'We're supposed to be doing this together.'

My temper flares momentarily, a reckless combination of fear and frustration clouding my judgement.

'Come on then!' I demand. 'Let's do it.'

It's hard to say who jumps first, I feel like we both do it at the same time but, oh boy, we're doing it. We're really doing it.

The seconds between my feet leaving the solid ground and hitting the water seem to last forever. The impact is jarring, surprisingly cold water enveloping me, plunging me into the world below the surface.

As I pop up, gasping for air and blinking the water from my eyes, Sonny surfaces nearby. He's laughing – a joyous, unburdened laughter that's contagious. Our eyes meet, and we can't help ourselves. I suppose it's adrenaline and relief surging through us. A simultaneous mix of shock and joy.

I glance back up towards the top of the cliff, squinting to try to see if anyone is looking down at us, but the sun is too bright.

'This way,' Sonny says, so I follow his lead.

We swim our way towards the shore, eventually swimming into a rock pool surrounded by massive natural structures, eventually finding some dry land inside a natural grotto with only bursts of sunlight shining through the small gaps where the huge boulders meet.

Hopped up on adrenaline, and delighted to still be alive, we snap together once again, rolling around on the sand together as we kiss. His lips taste salty, and I can feel my wet body attracting every grain of sand that touches it. It's a dirty kiss, in every way it can be, but a sober one this time. It's everything I want. He – annoyingly – is everything I want.

'We should do this inside sometime,' I suggest, laying my head on his chest as he lies back on the sand.

He laughs.

'Maybe that will be our kink in the UK,' he jokes. 'Assuming you don't start hating me again, the second we touch down.'

'We'll see, won't we?' I reply, although it's hard to imagine now, which is wild. 'Listen, there is something serious I need to talk to you about, though, before we go home.'

'What's up?' he asks, pulling himself up on his elbows so he can look me in the eye.

'I had a chat with Brittany earlier, during the – I don't know, the weird thing with the booths,' I babble, forgetting what silly name Hope gave it. 'She confided in me that it was her who went to the hospital for something, that Duane was covering for her. We have to protect her – from us, from Brett, from everyone.'

There's no need for me to tell Sonny exactly what happened to Brittany.

'Okay, so, what do we do?' he asks, not even asking for the details. 'We won't tell anyone. Their secret's safe with us.'

I am so relieved to hear him say that.

'Honestly, this place is fucked up, I just want to get out of here,' I say, squeezing him tightly. 'The things they have been making us do, in the name of therapy, is just bullshit. They're messing with us all, squeezing money out of us all, knowing that their genuine customers will be too embarrassed to ever tell anyone about what went on here, lest their secrets get out.'

'But we're not their genuine customers, we don't have anything to lose... You know what, maybe we should expose this place, the resort,' Sonny suggests. 'There's something so off about all this, and together, we can uncover the truth. We can bring Eden down.'

I feel the corners of my mouth pull into a big grin.

'Let's do it,' I say.

Even if it's the last thing I do – work-wise, of course, I'm not being that dramatic – I want to expose Eden and, most of all, I want to finally wipe the smug smile from Hope's face.

A loud horn sounds, one that we haven't heard before.

'Perhaps it's for the coastguard,' Sonny jokes. 'They sound the horn to let them know that there are guests loose in the ocean.'

I laugh.

'Come on, let's go tell them that we're alive, and then gather the last bits and pieces we need for our article.'

'Let's do it,' he replies with a smile.

31

As Sonny and I step into the dining room, the atmosphere is so heavy with... something, it's like walking into a brick wall – or crashing into the ocean from a great height.

Everyone else is here, sitting around the dining table, all smiling from ear to ear as they watch us enter the room. No one is smiling quite as widely or as brightly as Hope, though. She's grinning the smug grin to end all smug grins. Something seems different, though, something I can't quite put my finger on. Perhaps she's always this genuinely happy, when she realises she didn't murder any guests by encouraging them to *jump off a cliff*.

'Come, sit down, join us,' Hope invites us, beckoning us over with a hypnotic motion of her index finger. 'The final challenges are over. It's time to debrief.'

Sonny and I take our usual seats at the table. I wonder if he feels as uneasy as I do – he certainly looks uncomfortable.

'Looks like you guys have been for a swim,' Heath says with a chuckle, nodding toward our damp clothes.

'And you haven't,' Sonny muses suspiciously.

'Okay, let's talk,' Hope says as she stands up in front of us all.

'The final challenge here at Eden is the leap of faith, as you all now know, but something unusual happened today. For the first time, a couple actually jumped.'

Wait, what? I cock my head curiously as I try to process her words.

'Allow me to explain,' Hope continues – why do I feel like she is only talking to me and Sonny right now? 'Eden isn't quite what you think it is. Yes, it's a couples' retreat with therapeutic elements designed to mend broken relationships, but perhaps not in the way you imagined.'

A shiver runs up my back, causing my shoulders to wiggle. I look to Sonny, but it seems like he's just as freaked out as I am.

'Everything here at Eden, from the very moment you step off that boat, is meticulously designed to push you to your limits,' Hope continues. 'The hikes, the irregular mealtimes, the lack of familiar comforts, the hard work you undertake only to see it undone, the intentional mix-up with intimacy pods, the temptation of the secret rum bars, the jarring wake-up call of the drums the next morning – and let's not forget the obstacle course with the unbeatable first obstacle...'

'I knew it,' Heath interrupts, with a triumphant clap of his hands.

'So far, every single group has gone on to breakfast after the impossible obstacle course, regardless of whether they earned it or not,' she tells us with a smile. 'Human nature will always be second nature. And then, finally, the leap of faith.'

'That only we did?' I check with her.

'That only you have ever done,' she replies. 'By the time a couple is up there on that cliff, being instructed to jump, everything that has happened before falls into place for them. The roller coaster we've created has a way of getting couples back on track, of uniting them against a common adversary – me, and this place.

When I tell them about the contract they signed, allowing us to do whatever it takes, I inform them that if they don't jump, we push them, that's usually when the final barriers come down. And that's when the truth comes out.'

Sonny's expression mirrors my own – shock combined with awe.

'So, no one has to jump?' Sonny checks.

'No, no one has to jump,' she replies. 'But you two did.'

Oh my God, we did jump – why on earth did we jump?

'Telling people they need to jump is simply the catalyst for couples to confront their issues, to air their grievances, to finally communicate openly. It's been the mechanism that's helped countless couples find their way back to each other.' She pauses for a moment. 'It is a perfectly safe spot to jump from, though.'

I'm torn between relief that this was all a psychological exercise and an unsettling realisation that we were all being manipulated this whole time. My head spins as I try to get my head around this – oh, and the irony that I really don't like being lied to. That's rich coming from me, isn't it?

'So, now that we all know, how is everyone feeling?' Hope asks as she rubs her hands together excitedly. You can tell this is her favourite part.

Hope's question hangs in the air for a moment.

'We're doing so much better.' Izzy's voice breaks the silence, her tone the most hopeful it has sounded so far. 'We've realised that we've both been struggling with similar issues, and hiding them from each other, but now that we know, we can tackle them together.'

'And we might be skint, but honestly, we're not too fussed,' Danny continues, squeezing her hand. 'We fell in love when we didn't have two pennies to rub together. Plus, I'm a footballer, I can always make more money.'

'And people offer me money to take my top off all the time,' Izzy adds. Everyone turns to her. 'I'm kidding, I'm kidding.'

'Well, it's wonderful that you've taken steps to confront your challenges and find contentment with what you share,' Hope tells them. 'Well done.'

All of a sudden, I notice something different about Hope's voice. It's a subtle change, one that's hard to put your finger on. Her tone is more genuine, less programmed – as if the phoney veneer has been stripped away. For the first time, she sounds like a person, not something Heath would build in one of his robot factories. Okay, suddenly her yo-yoing personality makes sense. For the most part, it was all an act, a character she has invented to drive guests crazy. It's hard not to be impressed.

'I found out this one has been plotting something behind my back,' Kellee announces through a happy smile, with playful accusation, pointing at Heath.

'And this one,' he counters, nodding toward Kellee, copying her choice of words, 'hasn't been up to anything behind mine.'

Heath seems like a different man. Softer, with less bravado, and all of the traits that have been annoying me kept well under wraps.

'I wanted him to think I was cheating on him, because I thought he was cheating on me – he wasn't, he was working on some chip,' Kellee reveals. 'A chip called Lille, which it turns out is Danish for small, because this special chip is so tiny.'

'All right,' Heath says, laughing awkwardly. 'I didn't tell her because it's confidential. If my competitors found out ahead of the announcement – I have the market to worry about and so on. But I'm doing all of it so that I can take a step back from the company, so I can go on tour with Kellee, and we can spend more time together. I want to support her for a change.'

Wow, it's hard to believe Heath didn't jump, because a concussion is the only thing I can think of to explain this whole new man he's become.

'We're doing good too,' Duane says. He suddenly seems so much lighter, so much more comfortable talking to the group. His gaze shifts confidentially from person to person as he addresses us all. 'We needed this and to see what life was like without all the bullshit. We think we're going to take a long break from acting.'

'We're going to build a house,' Brittany says excitedly. 'And just go somewhere and be normal for a while. See how that goes.'

I smile. I'm so happy for them.

'And then we have our couple who jumped,' Hope says, prompting us. I look at Sonny and laugh.

'I can't believe what I'm hearing,' he starts as he searches for the words. 'I mean, what can I say? It works. It's worked for everyone here and it's worked for us. We were a mess before we arrived. Our relationship was complicated, we were making each other miserable but, yeah, good work.'

Sonny gives Hope a small round of applause.

Wow. He's right – we might not have stepped on to this island with the intention of healing our own wounds, but there's no denying the transformation we've undergone. Whatever they are doing here, it works like a charm. Sonny and I have confronted our decade-old issues head-on, bridged the gaps that had been widening between us over the years, and, incredibly, I think we've both had a lot of fun doing it.

'There is one thing, though,' I interject as my conscience catches up with me. 'Something you all should know about us. We're not actually wealthy. We're just regular people with regular jobs – we pretended to be rich, because we didn't think we'd be allowed to come here otherwise.'

'See, I told you they were too nice to be rich,' Kellee's playful voice chimes in. She digs her elbow into Heath's side, her grin infectious. 'You owe me $5,000, mister.'

As I look to the others at the table, I'm surprised by the lack of reactions to my revelation. No one seems to care. From the beginning, it's been as though we were all in this together, we formed genuine friendships during our shared experiences. No one cares that Sonny and I aren't rich. I suppose they probably would care, if they knew we were journalists, but we're not going to write anything about them. Telling them why we were sent here in the first place will only ruin the transformative experience they have all enjoyed. Everyone is on top of the world, their wounds healed, their optimism restored. Anyway, it's easy to say now, but I like to think that I never would have been able to go through with it, and that Sonny wouldn't have either. We can tell our new friends about our jobs later, when they can feel reassured that we were never going to use anything they told us against them.

'All is well that ends well,' Hope chimes in, her warm voice dispelling any lingering tension. 'As I'm sure you've gathered, today is your last day, but it will be one that you will never forget. Go to your suites and get yourselves ready. I'll be sending someone to escort you to the luxury spa we have here. Enjoy your time there before dinner – a proper meal, one that everyone can enjoy. You won't be disappointed.'

The room erupts in a genuine cheer – I imagine mostly because of the food thing, but a spa sounds nice too. We disperse, laughter and chatter filling the air as we gladly do as we're told for once.

'This place is amazing,' I murmur to Sonny, looping my arm through his as we walk.

There's a newfound closeness between us, a comfortable bond, as though we had got together at uni and stayed together ever since.

'It really is,' he agrees. 'It's hard to believe how much all of this actually helps people but it does. It genuinely does. Incredible.'

I nod, a smile tugging at the corners of my lips.

'Let's not write a word about it,' I suggest, my voice hushed. 'Or tell anyone a thing about the place. Eden helps people. Let's not ruin it. If we told the world how it worked, it would never work again.'

'I did wonder why none of us had to sign an ironclad NDA,' he muses. 'Everyone here is so happy with the results, they leave happy to be a part of it. And, yes, you beat me to it. Let's keep Eden's secrets along with everyone we've met while we were here.'

And so Eden's 100-per-cent success record not only remains intact, but Hope's secrets – and the secrets of the island – will stay hidden too.

It's so funny, all this time, I've spent the whole time thinking about what a quack Hope is, but it turns out she's right. Not just with her methods but about me and Sonny too.

Perhaps we really are meant to be together after all.

32

For the first time – since, well, the first time all those years ago – I wake up nestled against Sonny, our bodies intertwined in a way that feels different – more connected, more genuine. It's something that I never thought would happen in a million years and yet here we are. It's like we've reconnected, we both know where we stand, we are finally on the same page and suddenly life ahead of us feels like something that is worth getting excited about.

My head rests on his chest, the steady rhythm of his heartbeat beneath my ear, and it's oddly comforting, hearing the life inside him. I feel alive too, in a way that I haven't for a long time. I didn't know what to expect from the trip – other than the unexpected, I suppose – but I never could have anticipated this. I feel so happy I can't stop smiling to myself.

Sonny's fingers brush lightly against my back, and as I glance up, his lips meet mine for a sweet, gentle morning kiss.

'Good morning,' he murmurs, his sleepy voice soft and soothing.

'Good morning,' I reply, stealing another kiss.

'How did you sleep?' he asks.

I nestle further into him, never wanting to move from this position.

'That was probably the best sleep I've had in ages,' I reply. 'Maybe ever. Eden has done me so much good.'

It's true – something has shifted within me during our time here. I feel like I get to leave here a new person, one with new opportunities to be happy, and to do better.

'It's amazing how much perspective can change when you step out of your comfort zone,' he muses, his fingers tracing lazy circles on my back. 'I suppose that's the whole point of this place.'

'You're right,' I reply, stroking his chest. 'I suppose, when you think about it, you getting slapped was the best thing that could have happened to both of us.'

Sonny laughs, knowing that I'm joking.

'I'm not sure about that,' he replies. 'But I'm glad we came.'

His chuckle vibrates beneath me. I squeeze him tightly.

'Right, don't do that, because as much as I'd love to stay right here with you all day, we've got a boat to catch this morning,' he reminds me, a sexy sparkle in his eyes that I can tell is taking all his power to resist running with.

'I know, I know,' I reply. 'We're on the first boat, first thing, with Kellee and Heath. I'm surprised the loud horn signalling the boat's imminent departure hasn't echoed through the air yet.'

I pull a face. I'm not going to miss that horn.

'I'm starting to think that horn was all part of the torture,' he says as he climbs out of bed.

'It definitely worked,' I reply, grabbing Sonny's pillow, snuggling up to that in his absence.

After wrestling on the clothes he set out last night, Sonny leans over, planting a swift kiss on my lips.

'I need to pop out for a bit, take care of something,' he says with a secretive smile.

Something about his words, and the look on his face, gets me excited.

'Oh, yeah?' I say playfully, raising an eyebrow.

'You'll find out soon enough. I'll meet you at the boat,' he says with a wink before disappearing.

Okay, now I really am excited.

Alone in the room, I take my time getting dressed, my thoughts swirling with anticipation. I admire myself in the mirror, amused by how much I've come to appreciate the colour pink during our stay. It makes me look happier, somehow, less intense. Bizarrely, less like a journalist, which I like. It's almost like a reflection of the newfound optimism I seem to be high on today.

With some time to spare, I decide to treat myself to one final contraband cup of tea out on the deck. I open Sonny's packed bag, carefully navigating through his neatly folded things to find the secret pocket where the teabags live, but I'm surprised when my fingers land on something different, something unexpected – a small, unfamiliar device. Intrigued, I examine it, eventually realising it's some kind of satellite messaging device of sorts. A quick press of a button reveals a single message thread between Sonny and his editor, CJ.

My heart races as I skim through their conversation. Oh my God, I can't believe it, Martin Savage – the head of Mediworldwide – has died. He was old, in his late seventies maybe, but I think everyone thought he would live forever. As I read on, it knocks me sick. CJ reveals to Sonny that the Savage kids have taken the reins of the company already, and that the first thing they are planning to do is overhaul *Stylife* and *Mach*, scrapping the gendered magazines in favour of one bigger, better publication. CJ tells Sonny that merging the magazines means that there will only be room for one editor, and one showbiz editor, and that the two of them could secure the jobs if Sonny comes back from Eden with something extra, something I don't know about. And then I see Sonny's reply:

I'll see what I can do.

I drop the device, my hand flying to my mouth in shock. I'm surprised, but why? Sonny has clearly been working me this whole time, doing what he needed to do to land a bloody job, over me, again.

With a heavy heart, unsure what else to do, I quickly return the device to the bag, just as there is a knock at the door. I answer it and Lucian's friendly face greets me.

'Good morning, Lara. I'm here to help with your bags and take you to the boat,' he tells me.

'Thanks, Lucian,' I say quickly. 'You can take the bags, but I think I'll catch you up, if that's okay?'

He raises an eyebrow, concern flickering in his eyes.

'Are you sure?' he replies. 'It will be leaving soon. I wouldn't want you to miss it, although I suppose you could always take the next one.'

'Yes, that's fine,' I say, nodding perhaps a little too intensely. 'I just need to do something first, I'll be right behind you.'

Lucian reaches into his pocket, retrieving a small deck of cards. He hands one to me, and as I take it, I notice there's a small map of the island with a yellow line on it.

I raise an eyebrow, intrigued by the card.

'What's this?' I ask.

'It's the direct route to the boat,' he tells me. 'Just follow the yellow line on the map, and you'll get there without any unnecessary detours.'

I can't help but smile as I look at the card, recalling our hike here on the first day.

'You mean we could have just walked straight here from the boat when we arrived? We didn't actually need to hike around the island?'

He nods, pure amusement in his eyes.

'I think the hike actually leads you around in a circle,' he says. 'Sometimes you need to go the long way, but other times simplicity is the best path.'

I shake my head in disbelief, laughing to myself.

'I can't believe I'm still being Eden'd,' I joke.

'It's all part of the experience, isn't it?' he says. 'Anyway, make sure you take the shortcut this time.'

I thank him, give him the cases, and grab my Birkin like a woman who means business. I'm going to see if I can find Sonny, before we go to the boat, so that I can have it out with him straight away. Well, if I don't do it now, I won't be able to do it safely without an audience until we're back in London.

Passing by the pool area, I spot Brett, sunning himself on one of the loungers.

'Hey, Lara, come here,' he calls out when he spots me.

'Hi,' I say. 'Have you seen Sonny?'

'No, but he's who I wanted to talk to you about,' Brett says, his expression serious and his voice low as he leans in. 'I wanted to ask you – is Sonny holding something back from me?'

I furrow my brow at him.

'What do you mean?' I ask.

He sighs, clearly there is something on his mind.

'We struck a deal, he gave me the big scoop on Brittany and Duane, and in return, I provided him with whatever information I had on the other guests. It felt like he thought he was getting the better end of the deal, but honestly, I gave him what little dirt I had, but I'm still none the wiser about how this place works. Still, what he gave me, well, it's gold. But you know how it goes – if something sounds too good to be true, it usually is. And I've been wondering if he's keeping something from me. Maybe the two of you know what the deal is here and you're not telling me?'

He narrows his eyes at me suspiciously.

I'm taken aback by his confession, relieved that he seems to be unaware of Eden's secrets, how the place works, how they get results. But I can't ignore the sharp pang of betrayal as I learn that Sonny has made a deal with Brett, and that he's thrown poor Duane and Brittany under the bus, just to land himself a job. He's done it again. He's actually done it again.

'Lara!' I hear Carmen's voice coming from behind me. 'Lara, the boat is leaving soon.'

'Can I get the next one?' I call back, hoping my voice carries to her.

Carmen looks puzzled.

'Erm, yes,' she calls back, uncertainty in her tone. 'Shall I tell them to let Sonny know he should get off the boat or…?'

'He already knows I'm hoping to catch the later one,' I lie. 'You can tell them to set off when they're ready.'

'Okay, sure,' she calls back.

I turn back to Brett, a heavy feeling in my chest making every movement feel sluggish. I just can't believe Sonny would go behind my back, trading other people's personal secrets to secure his job. This time hurts so much more than the last time.

Brett laughs.

'Sometimes I forget that you guys are not a real couple,' he says.

'Sometimes I do too,' I say with a sigh. 'But not any more.'

If there is one thing I know for sure, now more than ever, it is that I don't want this stupid job. I could try to get more out of Duane, take it to our bosses, and hope to come out on top, but I'm not interested. All I care about right now is helping Duane and Brittany. I need to try to get Brett not to write this story about them. I do have something to offer him; when the secret that Brittany was the one who was in hospital gets out, it won't be long before someone is able to figure it out. I can't betray her trust like that, I owe her making this right.

'I might have more for you,' I tell him. 'Why don't you tell me what Sonny told you? When I'm certain you're not bluffing, I'll tell you what he missed out.'

Brett laughs.

'I respect how untrusting you are,' he tells me. 'I've got a lot of time for it.'

My mind races as I wonder how I'm going to play this. What can I give Brett that will be enough to make him back off Duane and Brittany? I don't want to give him any more than I have to – well, I don't want to give him anything.

'Okay, so Sonny told me all about what Brittany and Duane have been hiding, their big secret, that Brittany has been having an affair,' Brett says.

I try not to let my confusion show on my face. That's not true, at all, and Sonny knows it. He's made it up. I guess it's marginally better than him telling Brett the real story but, even so, he knows how this game is played. Even an entirely fake story will be printed, it will get the rumour mill going, and the accusation will follow Brittany around forever.

'Right, the affair,' I say. 'Did he give you all the details?'

'He told me that Brittany spent Christmas Eve in Paris, with the guy she was screwing behind Duane's back, causing a huge fallout between the two of them. And that's how they ended up here, to try to get over her betrayal. He even gave me her lover's name: Benedict Armhand. Sounds like someone with money.'

Benedict Armhand – Sonny's fictional source. Why would he use that name in this context? And the story about Christmas Eve – none of it adds up. Duane and Brittany were in Edinburgh, not

Paris, on that day. I know that because Duane told us all the story, the paparazzi almost running them off the road. And anyone with an internet connection could confirm that – they could see the pictures for themselves.

Oh, and there it is, the realisation that catches up with me. Anyone with an internet connection – so not Brett, who has been here since before Christmas, so he won't know what happened with Duane and Brittany in Edinburgh on Christmas Eve.

Sonny hasn't been scheming to secure a job at all. He's done it to trade every bit of information Brett has on the people who have stayed here, giving him nothing but a fake story in return, one that, if Brett publishes it, will immediately discredit him. Oh, that's smart. Smart, brilliant, so kind and… so Sonny. And I just sent him home alone, with no explanation.

'Oh, actually, I do need to catch this boat,' I tell Brett. 'Sorry. You have all the info I have, though.'

'Okay, sure, I'll believe you,' he calls after me. 'See you around, Lara.'

'Shit,' I mutter to myself under my breath as the guilt and regret render me suddenly unable to read a simple map.

I head to the dock, to try to make the boat, only to see it just off in the distance.

Double shit.

33

Fresh off the plane, back in a cold and moody-looking London, I'm plunged back into reality at once. No more sunshine, no more luxury. Just seasonal anxiety disorder and worrying about how I'm going to pay my rent. My time at Eden feels like a distant dream already, and I'm still flailing around in the fallout.

Now that I know what day it is, and what time it is, I know that it's a workday, so I'm taking the bull by the horns, heading straight to work, but only so that I can quit my job. Well, they did say that they would sack me, if I didn't give them anything good, so I may as well save them the trouble.

Yes, today is the day I quit my job, and it's a decision I've come to terms with. Well, sort of. Everyone needs a job to pay the bills and make life work, and I'll have to figure out how to do that, but I can't ignore the nagging feeling that this isn't the right path for me any more. Unless the universe delivers me one hell of a sign that I shouldn't, I'm determined to hand in my resignation right now.

The *Stylife* offices stretch out before me as I walk through the doors, but something isn't right. It's eerily quiet, like stepping into a ghost town. There isn't a single person here, it's as though they all just upped and left. God, don't tell me I've just walked into a bomb scare or something.

Confused, I call Lauren using the phone on my desk – because my phone is still at home. She should be in today, so she should know what's going on.

'Lara, hi,' she says. 'Oh my God, Addison told me she had sent you away on a top-secret project. My imagination has been going berserk. Are you back?'

'I am,' I say, smiling because it's so good to hear her voice. 'I'm at the office but no one is here. Where are you?'

She laughs. Wherever she is, it sounds busy.

'Oh, you're not going to believe this,' she starts. 'The Savage kids decided to throw a company fun day – as a wake for their dad, and to signify the new era of the company or something.'

'A fun day for a wake?' I blurt in disbelief.

'Yeah, there is an actual funfair,' she says. 'For a wake. Welcome back!'

I've missed her sarcasm.

'Where are you?'

'Folkham Park,' she tells me. 'They've hired the park, but they've got an employee register at the gate with photos, so you should be able to get in. Shall I meet you on the bridge?'

'I'll be right there,' I tell her.

'Bring a big coat,' Lauren warns. 'It's freezing out here. See you soon.'

'Okay,' I reply.

'Oh, and by the way, Sonny's here,' Lauren adds casually. 'He's with Jon. I thought I'd better warn you.'

'Okay,' I say again, my voice much higher this time.

Hanging up, I take a deep breath, and grab the coat that I left here before my, shall we say, interlude from real life. I need to go, find Sonny, and explain to him that I made a mistake, I jumped to the wrong conclusion, and hope that he forgives me for thinking the worst of him.

At a funfair. In January. Great.

34

Walking through the funfair, my eyes widen in absolute disbelief. It's absurd, it's tacky, it's out of place, it's disruptive, and it's everything that Martin Savage would have adored. I can't help but wonder if his kids might do a better job of running the company than he did, if their values might better align with society. I'm not sure they could be worse, and I'm not sure it would stop me from quitting either.

Lauren spots me from a distance and rushes over. She practically tackles me to the ground with a big hug, but she quickly drops me again, to look me up and down.

'Look at you, all tanned and pretty in pink,' she exclaims. Then her eyes home in on my bag and her jaw drops. 'Is that a Birkin?'

'It's all I had,' I say with a shrug, my words unintentionally sounding more la-di-da than I intended. 'I'm just borrowing it from work. I'll have to give it back now that I'm home.'

'Where have you been?' she blurts. 'I have so, so many questions.'

'I can't wait to tell you all about it,' I assure her – well, as much of it as I can tell her, anyway. 'But before that, have you seen Sonny? I really need to talk to him.'

She narrows her eyes at me and then smiles.

'Oh, yes. He's over there, with Jon,' she says, nodding in their direction. 'They're queuing up for the funhouse.'

'Thanks,' I reply, my heart skipping a beat as I psych myself up.

I head for the funhouse, following the line of people, but I don't quite make it in time. Sonny has just gone inside, Jon is just about to.

'Sonny, I need to talk to you!' I call out, desperation in my voice, but my words get lost in all the fun of the fair.

'No queue-jumping!' someone yells at me from down the line.

'She can have my place,' Jon says gallantly. He turns to the man running the ride. 'Can she go in instead of me?'

The man running the ride could not give less of a shit.

'Yeah, whatever,' he says with a nod.

'Thanks so much,' I tell Jon. 'I'll come find you and Lauren after.'

As I step into the funhouse, memories from my childhood come flooding back. I used to be terrified of stuff like this. The first obstacle is a motor-powered hamster wheel-like contraption that I'm supposed to walk through. I hesitate for a second, recalling the time when I was a kid and didn't dare pass through it, screaming and crying until someone in the control room turned it off for me. Then I remind myself that I jumped off a cliff yesterday – or the day before, maybe – depending on where we were, and what the time difference was.

Next is a ladder leading up to a balancing beam high above a ball pool. I spot Sonny on the beam and I feel both excited and sick to see him.

'Sonny!' I call out.

He turns, nearly losing his balance, but as he levels himself out again, a warm smile spreads across his face.

'I'll meet you on the other side!' he calls back.

I focus on the beam ahead – the only thing standing between me and Sonny. It feels like it wobbles and bends beneath my feet, but I take it a step at a time, one foot in front of the other, until I'm there. I think I've made it across when I stumble right before I reach the other side. Luckily, Sonny's arm reaches out, grabbing me, pulling me to safety.

'You missed the boat,' he eventually says, kind of casually.

'Yeah, in more ways than one,' I reply with a smile. 'Sonny, I messed up. I found that messaging device in your bag, and I jumped to the worst conclusions.'

'Shit, Lara, I'm sorry,' he says, sounding like he means it. 'CJ insisted I take it, and I got those messages from him at the beginning of the trip. I should've told you, but I thought the longer I left it, the harder it'd be for you to trust me.'

'I went to see Brett, after I found it,' I continue. 'He told me what you said to him, the information you gave him about Duane and Brittany.'

A smug grin beams from Sonny's face.

'If he prints that story, no one will ever believe a word he says again,' he tells me triumphantly. 'And honestly, he didn't have much on the other guests, but I doubt anyone would take him seriously if he tried to tell anyone about it now.'

'So that's why you snuck off this morning,' I point out.

'No, actually, I did that the night before,' he replies. 'This is why I went out in the morning.'

Sonny rummages around in his pocket before pulling out a creamy-coloured shell with the most intricate of patterns on it.

'For your collection,' he tells me.

I feel my bottom lip wobble slightly as I suck in a sharp breath of air.

'You're brilliant,' I tell him. 'And I'm so sorry for doubting you. But listen, I'm here to find Addison. I'm quitting my job, and if there's only one spot, I want you to have it. I'm taking myself out of the running.'

Suddenly, Sonny's expression turns to something more serious.

'It's too late,' he says simply. 'It's too late because... I already handed in my notice.'

'You did?' I squeak.

'Yeah, well, I've already got a new job,' he says – again, so casually, but with a big smile. 'They let me sit with Kellee and Heath on the flight back to London. I told him that I was a writer and he offered me a job working for him. He wants me to write the copy for this mysterious project he's working on. It means moving to Australia, though.'

I hold my breath for a second. No. No, no, no. Sonny is moving to Australia.

'I thought that while I was there, I could do a bit of exploring, see if I can get something going with travel writing in my free time,' he explains.

'Yeah, that makes sense,' I reply, trying to sound enthusiastic.

I notice that we're standing next to a steep slide, and dramatically wonder if I should throw myself off it, so that the (ball-covered) ground can swallow me up.

'I thought you could come with me,' he adds.

'What?' I blurt.

'I thought you could come with me, help me explore, maybe you could try to write your book, or figure out what else you might like to do,' he continues. 'Plus, Kellee said I wasn't allowed to go unless I brought you.'

All of a sudden, every drop of blood in my body feels like a fire surging around in me as the sheer joy gets ready to erupt.

I grab him and pull him close, kissing him like I've never kissed anyone before.

When I pull away, he smiles, but playfully searches my eyes for an answer.

'Is that a yes?' he asks excitedly. 'Fancy taking another leap of faith with me?'

I glance at the ball pool below us, then back at Sonny, a cheeky smile taking hold of my face. Taking his hand, I lead him towards the edge.

'What do you think?' I say, before we both step off into the unknown.

ACKNOWLEDGEMENTS

Thank you to Nia and to the rest of the team at Boldwood HQ for working with me on another book – I can't believe this is our sixteenth book together.

Massive thanks to everyone who buys, reads and reviews my books. Your support means so much to me and I really appreciate all the lovely reviews.

Huge thanks to Kim (who buys the best publication day presents), to Pino, and to Aud, my biggest fan, who has all my books on her shelf. Thank you to James for always being so helpful and supportive, and to Joey for always being there for me – and always having such good ideas. Thank you to Darcy for being my right-hand girl, and a shout-out to Sam and Wayne for always being so supportive – and for helping me name one character in particular.

Finally, thank you to Joe, my brilliant husband, for all his continued love and support, for always being there for me, always helping me in absolutely every way possible. I'm so fortunate to have such an amazing, supportive family – I love you all so much.

ABOUT THE AUTHOR

Portia MacIntosh is a bestselling romantic comedy author of over 15 novels, including *My Great Ex-Scape* and *Honeymoon For One*. Previously a music journalist, Portia writes hilarious stories, drawing on her real life experiences.

Sign up to Portia MacIntosh's mailing list for news, competitions and updates on future books.

Visit Portia's website: https://portiamacintosh.com/

Follow Portia MacIntosh on social media here:

facebook.com/portia.macintosh.3
x.com/PortiaMacIntosh
instagram.com/portiamacintoshauthor
bookbub.com/authors/portia-macintosh

ALSO BY PORTIA MACINTOSH

One Way or Another

If We Ever Meet Again

Bad Bridesmaid

Drive Me Crazy

Truth or Date

It's Not You, It's Them

The Accidental Honeymoon

You Can't Hurry Love

Summer Secrets at the Apple Blossom Deli

Love & Lies at the Village Christmas Shop

The Time of Our Lives

Honeymoon For One

My Great Ex-Scape

Make or Break at the Lighthouse B&B

The Plus One Pact

Stuck On You

Faking It

Life's a Beach

Will They, Won't They?

No Ex Before Marriage

The Meet Cute Method

Single All the Way

Just Date and See

Your Place or Mine?

Better Off Wed

Long Time No Sea

The Faking Game

Enemies to Lovers

Printed in Great Britain
by Amazon

37194192R00155